ACCLAIM FOR SARAH E. LADD

"My kind of book! The premise grabbed my attention from the first lines and I eagerly returned to its pages. I think my readers will enjoy *The Heiress of Winterwood*."

—JULIE KLASSEN, BESTSELLING, AWARD-WINNING AUTHOR

"Ladd proves yet again she's a superior novelist, creating unforgettable characters and sympathetically portraying their merits, flaws and all-too-human struggles with doubt, hope and faith."

—*RT Book Reviews*, 4 STARS, ON *A Lady at Willowgrove Hall*

"[E]ngaging scenes of the times keep the pages turning as this historical romance . . . swirls energetically through angst and disclosure."

—*Publishers Weekly* ON *The Headmistress of Rosemere*

"This book has it all: shining prose, heart-wrenching emotion, vivid and engaging characters, a well-paced plot and a sigh-worthy happy ending that might cause some readers to reach for the tissue box. In only her second novel, Ladd has established herself as Regency writing royalty."

—*RT Book Reviews*, 4 1/2 STARS, TOP PICK!
ON *The Headmistress of Rosemere*

"If you are a fan of Jane Austen and *Jane Eyre*, you will love Sarah E. Ladd's debut."

—USATODAY.COM ON *The Heiress of Winterwood*

"This debut novel hits all the right notes with a skillful and delicate touch, breathing fresh new life into standard romance tropes."

—*RT Book Reviews*, 4 STARS, ON *The Heiress of Winterwood*

THE CURIOSITY
KEEPER

Other Books by Sarah E. Ladd

The Whispers on the Moors

The Heiress of Winterwood
The Headmistress of Rosemere
A Lady at Willowgrove Hall

THE CURIOSITY KEEPER

A TREASURES OF SURREY NOVEL

SARAH E. LADD

THOMAS NELSON
Since 1798

NASHVILLE   MEXICO CITY   RIO DE JANEIRO

Published in Nashville, Tennessee, by Thomas Nelson. Thomas Nelson is a registered trademark of HarperCollins Christian Publishing, Inc.

Thomas Nelson, Inc., titles may be purchased in bulk for educational, business, fundraising, or sales promotional use. For information, please email SpecialMarkets@ ThomasNelson.com.

Scripture quotation used as inscription on brooch (Romans 8:28) is from the King James Version of the Bible.

Publisher's Note: This novel is a work of fiction. Names, characters, places, and incidents are either products of the author's imagination or used fictitiously. All characters are fictional, and any similarity to people living or dead is purely coincidental.

Library of Congress Cataloging-in-Publication Data

Ladd, Sarah E.
    The curiosity keeper / Sarah E. Ladd.
        pages ; cm. -- (A treasures of Surrey novel ; 1)
        Summary: "Born into two different classes, James and Camille shouldn't even know each other. But when the pursuit of a missing ruby brings them together, much more than a mere acquaintance is ignited. The daughter of a curiosity shop owner, Camille would never be considered a lady. Nor does she want to be. With a fiery personality, she dreams of adventures far beyond the walls of her family's modest business. But when her father thrusts a mysterious box into her hands and disappears, her whole world -- dreams and all -- shifts. James is an apothecary, tending to the health needs of the town of Bentworth. His father, a well-known explorer and collector, is quite wealthy from the spoils of his adventures until one risky gamble and a stolen gem leave him on the edge of ruin. Seeking his father's approval, James picks up the hunt for the stolen ruby, leading him to the door of Camille's curiosity shop. With both of their lives in danger as the ruby remains at large, James squires Camille away to the Bentworth School, believing that would be the last place her pursuers would look for her. They both find their hearts and dreams heading in a new direction, but before they are free to embrace their future they must solve the mystery looming around them. The more they uncover, however, the harder it becomes to know whom to trust. And they begin to realize that recovering the ruby may require a great sacrifice: their newfound love and maybe even their lives. "-- Provided by publisher.
        ISBN 978-0-7180-1178-9 (softcover)
    1. Precious stones--Fiction. 2. Man-woman relationships--Fiction. I. Title.
    PS3612.A3565C87 2015
    813'.6--dc23
                                    2015001997

Printed in the United States of America

15 16 17 18 19 20 RRD 6 5 4 3 2 1

I lovingly dedicate this novel
to my sister, Sally—
my first and best friend.

Chapter One

*C*amille Iverness met the big man's gaze.

Bravely.

Boldly.

She would not be bullied or manipulated. Not in her own shop.

Camille recognized the expression in the man's eye. He did not want to speak with her, a mere woman. Not when the owner of the shop was James Iverness.

But James Iverness—her father—was not present.

She was.

She jutted her chin out in a show of confidence, refusing to even blink as he pinned her with a steely stare.

"As I already told you, Mr. Turner, I have no money to give you," she repeated, louder this time. "Any dealings you made with my father you will need to take up with him. I've no knowledge of the transaction you described. You had best return at another time."

"I've seen you here, day in, day out." His voice rose in both volume and gruffness. "How do you expect me to believe you know nothing about it?" The wooden planks beneath his feet groaned as he shifted his considerable weight, making little attempt to mask his effort to look around her into the store's back room. "Is he in there? So help me, if he is and—"

"Sir, no one besides myself is present, with the exception of my father's dog."

It was in moments like this that she wished she were taller, for even as she stood on the platform behind the counter, the top of her head barely reached his shoulder. "If you would like, I will wake the animal, but if you have seen me here often, as you claim, then no doubt you have also seen Tevy and know he does not take kindly to strangers. You decide. Shall I go fetch him?"

Mr. Turner's gaze snapped back to her. No doubt he knew of the dog. Everyone on Blinkett Street knew about James Iverness's dog.

His whiskered lip twitched.

A warm sense of satisfaction spread through her, for finally she had said something to sway the determined man.

Mr. Turner's face deepened to crimson, and he pointed a thick finger in Camille's direction, his voice matching the intensity of his eyes. "Tell your father I've a mind to speak with him. And tell him I want my money and won't take kindly to his antics. Next time I am here I will not be so willing to leave."

He muttered beneath his breath and stomped from the store, slamming the door behind him with such force that the glass canisters on the near shelf trembled.

A shudder rushed through her as she watched him lumber away, and she did not let her posture relax until the back flap of his gray coat passed the window and was out of sight. How she despised such interactions. As of late, Papa seemed to be angering more patrons than he obliged, and he always managed to be conveniently absent when they came to confront him.

She needed to speak with Papa, and soon. Awkward conversations like the one with Mr. Turner needed to stop.

Camille tucked a long, wayward lock of hair behind her ear and drew a deep breath. Once again her father's dog had come to her rescue, and he was not even in the room.

"Come, Tevy," she called. In a matter of moments the massive brown animal was through the door and at her side, tail wagging enthusiastically.

"Pay heed!" she laughed as he nudged her hand, forcing her to pet him. "That tail of yours is likely to knock every vase off that shelf if you're not careful, and then Papa will blame—"

The door to the shop pushed open, jingling the bell hung just above it. She drew a sharp breath, preparing to deal with yet another customer, but it was her father who appeared in the doorway.

He was a short man, not much taller than she herself, but that was where their physical similarities ended. His green eyes made up in intensity what he lacked in stature. His hair, which in her youth had been the color of sand, was now the color of stone, and years spent on a ship's deck had left his complexion ruddy. His threadbare frock coat, dingy neckcloth, and whiskered cheeks made him appear more like a vagabond than a shopkeeper, and despite his privileged upbringing, he often acted and spoke like an inhabitant of the docks where he did much of his trading.

"Good day, Papa."

He ignored her welcome and bent to scratch Tevy's ears. After pulling out a bit of dried meat and handing it to the dog, he reached back into his coat. "This came for you."

He stretched out his hand, rough and worn. Between his thick fingers he pinched a letter.

Camille stared at it for several moments, shocked. Clearly she could make out her name—in her mother's handwriting. The edge of the paper was torn. She could not recall the last letter she had received from Mama.

He thrust the letter toward her. "Don't just stand there gawking, girl. Take it."

Camille fumbled with the missive to keep it from falling to the planked floor below, but for once, she found herself unable to find words. Unprepared—and unwilling—to deal with the onset of emotions incited by the letter, she blinked back moisture and shoved it into the front pocket of her work apron.

"Are you not going to read it?" Her father nodded toward her apron.

Of course he expected her to read it, for he himself devoured every one of his wife's scarce communications the moment they arrived. Though they both felt her absence keenly, they reacted to it very differently—and they never, ever discussed it. Over time, Camille had made the topic off-limits in her own mind, and a letter crafted by the very person who was the source of the pain was unwelcome.

"I'll read it later. There is far too much to do at the moment." She sniffed and gestured toward the curtain that separated the shop from the back room. "There was a crate delivered to you by cart in the alley, but it was too heavy for me to lift."

She was a little surprised at the quickness with which her father let the topic of the letter drop. "Why did you not have the men delivering it bring it in?"

"I tried, but they refused—said it was not their duty. They left it in the courtyard out back."

"When are you going to learn that such things are your

responsibility? You should have persuaded them to bring it in." Her father shifted through the papers on the counter, not pausing to look up. "Had you been a boy, this would not be an issue."

Camille folded her arms across her chest. "Well, I was not born a boy, and there is precious little I can do about that. So if you will fetch the delivery in for me, I shall tend to it. Or it can spend the night hours where it sits. But the sky looks like it holds rain, so whatever is inside that box will just sit there and soak."

After much grumbling, Papa disappeared through the back and returned dragging a large, awkward crate. Camille helped him bring it close to the counter, then pried the lid off and reached for one of the linen-wrapped items inside. Laying it on the counter, she carefully pulled back the fabric and revealed a canvas. Strokes of emerald and moss depicted a countryside set below a brilliant sapphire sky. She flipped through the next canvas, then the next. All boasted lush pastoral landscapes.

She clicked her tongue as she assessed the cargo. "They are all paintings. Why did you buy these?"

"I didn't buy them," he muttered. "I traded for them."

"That is the same thing, Father. Paintings do not sell well. You know that. They will sit on the shelves for months, I fear. And we haven't the space as it is."

"When will you learn not to question my ways? Sometimes such deals must be made to clinch future arrangements. You mind the counter and leave the dealings to me."

She ignored him and lifted another canvas out of the crate. "Speaking of dealings, Mr. Turner was just in looking for you."

At this he raised his head. "Did he make a purchase?"

"No, quite the opposite. He said you owe him money."

"You didn't give him any, did you?"

"Of course not."

Her father returned to his stack of papers. "Turner is a fool."

"Do you owe him money?" She leaned her hip against the counter. When her father did not respond, she continued. "If you insist upon doing these business dealings on the side, that is fine, but you must understand that you have put me in some very awkward situations. Mr. Turner was quite angry."

Her father disappeared through the doorway, signaling he was finished with the conversation. She sighed and lifted another canvas, assessing the delicate brushstrokes with a practiced eye. A lovely piece, expertly done. In another shop it might fetch a pretty penny. But not here. Their patrons wanted the unusual, the wildly exotic—unique treasures from far beyond England's shore, not calm renditions of their own British countryside.

But Camille's practical side could not quiet the beating of her heart as she took in the tranquil meadow and vivid flora depicted by the artist's strokes. Memories of her time in such a setting rushed her. She remembered running through the waving grasses, wading in the trickling streams, breathing air so fresh and clean it practically sparkled.

So long ago . . .

When she was small, Camille and her mother had lived on her paternal grandfather's country estate. At that time her father had been endlessly absent, either away on business or incessantly traveling the world to quench his thirst for the rare and mysterious. But after her grandfather's death, the lavish estate had been sold. Her father, the sole heir, had invested the proceeds into this shop. And life as Camille knew it had changed forever.

She longed to flee from the dirty confines of Blinkett Street and return to the countryside, to once more breathe fresh air and to bask in the golden sunshine that bathed the meadows. But Grandfather was dead, and Mama was far away, and Papa begrudged even her necessary outings to the greengrocer and the butcher.

She sighed as the door's bell signaled another customer.

Camille had not left London since she first came to the city eleven years earlier.

She was beginning to wonder if she would ever leave London again.

Chapter Two

Mr. Edward Langsby, superintendent at Fellsworth School, tapped with his knuckles on the sickroom door, which stood slightly ajar. "Mr. Gilchrist, you have a visitor."

Jonathan Gilchrist looked up from the bedside of his young patient. Despite the fever, the boy was sleeping soundly. Jonathan pressed a hand to the child's forehead before turning back to the superintendent. "Who is calling?"

"A footman from Kettering Hall. He claims it is urgent."

Jonathan drew a deep breath and adjusted his waistcoat. A footman from Kettering Hall. Again. "Did he say what brought him here?"

"No. Just that he needed to speak with you directly."

Jonathan looked toward the uncovered window. Rain pounded against the paned glass, and a howling wind rattled it in its casings. What could have so upset his father that he would send one of his footmen out at such a late hour and in such inclement weather?

Jonathan turned to Mr. Langsby. The older man was in a haphazard state of dress, and his disheveled hair and the circles beneath his eyes suggested that he had been roused from slumber.

"I will go down and see what he needs. It is a shame he had to wake you, but I am finished here. There is a powder on the table there. See that it is mixed with warm water and that he drinks it twice daily. I would prefer it if one of the teachers sat with him through the night, just in case there are any changes."

The superintendent nodded in agreement. "I shall ask Mr. Vingate to sit up with him."

"Thank you. And do not hesitate to contact me should he worsen. From the sound of it, I shall be at Kettering Hall this night instead of the cottage, so if you require my services I would start there."

Jonathan followed the superintendent down the narrow staircase separating the sick room from the rest of the building and through the kitchen to the front foyer. There stood a young footman, soaked from head to toe. "What is it, Thaddeus?"

The footman cleared his throat and blinked the water from his eyes. "Mr. Gilchrist says you are needed at Kettering Hall. There's been a robbery."

"A robbery?" Jonathan repeated, not certain if he had heard the young man correctly.

He had grown quite accustomed to being woken from sleep in the midnight hours. Sickness was hardly confined to daylight. At least once a week a patient would pound on his door seeking assistance with the onset of illness or a fever spike. And his father had few qualms about sending for him at any hour.

But never had he been summoned with news of a robbery. "Are you certain?"

Jonathan rubbed his hand across his face.

"Your father is certain." The young man wiped the rain from his face with his sleeve. "He says someone has broken into his study."

Jonathan refused to become alarmed at yet another of his

father's assumptions. "If it is indeed a robbery, perhaps you should ride for the constable. His services would be of more use to Father than mine at this moment."

"It was suggested, and Mr. Gilchrist says there is nothing a constable can do." The footman swiped his soaking hair from his forehead. "He said you need to be there."

Jonathan drew a sharp breath. There was little room for doubt in his mind that his father had indeed requested—no, ordered—his presence. The man was no stranger to overreacting and had been sending for him more and more since the death of Jonathan's older brother, Thomas, two years prior. As of late Jonathan was being summoned for tasks that could easily be handled by one of the servants. The last thing he wanted to do was to venture out in the rain, only to learn that his father had misplaced a trinket. Again.

A clap of thunder shook the school. Jonathan reached for his caped greatcoat, hanging on a hook next to the door, and leaned to the left to peer out the flanking window. Streams of raindrops streaked the wavy glass and veiled his view of the black night.

"I-I brought a mount for you," the footman stammered. "Thought it would be faster than walking."

Jonathan looked past the youth out the door. Sure enough, two horses stood pitifully hunched against the rain.

He pushed his arm through the coat's sleeve. "Tell me more about what has happened."

Thaddeus stepped next to Jonathan, water still dripping from his coat and plopping to the stone floor below. "Just before midnight there was a crash from the north of the house. Sounded like breaking glass. I heard the noise myself. When I got there Mr. Gilchrist was in his study, and he would not allow anyone in except for his valet. He was angry, shouting and such. He just kept saying, 'It's gone.'"

Jonathan frowned. "What is gone?"

"Don't know."

Jonathan groaned and reached for his hat—the wide-brimmed one he often used in weather—and stepped out into the night.

The rain hit Jonathan's face like icy pellets as he rode, and the late-spring wind pierced the wet fabric of his clothes. Fortunately, the ride to Kettering Hall was a short one—down the main lane through the village of Fellsworth and over the Leaflet Bridge. The road ran alongside Kettering's south orchard and then past a walled rose garden. At present all was masked in darkness, but he had made the journey so frequently that he did not doubt he could make it blindfolded.

Normally this time of night Kettering Hall would be as still and quiet as the grasslands and meadows that surrounded it. But not tonight. As always the ancient redbrick structure stood steadfast in the weather, a black silhouette against the midnight sky. But yellow candles now blinked from the windows. A dog barked, low and sharp, from somewhere in the east. Male voices battled to be heard against the wind and rain slamming to the ground below.

As his horse pranced to a stop in front of Kettering Hall's entrance, Jonathan slid to the ground. He handed the reins to another footman, who stood waiting, and climbed the steps toward the open front door.

The main hall was alive with servants dressed in nightclothes and robes. Candlelight cast odd shadows on their sleepy faces. How strange it was to see them in this stage of undress instead of the clean, stark uniforms they usually wore.

Such confused disorganization was uncommon at Kettering Hall. The atmosphere reminded him of another somber night, four years prior, when he had been summoned to his mother's deathbed. The servants had been awake and in nightclothes then as well, but instead of usual silence, the air had been full of soft crying and hushed voices.

He removed his hat and handed it to Abbott, the butler.

"I'm glad to see you, sir."

Abbott's familiar hoarse whisper was a welcome sound. He had known the man ever since he was a boy, and of all the staff at Kettering Hall, he placed the most trust in the aging butler.

Jonathan pulled his arm from the sleeve of his coat. "What has happened?"

Abbott took the coat. "According to your father, there has been a robbery in the study. But you know how he is. He will not allow anyone else—"

"Jonathan!" Ian Gilchrist's unmistakable voice rose above the hall's activity. "Is he here?"

Abbott cut his eyes toward Jonathan before responding. "Yes, sir, he has just arrived."

"Enter."

The study door, which remained locked most of the time, truly was a gateway to the mysterious unknown. Within those walls his father kept the bulk of his "collection"—an assemblage of all things strange and unusual, ancient and fanciful, gathered from every corner of the globe.

Jonathan's hand hovered over the handle. His father bellowed his name again, demanding that he enter. Yet Jonathan hesitated, for he was rarely invited into this room. But apparently tonight was different. Something had happened—an event significant enough to warrant an invitation into the inner sanctum. He found himself half dreading the impending conversation and half curious about what could have riled his father to such a state.

The door squeaked on antiquated hinges as Jonathan pushed it open. Stagnant air immediately filled his mouth and lungs, feeling almost too thick with dust to actually be of use. But then a brisk breeze, carrying with it bits of rain, gusted into the room through an open window, fluttering out the curtains and snapping him to the present.

Eerie darkness surrounded him, broken by the flickering light from several sputtering lights positioned around the room.

And what the candles illuminated was a shock.

Jonathan's gaze did not go directly to his father. Instead, trinkets and trunks of every shape and size captured his attention, momentarily halting his ability to speak. He struggled to make out the objects in the dark. Paintings and murals covered the walls, all but obscuring the dark-green paint. Mounted animals clustered in awkward groupings, their beady eyes glinting in the candlelight and faces frozen in various expressions. Trunks and tables, chairs and vases, all crowded together in dusty heaps.

Jonathan feared stepping further into the room, lest one misstep trigger an avalanche of statues and books. He inched to the right, and the movement incited a squawk from a creature in the corner.

"What in blazes?" Jonathan jumped and backed into a table, sending the contents tumbling to the wood floor. As his eyes adjusted to the dim light, he beheld a giant, brilliantly colored bird in a corner cage, staring at him with pale yellow eyes.

But his father paid him no heed. "They took it. Dash it all, they took it."

Jonathan gingerly made his way toward his father. He lifted the candle from the desk and looked around him, wondering how it would be possible to notice if anything was not in its right place. "Took what?"

"Garrett, leave us."

The aging valet, who had been standing next to his father, fixed his rheumy eyes on Jonathan before finally leaving the master's side.

Garrett pulled the door behind him as he exited. Jonathan stepped over to close the window, then realized it was not merely open, as he had thought. Instead, the glass was shattered. A few reflective shards lay on the wooden floor beneath their feet.

His father scooted the chair away from the desk with his foot and dropped into it. The light from the candle next to him reflected on the hard lines of his face, making him appear much older than his fifty-two years. The man slumped forward, motionless save for the tapping of his fingers on the chair's carved arm, and stared unblinking into the fire. His flinty expression was one Jonathan had not seen since his brother's death.

Jonathan waited. Ian Gilchrist was not one to be pushed. He would divulge his thoughts in his own time—and not a moment sooner.

In the passing silence, Jonathan picked up a small box from a table and lifted the lid.

"Touch nothing," hissed his father.

Growing annoyed with his father's moody vagueness, Jonathan let the lid fall shut and returned the box to the cluttered table. "You called me here, Father. I assume you have some reason other than desire for my company."

"I have been robbed, Jonathan. Make no mistake." His father

pointed to the window with a shaky finger. "That must be how the coward entered the room, for the door was locked. He must have left the same way."

Jonathan stepped over a pile of papers and toward the window. He braced himself with his hand on the window's frame and leaned out just enough to see the drive below. It would have been difficult to enter the house through this window. The rain had muddied any chance of finding footprints or evidence of a ladder. Jonathan turned back to the room, his back to the night's elements, and looked around, wondering how his father could have determined so quickly what was missing. "What has been taken?"

His father's response came as a whisper. "The Bevoy."

"What is the Bevoy?"

Jonathan regretted the bluntness of the question as soon as it passed his lips. His father was a secretive man, private in his affairs. He trusted very few, and Jonathan was not privy to that minuscule circle.

"The Bevoy," his father repeated, annoyance tingeing his words, "is a ruby of great worth." He pushed back from the desk as he said it, his graying hair wild from having been woken from slumber.

"A ruby?" blurted Jonathan. "All this fuss is over a ruby? A ruby can be replaced, Father. Is anything else missing?"

His father fixed his eyes on Jonathan, pinning him with the intensity of his stare. "It is not just a ruby, as you say. It is large as a quail's egg, still untouched and unpolished. And it is rumored to either bless or curse whoever possesses it."

Jonathan huffed. "Gems cannot be cursed, Father."

"Bah!" Ian Gilchrist threw back his head in a burst of sarcastic laughter. "Simpletons may think such things. But I have been collecting a long time, and I have seen things, I tell you—inexplicable events tied to various artifacts. There are mysteries in this world that cannot be easily explained. One may not be able to explain them, but that does not mean they are not real."

Jonathan tried to follow his father's logic. "Very well, assuming you are correct and the ruby is cursed, why would someone want to steal it?"

"Because it can carry a curse *or* a blessing. Some believe it will bring wealth to whoever possesses it. Not to mention the gem itself is worth a fortune."

Jonathan told himself he should stop asking questions—mostly because he was not certain he wanted to hear the answers. Long-held suspicions of his father's activities and the man's record of ill-gotten gains had caused Jonathan to hold his tongue and keep his distance for the past several years. No doubt it would be best to adopt a similar strategy now.

He moved away from the window and closer to the warmth of the fire. "If you are seeking my advice, I think you had best summon the constable and leave this with him."

His father stood and stepped over to the sideboard, where he poured himself a dram of brandy and shot it down his throat. He grunted a sigh before slamming the glass back on the table. "The constable won't be of any help. Not with the sorts of ne'er-do-wells that took this."

"How can you be sure?"

"I've seen my fair share of the world, boy." Ian Gilchrist poured himself another glass, pausing long enough to shake his finger toward Jonathan. "And I've seen my share of justice—or the lack of it. No, we do not need a constable."

Jonathan could not help himself. "If it is cursed, why is it so important that we recover it?"

"Because it is mine, and not a single soul on this earth has the right to take what belongs to Ian Gilchrist." The old man slapped the table, his jowls shaking, his agitation growing in volume and intensity. "Besides, I have made arrangements to sell it for a goodly sum."

"You? Sell part of your collection?" Jonathan gave a nervous laugh. "I've never known you to part with any piece, regardless of the amount."

But his father did not laugh. Instead, his lips curled downward. "I made a bad investment. I planned to sell that ruby to set things right."

Jonathan sobered. "Set what right?"

"If you must know, I made a wager on which I could not deliver. If I fail to meet the terms of the agreement, we could lose Kettering Hall."

Jonathan stared. Surely he had misunderstood. "What do you mean, lose Kettering Hall? There must be something else that can be sold to cover debts. Just look around here."

"I have already parted with many of the more valuable pieces. Without the ruby, what I have now is not of sufficient value to cover the debt." He picked up his glass and drained it. "Your sister's dowry is tied to that sum of money."

At this, Jonathan snapped his head up. His sister would marry within the year. "I thought her dowry could not be touched."

"There was a loophole, and I took advantage of it. It made good sense at the time." He looked up with a scowl. "I will not be judged, not by my own son."

Jonathan rubbed his forehead, trying to make sense of what

he was hearing. "But if the ruby was so valuable, why keep it here where you live? Why not under lock and key in London?"

"If I own something, it is mine. I will keep it with me. Your brother understood this. I do not see why it is so hard for you to do the same." He picked up a small statue and turned it over in his unsteady hands. "Time is short. Either death or my creditors will call soon. You are the heir of Kettering Hall. It is time you acted like it."

Jonathan felt the anger begin to boil in him. "What exactly is it that you expect me to do?"

"You must go to London. Henry Darbin is there. He works in a private capacity to solve such crimes. 'Tis his profession. No doubt he will assist us as well. Go find him."

"I will do no such thing," Jonathan protested. "This is a matter for the constable. I have no wish to get involved in your schemes."

"Is my own son such a coward?" his father challenged. "You are the heir of Kettering Hall. Would you abandon your birthright?"

Jonathan forced his voice to remain steady. "It was never meant to be my birthright, as you frequently remind me."

"And Penelope? Are you ready to seal her fate as well? We need her union with Alfred Dowden to recoup other losses. He is a fine man, but he is not a fool. He will not marry her without the dowry."

Jonathan could not help but wince at the mention of his sister. She was the one who would likely suffer the most as a result of their father's loss. But embarking on this fool's errand could hardly save her.

"You are trapping me, Father. I will not be trapped."

"You are a Gilchrist. You will not allow our family to face ruin."

"Then tell me how this happened. What dealings went bad?"

"That is not your business."

"You ask for my help, yet refuse to tell me how the situation came to pass?"

"Do not take that tone again in my presence. You are not master of Kettering Hall. Not yet. You are my son, and it behooves you to do what I say. You are to go to London. Find Darbin."

The old man barked the order, then turned back to the window. Clearly, Jonathan was dismissed, but he didn't move right away. He just stood there rooted to the floor, feeling the monstrous stacks of his father's collection close in around him.

He had never been meant to inherit Kettering Hall. That privilege—that burden—had belonged to his elder brother. But after Thomas's death Jonathan had been thrust from his lowly life as a village apothecary to the unwelcome position of heir. But a lifetime of failed expectations and broken promises had taught him prudence, so he had continued along his original path, planning his finances and his future as if he would have to survive on an apothecary's living.

Indeed, he far preferred his life as an apothecary. He relished being useful, an agent of healing, and dreaded spending his time and energy to manage family assets he cared little about.

But the harder he tried to separate himself from Kettering Hall, the tighter the cord connecting him to his birthplace coiled.

Chapter Three ————————————

Jonathan stepped out of his father's study and felt a rush of cool, breathable air. He filled his lungs with it and then quickly exhaled as if to cleanse himself from what he had just heard.

He was aware of the eyes on him. Garrett, the valet, stood across the hall, never too far from his master. Two footmen lurked in the shadows, no doubt whispering about their odd master and his ever odder obsessions. Jonathan cast a stony stare their way, and the men scattered.

But as he turned, he noticed another set of eyes.

Penelope's.

His younger sister was swathed in a silk wrapper. Her long hair, fair like his own, was bound into a plait that hung over her shoulder. But it was her eyes, wide and red-rimmed, that halted him.

"How long have you been standing there?" he asked.

"Long enough to hear Father. And you. Garrett did not latch the door." She crossed her arms over her chest, her gaze direct. "What are you going to do?"

He pushed his fingers through his hair, still disheveled from the wild ride, and leaned against the small table in the hall. "I don't know."

"How bad could it be to talk to Mr. Darbin?" she reasoned.

"You do remember him, do you not? He was always a good sort. I am sure he would help us."

Jonathan nodded. Yes, he remembered Henry Darbin. The man had been Thomas's best friend, and the older Gilchrist son and his school chum could not have been more alike. That fact alone was a cause of Jonathan's reluctance to involve him.

His sister continued. "At least speak with him. We both know Father can be a bit dramatic at times. But if the ruby is gone, really gone, and Father refuses to inform the constable, then Mr. Darbin may be our only hope of ever seeing it again."

"Our only hope?" scoffed Jonathan. "You seem to forget, sister, that the loss of this ruby means nothing to me, other than the fact that I am sorry that someone has violated our home." He began to pace, rubbing his hand over the back of his neck. "This is what we have warned Father about for years, is it not? That his collecting and his choice to keep company with unsavory sorts can only lead to trouble."

"Do you not wish to secure a better future for yourself as well? I cannot pretend to understand how you can be content in that dark little apothecary's shop day in and day out. But if you will not consider it for your own sake, please then, at least consider it for mine."

When Jonathan did not respond, she cut her eyes toward Garrett to ensure he was not listening. "If you do not go handle this matter, then I fear that Father will try to travel to London himself. His health is declining. You know as well as I that the journey would not be good for him. And given how impatient he has grown, even if he did manage to track down the right people, he could make things much worse."

She reached to grip his arm. "Please, Jonathan. Please, for

me. If there is no dowry and I am unable to marry, and if Father really does lose Kettering Hall, what will become of me when Father dies?"

Penelope's lips formed a pout, but it was not her typical pout, set intentionally to get her way. No, genuine emotion welled within her.

He knew the dangers for a woman in Penelope's situation. At twenty-three, she was already approaching the upper limit of marriageable age. She was hardly a spinster, but how much longer would she be able to rely on her pretty face to attract suitors? Without a dowry, her chances of making an advantageous match would decline. She had her heart set on Mr. Dowden. Unfortunately, he surmised Mr. Dowden had his heart set on her dowry.

He clenched his jaw. How quickly, in the span of an hour, everything could change.

Penelope's eyes began to fill with tears. This, too, was in her bag of tricks—tears that she could initiate at a moment's notice. But he knew his sister better than anyone else in the world, and he believed the tears were genuine.

His resolve began to waver. Besides Penelope, he felt no steady connection to anyone in the world. She was the one thread that tied him securely to Kettering Hall. All other cords of attachment had frayed with time.

"Very well," he said reluctantly. "I was going to go to London in a few days' time anyway. I shall call on Mr. Darbin. But I will make no promises on the matter."

Chapter Four

*C*amille pinched the bridge of her nose, then pressed the palm of her hand against her eye.

Night was falling. No longer did the gray daylight reach in through the shop's wide front windows and illuminate the back wall. Instead, a single candle shed light on the leather-bound ledger in front of her. She lifted the brooch pinned to the bodice of her pale linen gown and angled it so she could see the small timepiece dangling from the silver clasp. There was still much to do before she could rest.

She dipped her quill in the inkwell and scratched it across the rough paper, carefully recording the numbers of the day's transactions.

She added them. But the numbers did not make sense.

She added them again in her head, then she wrote them out on a spare piece of paper. Still they did not balance.

With a frown, Camille resumed the task of finding the mistake.

For it had to be a mistake.

She oversaw the daily transactions personally. Indeed, she was the one who collected the money each day. That day she had sold the snuff grater, the Italian watercolor box, the Chinese tea box, and the bolt of Indian silk. She had traded for a set of dueling pistols. Those along with all the day's other sales should have amounted to more.

Sarah E. Ladd

The shop's one-eyed cat, Link, nudged her arm. Surprised at the touch, Camille jerked, and when she did, he jumped, unsettling the bottle of ink and nearly sending it to its side.

At the clatter, the curtain closing off the back room fluttered, and her father poked his head over the threshold. "What was that?"

"Oh, nothing," muttered Camille. She returned her quill to its holder and lifted the fat gray cat to the floor. "Link is merely attempting to assist me, 'tis all."

"That cat needs to be out of doors. I've said it before. It doesn't do to have him wandering about. This place is in enough of a disarray. Too many things could be broken."

Camille bit her lip at the reprimand. It felt as if he were blaming her for the disorder and the animals in the shop. She wanted to remind him that Link kept the cluttered store free of mice and that, even if she did shoo the cat away, he himself would only bring another into the store. But there was no reasoning with him.

He stepped through to the shop and started toward her, but then paused and whirled around. "Did you sell the Persian vases?"

Camille lifted her attention, the immediate need to defend her decision rushing to the front of her mind. "No, I moved them over there, by the wall. I only meant to make the shop tidier, Papa. It is nearly impossible for anyone to walk through."

He cursed under his breath. He hated when she moved his merchandise. He retrieved the vases and placed them back on the counter. "Did you ever read the letter from your mother?"

Camille looked down to the ledger. He had asked her about the letter daily since it arrived a week prior, yet it remained

24

unopened in the pocket of the apron she donned each day to protect her gown. "No."

"I don't understand your delay. Your mother took the time to write you; the least you can do is read what she wrote. Tsk. I never saw the like. Not answering her letters will cause a bigger rift than the one that is already there—mark my words."

She ignored his lecture. The last thing she wanted was another discussion about her mother. It was easiest to pretend the situation was nonexistent.

He stepped closer, the scent of brandy, tobacco, and the nearby forge accompanying him, and he plopped a small item wrapped in linen on the counter. "I want you to take this to Maxwell first thing in the morning. He is leaving for the continent in the next day or so. Instruct him to see this gets to your mother."

Camille sighed as she lifted the small package and held it up. "Another one? Papa, I don't think—"

"I didn't ask you what you thought about it," he snapped. "I told you to take it to Maxwell."

Camille shook her head, took the gift, and tucked it in the front pocket of her work apron along with the letter. Ever since her mother left London to go to Portugal nine years ago to care for her own ailing mother, her father had been anxious for her return. But weeks slid into months, and months swelled to years. Initially, her mother wrote promises of a quick return, but over time, the frequency and the warmth within the letters subsided. And yet, her father continued to write and send little gifts as if her return were imminent.

Camille wondered if the items her papa sent ever actually made it to her mother's hand, with the war and the sea travel. At first it had saddened her to see how her mother's selfish actions changed her father. But now his behavior was beginning to frustrate her.

She shook her head. "These trinkets you send her will not bring her back."

Her father ignored her and bent to scratch Tevy's ears.

Camille stepped out from behind the counter. "How can you be certain it will even reach her?"

James Iverness reached to snatch his hat from a hook by the door. "Just do as I say."

Camille drew a sharp breath. Her mother was the one topic that had the power to drive a wedge even deeper into her and Papa's strained relationship.

Instead of arguing, she nodded to the garments in his hand. "It's going to rain. Where are you going?"

"To the docks. Shipment from Africa came in today, and I want to make my offers before the goods are sent to the auction house."

She looked to the dark sky out the window. "When will you be back?"

"When I've finished my business. Tevy's coming with me."

"What?" Camille looked at the dog, who sat calmly at his master's feet. "Usually you leave him with me."

"Can't be helped, I've important business to tend to, and I need the dog for protection." He reached for his coat and pushed his arm through the sleeve.

She jumped up from the chair, eying the muscular dog. "You know how raucous the street can get at night. I would feel safer if Tevy stayed here."

"I told you I need him. That's the end of the matter."

Tevy followed Papa through the door, his tail thudding

against the thick door frame. The door banged shut, and she was alone.

Link nudged her elbow again, seeking attention, and she gathered him under her arm. His rhythmic purring filled the silent room, and she ran a hand over his warm fur.

On the street outside, a crash and an angry shout gave her reason to jump. She lit another candle and looked to the shop's only working clock, which shared a cluttered shelf with a stack of leather-bound books, a silver tea set, and a jar of old keys. A long evening stretched before her—a long, lonely evening. Or perhaps more, as her father's excursions had been known to last through the night and sometimes for days on end.

She sighed and scratched Link under the chin. "Looks like it is just you and me, old man."

Chapter Five

*D*rizzle floated down, sinister and dirty. Cold drops splatted on Jonathan's greatcoat, his cheeks, his eyelashes. He didn't bother to wipe them away, but only tipped his hat lower over his brow. With every step, muck and mire splashed from the grimy surface of Blinkett Street, marring his riding boots and dampening his buckskin breeches.

He and Henry Darbin had been here for more than an hour—watching, waiting. When they first arrived on the crooked street, people had bustled to and fro, lending a sense of security, but as evening's mist cloaked the scene, an unease— and a distinct chill—had crept in. Darkness now shielded the passing faces. The haphazard glow of orange torchlight had replaced the sun's gray glow, reflecting from the wet cobblestones like splinters of broken mirror. The onset of music from a nearby public house compounded the bedlam, and streaks of lightning raced across the sky in broken ribbons, threatening to bring more weather.

Jonathan did not want any part of traveling to this notoriously deviant section of London's south side, but his eagerness to put the business of the ruby behind him overpowered his present discomfort. Almost a week had passed since the gem was stolen, and it had been just a day since Jonathan arrived at Darbin's dingy quarters in London to explain the situation. He should be pleased, for already Darbin claimed to have a sense of where the ruby was and how to retrieve it.

"You were right to come to me when you did, Gilchrist. I've helped dozens of theft victims recover stolen goods—so many, to be honest, that I have stopped counting." Darbin stated his opinion as if it were fact as he leaned against a stone wall, fiddling with the latch on his silver snuffbox. "It is clear you doubt my abilities, but I speak the truth."

"That remains to be seen, does it not?" Jonathan adjusted his collar and glanced at two questionable characters as they passed. "The way I see it, a great many things must come to pass for us to have the Bevoy back in our possession."

Darbin wiped a smudge from the little box and held it up to catch the weak light. "So cynical. Your brother would have seen this excursion as an adventure."

Jonathan did not want to speak about Thomas to anyone, let alone to his brother's best friend. "Not cynical. Just practical."

Darbin returned the box to his coat before fixing his gaze on the street before him. "I do wish your father had changed his mind and accompanied you and your sister to London. Now, there's a man always up for a rally of any sort. How fortunate you are to come from such a family. I come from a family of women. Six sisters. Six, I tell you." He smirked as he adjusted a leather glove. "No adventure there whatsoever, save for the occasional hunt for the perfect length of ribbon or an ostrich feather to adorn a bonnet."

Jonathan had no interest in learning about Darbin's family. He changed the subject. "Are you sure this is the right place?"

"I'm sure. I know these streets like the back of my hand."

Darbin pushed himself off the wall and strolled along the

street as confidently as if he owned the businesses flanking each side. He motioned for Jonathan to follow. "Best for you not to make eye contact with anyone. You're the spitting image of your brother, with those smart clothes and golden locks. We don't need anyone asking questions or, worse, starting the rumor that old Thomas Gilchrist has come back from the grave."

Jonathan fixed his gaze on the shadows in front of him, but he did not divert his eyes from those they passed. Even in death, his brother's ability to dominate taunted him. He would not keep his eyes down, nor would he adjust his hat to further cover his hair. He was here for one task, to find the ruby. And if his presence incited conversation that his brother had returned from the grave, what did he care?

Jonathan had known Darbin most of his life. He and Thomas had gone to school together from the time they were boys. Darbin's family was from the far north of England, and since Kettering Hall was much closer to the school, Darbin had often accompanied Thomas home for breaks. He had quickly become a favorite of their father's, his lust for adventure complementing that of Ian and Thomas Gilchrist. After Thomas's death, Darbin's visits to Kettering Hall had ceased. He had called once to offer condolences, but Father, in his grief, had refused visitors. After that, there had been no reason for Darbin to be invited back into their lives.

Until now.

Darbin's intention, like Thomas's, had been to study the law, but his desire for more exciting—and profitable—pursuits had moved him in another direction. He now acted in a private capacity to investigate difficulties that the overtaxed military and local constabularies were unable to handle. At Penelope's urging, Jonathan had visited Darbin in the days following the robbery. And just the previous morning, Jonathan had received notice that Darbin had uncovered information regarding the Bevoy and requested that Jonathan accompany him on the recovery.

Darbin's crooked smile cracked. "You aren't getting nervous, are you?"

Jonathan squinted, and from the corner of his eye he watched a lady of the night entice an intoxicated man. Nervous? He rarely felt nervous. But was he uncomfortable? Yes.

Of course he regretted the decision to come. What did he know about recovering a stolen anything?

Now Jonathan teetered on the edge of this precarious world, uncertain how to function within it. The boy within him was eager for his father's approval, for a nod of acceptance and confirmation, but the reasonable man in him knew the dangers of such an environment. And yet he could not turn back.

"Not nervous." Jonathan muttered his response after a long pause. "Just not accustomed to such pursuits."

Darbin's hearty laugh echoed from the crumbling facades that lined the street. "Of course you're not nervous. You've got the same blood flowing through your veins as your brother. Never saw a more fearless man, God rest his soul. Mark my words, Gilchrist. We'll find your father's trinket and the man who nabbed it."

Jonathan winced as Darbin's laugh sliced the night. "Do you not think it wise to be more discreet? We are trying to go unnoticed, not send him our calling card."

"You are wound far too tight." Darbin's heavy hand slapped Jonathan's back, the smacking sound intensified by the wetness of his coat. "Don't forget, I know these parts well. Leave the worrying to me."

They continued down the narrow street with its sharp juts and uneven surface. The scent of dung and smoke thickened, mingling with the damp mist settling around them. Jonathan sidestepped a man lying on the road and considered pausing to offer assistance, but Darbin reached out his arm, stopping Jonathan in his tracks.

"There. That's the shop—right there."

Jonathan's gaze followed Darbin's nod, and then he frowned as he assessed the shabby storefront with its dirty paned windows. A faded sign hung askew from the shabby shutters, with the words "Curiosity Shop" barely visible.

"Your father purchased the Bevoy several years ago from the man who owns that shop. It was a quiet transaction, no doubt. Every thief worth his weight knows of the Bevoy, so 'tis best for the owner to keep quiet about its whereabouts. From the moment you told me it was the Bevoy that had been stolen, I had a suspicion James Iverness was involved."

"How can you be sure?" Jonathan breathed, unable to take his eyes from the odd little shop. "If he sold the ruby to my father, it doesn't stand to reason that he would steal it back."

"Ah! That is where you are wrong. It does stand to reason. You have to think like a criminal." Darbin tapped his finger against his head. "Iverness is a crafty fellow, and he knows your father—his habits, his collection. More important, he knew your father had the Bevoy. Undoubtedly its location has been shrouded in secrecy for years to all but your father and Iverness. And Iverness is in a perfect position to resell the gem at a profit. No one would be the wiser."

Jonathan assessed the tiny shop in question. "From the looks of his shop, it does not appear he's overly concerned with acquiring wealth."

"That's the way he operates. Rumor has it that he is one of the richest merchants on this side of town, but you would never know it to look at this place. Keeps a low profile, this one."

"I trust you have more reason to suspect this man than merely a hunch?"

"I do. I have an informant who works in the auction houses, keeps me apprised of the traffic through there. There's been a man inquiring about gems recently—McCready is his name—and apparently he has inquired specifically about the Bevoy. Word is out that McCready intends to purchase the Bevoy at this location tonight."

Jonathan felt optimism flare within him. Perhaps it was good they had engaged Darbin's help after all; the man seemed to have everything figured out. Eager to put this whole mess behind him, he rubbed his own gloved hands together. "So what do we do now?"

"We wait." Darbin's steps slowed, then stopped. "Sometimes these sorts of situations pan out. Sometimes they don't. Patience is key. But I am not about to let him slip through my fingers."

They stood in silence for several moments. Then, as if on cue, a young woman appeared, a crooked broom in hand. She flitted over the threshold, her light-colored skirt swishing through the doorway, shadows muting her features. She brushed her hair away from her face before propping her free hand on her hip.

Jonathan watched her sweep off the front stoop. "Who is that?"

"That's his daughter."

"Iverness's daughter?"

"Yes. She helps him in the shop. Has for years."

The news took Jonathan aback. He had not considered that the man might have a family. "Do you think she knows about the Bevoy?"

"Hard to say, but unlikely. From what we can tell, Iverness operates alone, though he has extensive connections. We must be careful. He's a sneaky devil."

The young woman, petite and slender, paused in her task and looked up at the sky, shielding her eyes with her hand. She wiped her face and patted her uncovered hair before returning inside.

Jonathan smoothed his wayward neckcloth back into place. He couldn't shake the eerie sensation that tonight was a turning point, regardless of whether or not they recovered the ruby.

If he and Darbin failed, Kettering Hall—and his family's entire fortune—might be lost forever.

If they succeeded, he would surely be plunged ever deeper into his father's mysterious involvements.

And he couldn't tell which he dreaded most.

Chapter Six

amille jerked her head up as the sharp crack of a breaking bottle echoed off the cobbled street near the shop's entrance. Then a shrill yell, followed by boisterous laughter.

Would she never cease to jump at the sudden noises of Blinkett Street at night? After almost ten years, she doubted it. After darkness fell, the cadence of shouts and music from the tavern across the street felt like an assault. Of course, the commotion could be heard from the rooms she and her father occupied above the shop, but downstairs the sounds seemed more threatening, the danger more real.

She lifted her eyes. Silhouettes of men with uneven gaits blackened the window.

Her heart pounded, and she shook her head. The noise—and uncertainty—made her lose count. She returned her attention to the money box in front of her and started counting afresh.

How she wished Tevy were here by her side. Gentle as he was with her, his growl alone would halt an intruder in his tracks. But he was with her father, and there was no way to tell when they would return.

She looked up and let her eyes rest on the painting she had propped nearby, drawing hope from the pastoral scene it depicted. One day she would leave Blinkett Street, escape the sullied streets of London, and return to the tranquil countryside of her childhood. She had no intention of spending her life in this dreary shop. But now was not the proper time. Her father needed her. They might not be close, but he was all she had—apart from a mother who had all but abandoned her.

She took the key to the money box from the string around her neck, locked the box, and reached for her shawl. Her candle, burned nearly to a stub, cast long, flickering shadows on the walls of the shop and its scattered contents. She paused to note how it reflected off the sharp beak of a stuffed raven.

In the back corner of the shop, a narrow staircase led to the three upper rooms—a small parlor, her bedchamber, and Papa's chamber. Meals were always taken in the back of the shop, where the large fireplace afforded a place for cooking. Normally she ate alone. The fire had waned to nothing more than flickering embers, and the room's only light came from her candle. She inched her way around the long, uneven table, scooted the wobbly wooden chair to the side, and lifted the lid from a pot of stew. No warmth radiated from it. The scent wafted flat.

She returned the lid to its place, reached for a bit of bread, and took a bite of it as she headed toward the stairs. But as she did, a sound at the front of the shop commandeered her interest. Someone was fumbling with the door lock.

Papa.

He had a key, of course. But his state of mind on such evenings often made even simple tasks troublesome.

She put her candle to the side, clutched her shawl about her, and hurried to the door. She unlatched and opened it, just as she had a hundred times before. Then her breath caught.

The man was not her father. A stranger was trying to enter. She slammed her weight against the door, pushing with all her might to close it against the intruder and latch it again. But she was too late. The trespasser stuck his thick boot against the door frame, prohibiting the door from closing.

Moments slowed. Then sped. Camille's heart pounded and her vision blurred. She wanted to say something, she wanted to cry out, but her mouth was too dry.

She charged the door again, scrambling for control, but he grabbed it with a gloved hand and pushed against her, her strength no match for his.

He forced his way in the shop, bringing with him the wet and cold of night, the flickering torches on the street pushing his shadow before him.

Camille retreated, stumbling backward against the shelves of writing kits and silver services. Now that he was in, she wanted as much distance as possible.

"We are closed." Her voice sounded impossibly small.

The intruder smiled too confidently, his teeth stark white against the dark angles of his broad face. "Pardon the interruption, Miss. I've no wish to impose, but I'm looking for James Iverness."

His mock formality alarmed her further. Surely this intruder could hear her heart thumping within.

Calm. She had to stay calm. "He is not available."

He inched closer, slow and steady, like a fox stalking prey. His dark eyes flashed from right to left as if searching. As he approached, the hem of his long cape dragged against a low-lying shelf, clanking the glass bottles into one another and threatening to overturn them.

"Not available?" he repeated. "I would never accuse such a lovely creature as you of lying, but you don't really expect me to believe that, do you?"

She shook her head. Every bit of space that closed between them incited panic. "I swear to you, I do not know where he is. Y-you must leave."

He stopped an arm's length away from her. The candle behind her cast odd shadows on his whiskered face, and the scent of old brandy and tobacco encircled her. She wanted to look away from the wide-set, beady eyes that held her gaze captive. But fear, or perhaps disbelief, forbade her to look away.

"Show me where it is"—his thin lips curled in a sneer—"and I'll be on my way."

Tears pooled in her eyes, but she raised her chin. She would not show fear. She could not. She forced every ounce of her energy into keeping her voice level. "What is it you are looking for?"

"The Bevoy."

She continued to creep backward. The edge of the counter pressed into her hip. The heat of the candle sitting atop it warmed her back. "I do not know what that is."

The man picked up a jar from the table next to him and rolled it in his hands. "Well, that is a problem. For I have already paid half of what I owe on it, with the understanding that I would pay the rest when I return. Iverness was to meet me here. He's not here, but you are. And I want the Bevoy."

She swallowed hard. "If you would just come back at another time, I am sure my father would—"

Before she could finish, the man dropped the jar in his hand to the planked floor, shattering it into a thousand tiny shards.

Camille jumped at the sound and let out a little cry.

Then the man's massive arm reached toward her.

She did not think; she only acted. Reaching behind her,

she seized the candleholder and flung the lit candle toward her intruder. The light immediately extinguished, but the hot tallow landed on his face and neck. He howled in pain and spewed profanities, distracted long enough for Camille to twist around.

Behind her on a shelf was a stack of timeworn swords of every shape and length. She had no idea whether they were sharp or not. But she needed something, anything, to give the impression that she was capable of defending herself.

They were in mostly darkness now, the shop lit only by the flickering glow of street torches outside and the candle lamp next to the stairs. She had the advantage. She was familiar with the layout of this disheveled space. One wrong turn, and her perpetrator would send a pile of artifacts cluttering to the ground.

But her sense of confidence was short-lived. The man shook his head, and the weak candle lamp revealed that all trace of his smile was gone. He pushed the back of his hand across his face. "I had hoped we would be able to find some sort of middle ground, but since you are unwilling to cooperate—"

Camille's breath caught in her throat as the man reached into his coat and produced a blade. The candlelight caught on the bright metal and shot slivers of light into the air. Camille gasped, the air around her inadequate to supply her lungs. The sword in her hand felt impossibly awkward and heavy. She hadn't the first idea of what to do with it, especially when standing eye to eye with a man twice her size and double her strength.

She gripped the sword's handle so tightly that her fingers numbed and she adjusted her stance, holding the weapon before her. But in two fast steps he closed the space between them. His huge, gloved hand snatched her arm, and the sword clattered to the ground.

She whimpered as he yanked her closer, his strong fingers squeezing the soft flesh of her arm. She jerked and attempted to pull free, but the more she strained, the harder he tugged. Then he pulled her close, tightening his forearm around her shoulders and forcing her back against his chest, the blade before her face.

At the sight of the blade so close, she shrieked. Panic bubbled within her, fresh and hot. She wanted to look around, to search for an escape, but her eyes seemed fixed to the blade. "Please . . . please let me go."

"Now perhaps you take my questions a bit more seriously."

She could feel the muscles of his chest flex against her back. She was acutely aware of every sensation—the pinch of his hand on her shoulder, the heat of his breath, the spicy scent of brandy.

She swallowed, attempting to control her trembling. "Take whatever you want. Just please leave me be."

"Your father owes me. And I will get what is owed, one way or the other." He shifted the blade.

"I-I don't know anything about any jewel. Please, I promise you—"

"I saw him come in here earlier. Do not lie to me." His voice dripped with mock formality. "You'll regret it."

The idea that this stranger had been watching her shop sent icy shivers down her spine. She did not doubt the sincerity of his promise.

Then she heard a familiar squeak—the sound of wood against wood and the ancient door hinge giving way.

Chapter Seven ————————————————

Several hours had passed since Jonathan and Henry Darbin arrived at Blinkett Street. A misty veil still shrouded the neighborhood, and the rain continued to fall. By now it had seeped through his coat and chilled his skin.

And yet they continued to wait.

Earlier that evening, Iverness had entered the shop, and for a moment they had thought the exchange was imminent. But then, not long afterward, he had left with a big dog by his side.

Jonathan and Darbin were about to abandon their quest, assuming their information had been incorrect. But then they saw him—a tall, broad-shouldered man, alone, and concealed under a dark cape.

"There!" Darbin's tone sharpened and he shifted his position, turning his back to the shop. "Do you see him? That's McCready, there in the cape."

Jonathan nodded, careful not to make any motion or movement that might attract attention. "Yes, I see him."

They watched the man from their location across the street as he stopped before the shop's main entrance. The shadows hid the actions, but after several moments the door seemed to open. The man disappeared inside.

"Let's go." Darbin took several steps forward.

"Wait." Jonathan grabbed him by the arm. "What are you doing?"

"We are going to go get your ruby."

"You mean just walk in and ask him politely?" Jonathan made no attempt to hide his sarcasm.

"No. We are going to take it." Darbin pulled a knife from his belt and thrust it in Jonathan's hands. "You might need this."

Dumbstruck, Jonathan took the knife.

"Think you can handle that?" Darbin raised an eyebrow.

Jonathan swallowed. "Of course I can."

"I know you Gilchrists prefer to arm yourselves with pistols. Your brother was the best shot I ever saw." Darbin chuckled. "But I don't suppose a man in your profession has much to do with firearms, eh?"

Jonathan stiffened. When he did not respond, Darbin nodded to the knife. "Tuck it somewhere safe, out of sight."

Jonathan stared at the weapon in his hands. The sensation of danger throbbed fresh within him. The idea of using a knife as a weapon flew in the face of everything he believed in. He was a healer, or at least that was what he tried to do. He could not use a weapon against another man.

Or could he?

Darbin retrieved a pistol from his coat and tucked it in his breeches, oblivious to Jonathan's concerns. "Come on, then. Don't just stand there like a lump when there is a task at hand."

Jonathan opened his mouth to protest. Then a strange energy surge through him. Now was the one time he needed to step away from what was comfortable. He slid the blade into his boot.

Jonathan hurried to keep pace with Darbin as they crossed

Blinkett, ignoring the filth splashing up from the cobbled street with each step.

Darbin stopped just to the right of the shop's window, his back against the stone wall. Jonathan pressed in beside him.

But then, as they stood there, the sound of breaking glass echoed from the confines of the shop, followed by a scream.

Jonathan jumped. He had almost forgotten about the young woman he had seen earlier in the evening. They had seen Iverness leave the shop, but no one else, so the woman had to still be inside.

Another loud cry from within, followed by a stream of threatening obscenities. What was going on in that shop?

Jonathan started for the door, but Darbin grabbed his arm. "What are you doing?"

"Do you hear that woman?"

"Yes, but be patient," Darbin whispered.

Another shriek sliced the air.

Jonathan turned to his side, just enough to look through the dirty windows. Dim candlelight showed a large, shadowy figure grappling with a woman of much smaller stature.

A fire lit in his belly. He could not just stand here waiting, pretending he did not see. He stepped around Darbin and headed for the door.

"What in blazes are you doing?" Darbin hissed, his face twisting with frustration.

Jonathan did not respond.

"Don't be a fool!" warned Darbin. "You'll ruin everything."

Jonathan hesitated. "But surely she's no match for him. We must do something."

"Camille Iverness can take care of herself. Interrupt now,

and McCready will know we are on to him. Do you want your ruby back or not? We must act rationally."

"I am." Jonathan bent to pull the blade from his boot, then reached for the door handle.

Camille drew a sharp breath as the door burst open. Her attacker noticed the sound as well. His grip slackened slightly as he looked toward the front of the store.

Camille seized the moment.

She held her breath and pushed her arm out with all her might. The distraction allowed her just enough room to duck out of the man's grasp. She threw her weight forward, slamming into a cluttered table. The din of glass shattering and metal objects clanking against the floor was almost drowned by loud male voices.

She didn't even try to listen to what they said. She had to get out.

Someone grabbed her arm from behind. She was trapped, pinned by the table and the darkness. She glanced toward the door. The sight of two shadowed figures fueled her fear and ignited her strength.

Then she heard a pistol cock.

She jerked and twisted, trying to wrench herself free, and then pain, hot and searing, sliced into her other arm, just above her elbow. The pain blurred her vision. Had she been shot? Cut with the knife? She couldn't tell. She had never felt either. The only thing that mattered now was breaking free and getting to safety.

She grabbed a metal candlestick and hurled it behind her. A thud and a grunt told her it had hit its mark, and then she was free. She grabbed her arm as she lunged away from her attacker. The sleeve felt sticky. Wet.

She knocked more items from another table to make it even more difficult to be followed.

Memory of the store's layout guided her through the darkness and toward the back room. But with each step she felt less steady and the pain increased. She pulled the curtain aside and stumbled through the space until she fell against the back door, the knob jamming into her side. A little light filtered in through the small back window. Only a few more steps and she would be free.

Chapter Eight

Camille's legs wouldn't move quickly enough. She felt as if she were running in quicksand, as if the shop's floor was grabbing her ankles and refusing to allow her passage. Pain still seared her arm, and the warm, sticky wetness had covered her palm. She pressed her other hand hard against the wound. She dared not stop to tend it now.

Behind her, the shouts and crashing noises continued. Blood pounded in her head, crying out a warning cadence. Then the sound of footsteps filled the dark room behind her, echoing a threat with each footfall.

A cry escaped her lips, whether from the pain or the fear she did not know. She fumbled with the doorknob, but her sticky hand slipped on the cold metal. Frantic, she jerked and twisted it with both hands until it finally gave way.

Night air, damp and thick, rushed her, filling her lungs. She lurched from the doorway. Rain pummeled, confusing her senses all the more. The tiny walled courtyard behind the shop, which should have seemed so familiar, loomed alien and sinister.

"Wait, wait!"

She did not look back to see who called to her. She lifted her skirt and ran toward the gate that led to the alley. A battered crate blocked her way. She tried to push it aside, but someone grabbed her arm again, pulling her backward.

Infused with sheer terror, Camille flailed and fought, desperate to free herself from the strong hands that held her.

"Stop." The voice was calm and deep. "I'll not hurt you."

She heard the words, but the meaning did not penetrate her alarm. She flung her fists at the man, beating with all the strength her frame could muster. But the more she fought, the stronger he seemed to become, and the more she despaired of escape.

Only as her fortitude and breath waned did she begin to realize that this man's voice was different from that of the stranger with the blade.

She ventured a glance and saw a broad-shouldered man with a white neckcloth. Light hair. No cape.

It was not the same man.

But who was it?

Chest heaving, her lungs starved for air, Camille slowed her movements. Still he did not fight her.

When she was certain she could speak, she dug deep for her customary bravado. She had to sound confident, in control. "Let go of me."

The stranger complied, holding his gloved hands up as if proclaiming innocence. "I am here to help." He glanced behind him at the gaping back door of the shop. "He is gone. At least I think he is."

Camille looked to the door. All was quiet save for her gulps for air. No more shouts. No more breaking glass.

Relief rushed her, but she could not relax. She trusted no one—especially someone who would be on Blinkett Street after dusk.

"Who are you?" she gasped.

"Jonathan Gilchrist." The man's voice was soft. Soothing. "But your arm. It must be tended to."

She looked down at her limb as if the injury was an after-thought. The moonlight was faint, but even in the dim glow it afforded, she could see the dark stain on her sleeve. On her hand.

A different kind of panic rushed her as the stain registered.

Blood.

Her blood.

The arm began to shake uncontrollably.

As if sensing her trepidation, he reached for it, his move-ment slow. But she snatched her hand back. "Leave me."

"I can help," he offered. "I am an apothecary."

She looked up at his shadowed face, several inches above her own.

He was too close. She stepped back but continued to stare, trying to make out his features, as if by doing so she could in some way judge his trustworthiness.

But her injury would not wait. Each heartbeat thrust fresh pain through her arm. Her chest grew hot, her head light. She could feel the blood dripping from her fingers. She needed help, and where else would she find it on Blinkett Street now that night had fallen?

She bit her lower lip and, fighting reluctance, extended her arm toward him.

At her motion, the man snapped into action. He pulled the torn sleeve away from the wound with a gentle touch and angled her arm to try to see it better in the moonlight. But then he shook his head. "It's too dark here."

Pulling off his neckcloth, he pressed it against the wound

and wrapped it tight. Camille winced in pain, trying to fight back the tears that welled with each movement.

"I know it hurts," he said, "but this will help slow the bleeding."

She nodded in the darkness.

"Come with me," he continued, tying off the knot. "We must get you out of here and to somewhere we can tend it properly."

Camille stiffened. She couldn't leave the shop—and with a man she did not know? The very thought was foreign.

But the next thought came with equal fervor: *Why would I stay?*

Her life had been threatened. Her father had left her alone—again—to pursue one of his clandestine business arrangements. He'd invited the murderous stranger to their door and not bothered to meet the man there. He'd even taken Tevy, her one defense against anyone stronger than her. Why should she risk her life to stay and guard his treasures?

"Where will we go?" she asked.

"Is there somewhere safe I can take you—a friend or family member, perhaps?" When she didn't respond, he spoke. "I'll take you to my family's house here in London. My sister is there, she will be able to help."

But Camille hesitated, tied to the shop in spite of herself. "I cannot go. This is my shop, this is my—"

Urgency heightened his voice. "Miss, I don't know if that man is coming back. But I would advise you not be here if he does."

"But my father—"

"Your father is not here. And I cannot, will not, leave you here alone."

She tried to process his words, to figure out a sensible plan, but her brain felt foggy. The thoughts running through her head did not seem to make sense.

She could not leave. The door was open. Things were broken. She needed to be there when her father came home.

But that might not be until morning.

Her head spun.

"It isn't far," he was saying. "And I have a carriage waiting a few streets over. Can you walk?"

She should protest. She should try to find her way to safety—wherever it was that safety lay. Or she should go back inside, lock the door, secure the money box . . .

Another crash echoed from inside.

She jumped in fear, alarm coursing through every vein in her body.

He held his finger to his lips and nodded toward the alley gate.

Chapter Nine

$\mathcal{J}$onathan offered the young woman his arm, and Miss Iverness laid a paper-light hand on his sleeve. Her wet hair clung to the curves of her face, and the stark white make-shift bandage seemed to glow in the murky darkness. He winced to see that blood was already seeping through.

It was not so much the sight of her blood that affected him. He had tended far more grievous injuries. But knowing his actions might have played a role in her injury tore at him. Darbin had warned him about acting brashly—and he had done just that.

He held his finger to his lips to signal her silence. The last thing they needed was to attract attention. She nodded, then looked straight ahead.

He guided her across the courtyard, assisting her as she stepped over the crate. The gate at the end opened to a narrow alley. Leaning out to look, he realized it led to Blinkett Street. He listened for further sounds of trouble, but no angry shouts met his ears, no pounding of boots on the cobbled surface— only the music from the public house and the occasional bout of laughter.

As they emerged from the alley onto Blinkett, Jonathan peered back down the street, squinting to make out figures in the deepening mist.

Where was Darbin?

After the initial confusion in the tiny shop, Darbin had chased after McCready, and Jonathan had followed Miss Iverness. He could only guess as to Darbin's whereabouts now.

The woman's hand trembled on his arm. Her lower lip was quivering. She was injured and no doubt frightened. She leaned against him, heavy now. Ruby or no, he could not abandon her. He would have to catch up with Darbin at another time.

"Where is your father's house?" Her voice was barely more than a whisper.

"Chire Street. The carriage is this way."

They walked along the lamp-lit street. Jonathan blinked as rain ran down his face. His hat had been lost somewhere in the skirmish, and the drops clung to his hair and dripped down his neck.

They continued in silence, until he noticed that her steps had started to slow. She swayed toward him. He held out his hand to steady her. "Are you all right?"

She did not answer him. Her steps started to swerve.

"Miss Iverness, can you answer me?"

She stopped and turned as if confused. She looked up at him and opened her mouth, but then she started to collapse before she could say a word.

He caught her as she fell. Quickly he swept her up in his arms, her wet skirts twisting around him, her head rolling against his shoulder.

"Miss Iverness," he breathed. "Miss Iverness!"

But her head fell forward unresponsive, locks of black hair clinging to her face.

He had to get her somewhere safe and out of the night air. Out of the danger.

He looked around to see if anyone had noticed, but the men lining the street paid little heed—as if the occurrence was so commonplace it was not worthy of breaking a stride.

Jonathan carried her the two blocks to the carriage. He lifted her inside, then signaled to the driver to pull out. As he had apprised Miss Iverness, the drive was quite short. It was unsettling, in fact, to realize how close unsavory Blinkett Street was to the more fashionable London neighborhoods.

Miss Iverness was still unresponsive when they arrived at his father's London address. Not wanting to attract attention, Jonathan did not call for assistance, but carried her from the carriage to the door himself. Upon realizing the door had been bolted for the night, he used the toe of his boot to knock.

At length Winston, the butler who oversaw the London home, answered the door. He opened it cautiously at first, but when he saw Jonathan with Miss Iverness, he flung it open fully, his eyes wide.

"Shh," Jonathan whispered to the butler, quickly scanning the interior rooms. "Is anyone awake?"

"No, sir. The staff has all retired for the night, as has Miss Gilchrist. I was waiting up for your return."

"Good," replied Jonathan. The last thing he needed was talk among the servants. "Wake Meeks, but no one else. Ask her to wake up my sister, then prepare tea and bring it as soon as she is able. But first I need you to help me."

The old butler nodded, his expression concerned.

Jonathan carried Miss Iverness to the parlor and reclined her on the sofa. He stood, breath heavy from the exertion. "Light those candles before you leave, will you? Then will you see to the fire and find something to cover the young lady? She might have caught a chill."

"Very good, sir."

The butler set about stoking the fire, bringing the room from cool darkness to a much warmer glow. Jonathan hurried to the study to retrieve his apothecary's box. He rarely went anywhere without it. He returned to the parlor and knelt next to the sofa. Miss Iverness's head rested against the sofa's arm. Her eyes were closed. Black lashes fanned her cheeks, and her pale lips were slightly parted.

He lifted her limp hand, taking note of the ink on her fingers. He felt her pulse and then untied the neckcloth from her arm, gently pulling the fabric away from the wound to expose a nasty gash.

At this she groaned, and her eyes fluttered, but she did not wake. The thick lashes closed over her cheeks once again, and he set quickly to the task of cleaning the wound.

By this light, the extent of the cut was clearer. It was deep, but she would recover. No doubt her fainting spell was due more to heightened emotion than to the severity of the wound. He quickly mixed powder and spread it on the wound, then reached to the bottom of a drawer in his box for clean bandages and rewrapped it.

He made quick work of the task, and by the time he had completed it he heard the shuffle of slippers, hurried and anxious, on the planked floor. He recognized Penelope's footsteps before he even saw her.

He scratched his head and ran his hand over his face. Nothing about this night had gone as planned, and the last thing he felt like was the lecture from his sister that was sure to come. Thomas may have been able to take such events in stride, but Jonathan was certain he would never develop a taste for the adventure, as Darbin had put it.

But like it or not, adventure had found him, and Penelope would not be happy about the outcome. He gritted his teeth as the parlor door opened. His sister appeared with the force of a gale, her night robe billowing behind her, her light hair fluttering, loose and untethered.

Her steps slowed as her gaze fell on the woman on the sofa. "What is this?"

"There was an accident," he said, not knowing where to start.

"She's covered in blood," Penelope's voice shrilled. "Just look at her arm."

"She will be all right." He said it as much to convince himself as Penelope. "The wound will heal."

"But where did she come from?"

"Blinkett Street."

"And where is Blinkett Street?" His sister's voice continued to climb octaves. "I thought you were going to get the ruby?"

"Darbin and I went to Blinkett Street to recover the ruby. But then, well, there were complications."

She fixed her deep blue eyes on his as if waiting for a more complete explanation. A muscle in her lip twitched, and he was uncertain if she was going to yell or cry.

She finally spoke. "Complications?" She began to pace. "No,

no. A complication is an unexpected guest for a dinner party. This is a . . . disaster. The woman is bleeding, Jonathan. Bleeding. And her gown is soaked."

"Please, keep your voice down."

"Who is she?" Penelope demanded.

"Miss Iverness. She is the daughter of a shop owner. We—"

"You weren't the one who harmed her, were you?"

"Egad, Penelope. Do you really think I am capable of something like this?"

"Well, what am I supposed to think? I certainly never, in my wildest dreams, would have ever thought that my fine, upstanding brother would bring a woman like this to our home in the dark of night."

He drew a deep breath and blew it out before trying again to explain. "Darbin and I were attempting to recover the ruby. We found our man and thought it was going to change hands at her father's shop. But apparently the scoundrel attempted to rob her . . . or worse. He assaulted her with a knife."

She folded her arms across her chest. "And where is Mr. Darbin now?"

Jonathan looked back to Miss Iverness's still form. "I am not certain. We were separated."

"Well this is splendid, just splendid. Did anyone see you bring her here?"

"What difference does it make?"

"It makes a great deal of difference," she hurled back at him. "Our family's name is already in shambles. The last thing we need is a scandal connecting you to some shopgirl who accompanies you to our home in the dark of night."

"You are making much more out of this than the situation

warrants. Trust me. My interaction with a young lady is the least of our worries."

"You are being very cavalier about this."

He looked to the door to make sure their conversation had not woken any of the staff. "It would help if you would not become overwrought. The evening has been trying enough."

"Overwrought?" she squeaked. "Overwrought? My brother brings a woman, unconscious and covered in blood, into my parlor and then tells me not to become overwrought? For all we know, she could be involved in this theft, and you invite her to our home."

"As I explained, this young woman was being held at knifepoint when we arrived, and then she was injured. I don't care who she is or what role she has in this situation, I could not leave a woman in peril."

"What about me? Am I now not a woman in peril?" His sister's expression immediately turned to a pretty pout, a practiced expression she could call upon at any time. "I was already the object of stares from the women at dinner at the Dowdens' house tonight. Miss Marbury, who as you know is my most trusted friend and would never intentionally hurt me, informed me that our family was the unfortunate topic of conversation at tea the other day. If news of this should fully come to light, I stand to lose my fiancé. My friends. My entire future is at stake."

"I do think you are exaggerating."

"Am I? And did you consider whether or not whoever did this followed you here? Do you even consider our safety?" Penelope's attention focused. "And what do we do with this Miss Iverness in the meantime?"

Jonathan ignored the onslaught of questions and focused on the last one. "We will put her in a guestroom for the night."

"A guest in our home?" Penelope fiercely shook her head from side to side. "No, Jonathan. No, no, no."

"I insist." He'd seen the fear in Miss Iverness's eyes. Heard the desperation in her voice. Even felt the force of her terror when she fought against him in the courtyard. And his actions had no doubt contributed to her plight. He was responsible now. He could not turn away. "She is in no condition to leave."

Penelope's jaw clenched, and her eyes narrowed. "I will not have a shopkeeper's daughter under the same—"

"Enough." Jonathan had to put a stop to this. "She will stay here until she is well, I don't care if she is a pauper or a duchess. And I expect you to be civil to her. She is a guest in our home, and you will treat her as such."

Penelope diverted her eyes. Jonathan was well acquainted with her tendencies. His sister possessed a kind soul, but her concern for the opinion of others had the tendency to influence her treatment of others.

"Of course I will be civil, Jonathan," she huffed, obviously offended. "I am not a monster. I would hate to see another woman in danger of any kind. But Father will be furious."

"Father is not here."

"He will find out. And what of the servants?" She tightened her robe around her. "There will be talk."

"We shall tell them a friend of yours is visiting. They will not ask questions."

"I doubt they will believe it." Penelope stuck her nose in the air, reminding Jonathan of when she was ten years of age. "If you and I are to have any future at all, we had best find out what we can about the ruby. For without it, I have no dowry, and you have no estate."

Chapter Ten

Several moments later, Camille came to consciousness with a start.

A strong ammonia scent wafted below her nose. She shook her head and opened her eyes.

Her surroundings were blurry. Foggy. Warm light shifted long shadows into focus.

She stirred ever so slightly. She moved her leg. Turned her head. But when she adjusted her arm, pain sliced through her. She bolted upright and cried out. At the movement, black stars darted across her vision, plunging her further into confusion.

"Shh. Be still. Do not move yet." A female voice, soft and calm.

Camille's heart thudded at the unrecognized voice, but eventually her vision cleared. A young woman with vibrant flax-colored hair sat next to her, leaning close.

Camille's gaze darted from the blazing fire to the murals on the wall to the heavy velvet curtains obscuring the room's two large windows. "Where am I?"

The woman smiled. "You are at the Gilchrist home. There now, be still."

Camille looked down at the source of her pain. A tidy white bandage wrapped around her arm. The sight of it brought vivid memories of the night's events rushing at her. She closed her eyes and drew a deep breath as she relived the terror.

"You poor dear. You are quite pale." The pretty blond woman's lips turned downward in what appeared to be genuine concern. "Does it hurt so very much?"

Camille swallowed. Hurt? Each heartbeat brought agonizing tingling to her upper arm. The mere act of breathing seemed to send knives to her wound. And though a light rug covered her, her clothes felt wet and clammy. Why?

She needed to get home—to be somewhere alone with her thoughts and resolve in her mind how this all happened. She ignored the woman's plea for her to remain still and struggled to sit up, gritting her teeth at the pain. "I will be fine, I am sure."

"Yes you will." A male voice, somehow familiar. Camille looked beyond the woman to a tall, fair-haired man. The sight of him kindled recognition.

This was the man from the alley. She had forgotten his name. She could not recall exactly how she had arrived at this house. But she did remember his kind tone.

"I fear the pain got the better of you," he continued, stepping closer. His hair was wet and hung over his forehead, and his clothes appeared damp. "That or the blood loss. I'm afraid you lost consciousness. But do not concern yourself too much. All will be well in the end."

Camille attempted to sit up once more, but her own wet clothing seemed intent upon keeping her captive. As she regained her senses, she became aware of how she must appear. Her gown and apron hugged her person, and her hair had come loose from its pins. She could feel it clinging to her face.

She glanced around the elegant room. She clearly was no longer on Blinkett Street. Mr. Gilchrist had brought her to the kind of place to which she had not ventured since her youth—a home of gentility and wealth.

A place where a shopkeeper's daughter did not belong.

She was not one to care what others thought of her—or at least she liked to think she did not. But as she took notice of her bloodstained sleeve and a tear in her skirt, hot tears began to burn. The thought that she—bloody and dirty—was marring this pristine home with these well-dressed people mortified her in a way she was certain she had never experienced.

"I am Penelope Gilchrist." The woman's voice was smooth, her gentle accent confirming that she was well-bred. "You know my brother, I believe."

Camille snapped her head back up and nodded a greeting. "Yes, we met. Briefly." The sense that she should be saying something polite—or at least introducing herself—nagged her. "I am Camille Iverness."

"It is a pleasure to meet you, Miss Iverness, but I do wish it was under more pleasant circumstances."

Camille returned her attention to the man, trying to wrest her mind away from her awkwardness long enough to make sense of her circumstances. "Can you tell me what happened?"

He stepped forward and took a chair next to the sofa. He rested his elbows on top of his knees and leaned forward. "When we were walking here, you collapsed. I have tended to your arm. It is unfortunate, but not serious. You will recover."

"No, I mean, what happened at the shop? There was a man, and we fought. Then someone else came in, and—"

"All that can wait until morning." Miss Gilchrist cut her eyes toward the man. "You are safe and well now, and that is all that matters, is it not? The last thing we want is for you to catch your death in that wet gown. Come with me. We will get you something dry and warm to wear. Then we can get you settled in a room for the night."

Camille quickly shook her head. She might be afflicted at the moment, but she did not need this sort of help. "Oh no, I could not."

The woman looked offended. "Of course you can! It is raining hard out there. The hour is quite late. And from what my brother has told me, it is unthinkable for you to return to your shop alone."

Camille looked past Miss Gilchrist to her rescuer. She half expected him to agree with her, to agree that it was best for her to go back where she belonged. But he simply sat staring at her, his square jaw set and his expression impossible to read. His hair was every bit as blond as his sister's, but his deep-set blue eyes were much lighter. Much more piercing.

Something about him teased her memory, as if she had known him long ago. But to her knowledge they had never met before tonight. He didn't seem the type to visit her shop.

Miss Gilchrist snapped her back to the present. "Please say you will stay the night. I would not be able to sleep for fear that something dreadful would happen to you."

For a moment, Camille's weary body was ready to accept. Outside those sumptuously dressed windows, thunder growled. Fear of what waited for her at home tightened her stomach.

But she could not stay. The shop had been left open. Unattended. What if her father returned to find it in such a state?

As if reading her thoughts, Mr. Gilchrist spoke. "Surely you cannot be considering returning there tonight after all that has happened."

Camille managed to swing her feet to the floor. "My father will be returning home soon, and he will be concerned about where I am."

She stood up. The room swirled. She swayed, and in two steps Mr. Gilchrist was at her side, taking her arm to steady her.

"You have lost blood, Miss Iverness, not to mention endured a trying experience. Please reconsider. You can sleep here tonight, and we will return you home safe and sound in the morning."

"Yes, please reconsider." Miss Gilchrist added.

Camille lifted her eyes to the portrait above the chimney-piece. A pastoral countryside, warm in shades of green and brown, called to her, and she realized she desperately wanted to stay. She certainly did not want to return to Blinkett Street. For what, after all, would she be returning to? A ramshackle shop full of broken merchandise? A father who might or might not even be there?

Her stomach gave a lurch, protesting the evening's events. Her skin broke out in gooseflesh, and the wet linen of her gown felt rough against it. Tears, hot in contrast, burned her eyes. She would not cry. She never cried. She just needed time to consider what to do. And here, she supposed, was as good a place as any to do just that.

She forced a smile. "Thank you for your hospitality. I would be happy to accept your kind invitation."

Chapter Eleven ————————————————

amille slowly made her way upstairs in the wake of Miss
Gilchrist and her lady's maid, a plump woman called Meeks.

It was not an easy trek. Her arm and head throbbed. Concern
for the state of her father's shop weighed on her mind. Thunder
cracked continually, lancing her already tense nerves.

If Miss Gilchrist was aware at all of Camille's discomfort,
she gave no indication of such. She chattered on about how
shocking the night's events had been, leaving Camille to wonder how much Mr. Gilchrist had shared with her regarding the
evening's events. But Camille didn't ask. All she wanted was to
be left alone so she could sort out the situation.

They entered a prepared chamber. Its warmth immediately
welcomed her into the opulent room. The dancing fire and the
canopied bed beckoned, and a soft carpet cushioned the hard
floor beneath her soggy kid boots.

"This will be your chamber for the night, and I hope you will
be comfortable in it." Miss Gilchrist swept around the space as if
assessing its suitability.

It was certainly finer than any place Camille had visited for
quite some time. She watched Meeks scurry from the bed to the
chair, fluffing linens and pillows. The sight brought to mind her
own childhood, when her governess had fussed over her in such
a manner.

"This is lovely," Camille breathed. "I am most grateful."

"Tomorrow we can find out what you know about the Bevoy, but first you must rest."

Camille frowned. The Bevoy? Was that not what the man who attacked her had asked about?

"The Bevoy?" Camille repeated, wanting to be certain that she had heard the woman correctly, that she wasn't merely hearing things in her afflicted state.

"Yes, of course. The Bevoy. But we can talk about that tomorrow. You have had enough for one evening."

Mr. Gilchrist had made no mention of anything called a Bevoy. Camille searched her memory and was sure of it. A sickening wave swept over her. Perhaps Mr. Gilchrist's intentions in helping her were not as innocent as they appeared. Was his kindness merely a cover for a hidden intention? Was this elegant house the refuge it appeared to be?

Worrisome thoughts continued to plague her as she shed her wet garments and donned the warm flannel nightdress the lady's maid provided. Even with dry clothing and a warm fire, an incessant chill coursed through her, refusing to let her forget the evening's frightening turn. Her thoughts jumped in quick succession from her pain to the shop to her father and then back to her pain.

"Meeks will take your dress and wash it for you. I fear the blood may not come out, but she can work wonders, even with the most delicate fabric. Your apron, though, seems no worse for the wear—but wait, what is this in the pocket?"

Camille had quite forgotten about the contents of her apron. She rubbed her arms, panicking slightly. For some reason, the idea of someone else—anyone else—touching her things seemed more than she could bear at the moment. "I had quite forgotten there was anything in there."

"'Tis a letter. And some coins. A pair of scissors and a small package of some sort. I'm afraid the wrapping is a little damp—oh well, cannot be helped."

She handed over the items, and Camille took them in jittery hands, eager to have them back in her possession.

"And here is the watch that was pinned to your gown." Miss Gilchrist held the silver brooch up to the light. "Oh, it's quite a lovely piece."

"My grandfather gave it to me," Camille blurted as she eagerly took the piece from her host.

Miss Gilchrist merely nodded, her attention shifting quickly. "We will leave your underthings here by the fire to dry. I should think they would be dry by morning. Do you not agree?" Miss Gilchrist. She pointed to a gown and shawl laid out at the foot of the bed. "Meeks brought these for you to wear tomorrow. I fear I have grown too big for the dress. Meeks tells me it is because of all of the scones I eat. Nonetheless, I can wear it no longer, but you might be able to."

Camille ran her finger over the pale-yellow silk dress. Tiny pink and yellow flowers bordered the scalloped hem of the neck and sleeves. How different it was from the linen or cotton she normally wore. It was much more like the silk she sometimes sold in the shop—too fine and priceless for everyday use. The shawl, woven of gossamer wool in a golden hue, shimmered in the candlelight.

Under normal circumstances, Camille would never accept such offerings. Even as her eyes admired the satin ribbon adorning the bustline, she was searching for a way to refuse it. But what choice did she have? She forced words from her mouth. "I thank you."

"Do not thank me. I only hope you are well." Miss Gilchrist's smile seemed genuine as she folded her hands in front of her. "I will leave you now. The hour has grown quite late. There is a cord there by the door that you can pull should you need anything during the night. Meeks will come you to straightaway."

Camille watched as the woman and her lady's maid left the room, then she hurried to close the door behind them.

Finally alone.

Finally quiet.

But her mind raced with unrest.

As if the evening's events were not odd enough, how did Miss Gilchrist know of the Bevoy? And what in the world was a Bevoy anyway? Odd how an item she'd never even heard of before could suddenly loom so large in her life.

Realizing she still held the brooch, she opened her hand and gazed at it. Such memories it held. Her grandfather had been dead a very long time, but every time she looked at the brooch or heard the soft tick of the watch, memories of his goodness and kindness flooded her mind.

Even though her mother had lived with them on the estate, it had been her grandfather who took an interest in her. He who taught her to ride a pony, who read stories to her by the fire. He had taken her to church in the nearby village and even sneaked tarts and chocolates from the kitchen for her.

He had made her feel loved.

She placed the brooch on the bureau. She did not need to read the inscription to call the words to mind.

"All things work together for good to them that love the Lord."

Grandfather had been a man of great faith, and no doubt he had believed the words wholeheartedly. But try as she might, Camille could not. When she considered her present situation, the words rang hollow.

It was pleasant to think that everything would work out in the end. But as far as she could tell, nothing could be further from the truth.

Later that night, after his sister and their unexpected guest had retired for the night and he had changed into dry buckskin breeches, cotton shirt, and wool coat to ward off a chill, Jonathan found himself unable to rest. So he retreated to his father's study.

He had never cared for their London home. He much preferred Kettering Hall and the calm stillness of Fellsworth. In fact, he avoided this house whenever possible, but soon avoiding it would not be an issue. As a result of his father's financial troubles, efforts were already underway to find a buyer for the London home.

It would not take long for the property to sell. Chire Street was a hub of social activity. But for the time being all was quiet, at least during the midnight hours.

Jonathan dropped into the chair behind the broad oak desk and reached for the sealed letter that sat atop it. He balanced the letter in his hands, tapped it against his palm, then tossed it back on the desk.

Even from a distance, his father had the ability to impose his will.

Jonathan did not need to read the letter to know what it

contained. His father's gout might prevent him from traveling, but it did not stop him from sharing his mind. Ian Gilchrist had become a man obsessed with recovering the ruby—he'd spoken of little else since the robbery. And he was dead set on the idea that Jonathan should be the one to recover it.

Jonathan wanted to be away from this—to go back to the simplicity of his life as an apothecary, tending to the villagers and the children at the nearby school. But this ruby, this ridiculous ruby, and his father and brother's ties to a world he did not understand prevented it.

If it were only for his sake, he would abandon it all. He did not need Kettering Hall. But he worried for his father, even though the man had brought much of his trouble upon himself. And his sister . . .

Childish and dramatic she might be, but their bond had always been strong. And without the recovery of this ruby, her future could indeed be bleak. Most of the estate's furnishings and his father's collection would stay with Kettering Hall were it to be sold, with almost nothing left to support Penelope if she remained unmarried. And without a dowry, her chances for making a good match were small indeed. Jonathan was well acquainted with Alfred Dowden. The man was not likely to go through with the marriage if the money vanished. The same was true for most men in their social circle.

Jonathan stood from the desk and moved to the fireplace. He stoked the orange embers and revived the dying fire. He could not help but think of Miss Iverness. Everything about the past several days had been unusual, but bringing her to their home had to be the most out of the ordinary.

He recalled how light and delicate she had felt in his arms, but there was a spark to her that he found intriguing. He tried to imagine Penelope fighting an intruder. Miss Iverness's spirit was tenacious.

Darbin had mentioned that Miss Iverness was a woman who could defend herself. A woman accustomed to the rougher ways of the street. And perhaps Darbin was right.

But whatever her personality, whatever her demeanor, Jonathan was still haunted by the feeling that he was responsible for her injury. If he had not rushed in and startled McCready, would Miss Iverness have escaped the tussle without harm?

A sharp pounding on the door interrupted his musings. A quick glance at the mantle clock confirmed it was past the midnight hour.

His pulse pounded.

The night's encounters with unsavory characters had left him leery. But in spite of the evening's dire events, he did not want Winston or anyone else opening the door at this hour.

He jogged from the study and looked out the window into the night.

Darbin. There could be no mistaking that lanky frame and those wide side-whiskers.

Jonathan flung the door open, ushering in a swirl of damp air.

Annoyance tightened Darbin's face. "I thought I'd find you here."

Jonathan stepped back, allowing Darbin room to enter. "Did you get it?"

"Did I get it?" Darbin snatched his hat from his head and shook it, spattering rain onto the polished wood floor. "No, I didn't get it."

Jonathan ushered Darbin to the study. "What happened?"

"I chased him as far as I could, but I lost him in a public house. Didn't want to cause a scene, attract attention to myself. But a man like that can't lay low forever." Darbin dropped his hat and coat onto one of the chairs flanking the fire. "What was that little stunt you pulled?"

Jonathan closed the study door. "What do you mean?"

"Oh, do not play innocent. I tell you to hold tight, and you go barreling in like some crazed knight in shining armor." He narrowed his eyes and pointed his finger at Jonathan. "Your little act of chivalry may have just cost us our only chance to learn about the ruby."

Jonathan was in no mood to argue—or to be put on the defensive. "I was not about to leave a defenseless woman—"

"Camille Iverness is hardly a defenseless female. Do you think that the daughter of James Iverness doesn't know her way around the sharp end of a blade? She doesn't exactly reside in Grosvenor Square, in case you didn't notice."

"Think what you will. I prefer to sleep with a clear conscience." That much was true, he told himself. If only his conscience really was clear.

"Well, isn't that lovely," Darbin said. "You can slumber with a clear conscience while I am out chasing some rogue with a knife."

"Come now, Darbin. I've never known you to turn down a good chase."

"Never known a Gilchrist to give in to a woman, either." Darbin stepped to the sideboard and grabbed a decanter. "Where is she, anyway? I went back by the shop, and all was quiet. Place looked to be ransacked, but maybe that was just a result of the skirmish. I'd hoped to find Iverness there himself. But no such luck. If he's involved in the theft, as I suspect, both he and the daughter may be in the wind."

Jonathan stepped to the sideboard and handed a glass to Darbin. "Miss Iverness is here."

Darbin sobered. "What do you mean, 'She's here'?"

"She's upstairs. Sleeping, presumably."

Darbin dropped his arm to his side, his incredulous expression darkening. "You brought Camille Iverness back to your home? Where you live?" He shook his head and shoved long fingers through his dark hair. "Did you drag her here kicking and screaming?"

"Of course not." He cleared his throat. "She came of her own accord."

Darbin shook his head. "I can't believe she agreed to come. Does your sister know?"

"Yes, she knows."

"Perhaps you see the wisdom in your actions. I do not."

Jonathan shrugged. "There really were no other options."

"There are always options." Darbin poured the brandy and indulged in a long swig. "Did you ask her about the Bevoy? Does she know anything about it?"

Jonathan shook his head. "I did not even mention it. She was injured and quite shaken."

"Don't be naïve, Gilchrist." Darbin dropped in the chair next to the fire. "I see you don't know that much about women like her. She'll use that pretty face of hers to charm the money right out of your hands." He finished off his brandy and looked up. "Still, it might be good that she's here. She could be your only chance to find the ruby."

Chapter Twelve

amille pushed the curtains away from the window.

Dawn had broken, and the first tendrils of gray light swirled into the room. The bedchamber was warm, and she marveled at the experience of waking in comfort instead of shivering in her little room above the shop. The room was lovely too. Even in the dim morning light she could see the details that the shadows had muted the night before—the lovely fabrics of yellow and green, the beauty of the gold-striped wallpaper.

How often had she dreamed of having just such a chamber for herself? But at the moment she could think of nothing besides getting out of this one and returning to what was normal.

Clarity of mind had arrived with the morning. Her arm ached and her head throbbed, but sleep had revived her spirit. She drew a deep breath, and the act of filling her lungs with air invigorated her resolve.

What had she been thinking to accept such an invitation—to spend the midnight hours in the home of complete strangers? Her decision to stay here had been brash, brought on by fear and uncertainty. And she knew one thing for certain: she would not be here when they woke.

She knew her hosts had questions for her, but she had no answers, and she could not face them again. How awkward the previous evening had been. She never wanted to feel that embarrassment, that sense of inadequacy, again. The memory of her burning humiliation urged her to exit the house more quickly.

Camille stepped over to the bureau. The contents of her apron pockets sat on the smooth service. She ran her thumb over the brooch and looked at the hands of the watch. The hour was still very early. If she hurried, she might make it home before Papa returned. Then she could at least attempt to mitigate the damage that had been done before he saw it. She shuddered to think what the shop might look like. She recalled breaking glass. Overturned shelves. And the door had not been secured, so who knew what she would find?

Her biggest obstacle was going to be dressing herself. Her arm screamed with pain, protesting each movement. She tested each finger, wriggling them one by one, doing her best to ignore the stinging of her wound. Blood had soaked through the bandage that Mr. Gilchrist had fashioned the previous night, but the surface appeared to be mostly dry. The dressing probably needed to be changed, but there was no time to concern herself with that now.

Her own gown was nowhere to be found. Miss Gilchrist's lady's maid had taken it to clean. But the borrowed dress of yellow silk was on a nearby chair.

She winced as she slid the gown over her arm. Fortunately it fastened by a series of ties instead of buttons and had an overdress that fastened in the front; otherwise she could never have managed on her own. Her dressing was not tidy, her stays far from tight, but they did not need to be.

She wrapped the borrowed shawl around her to hide any dressing missteps and turned to assess her reflection in the gilded mirror in the corner of the room. Her black eyes appeared haunted in her pale face. She looked as if she had encountered a major illness. But at least she could stand without the room spinning—a distinct improvement over the previous night.

She pinned her hair off her shoulders as best as she could manage and gathered her things, wrapping them in her still-damp apron. She could feel her energy returning. Her fight.

Jonathan propped his feet up on the desk. He laced his fingers together, rested them behind his head, and stared up at the leaves carved into the plaster ceiling. Sounds of the street were beginning to creep through the window, and first light danced amongst the shadows of the intricate curves.

It was one of his favorite things to do—greet the dawn after staying up all night. But this particular dawn brought him nothing but worry.

Darbin had stayed until the wee hours of the morning. The investigator certainly reminded Jonathan of his own older brother. Both men harbored the same lust for excitement and fascination with the unusual—a combination that Jonathan found both enviable and irritating.

Jonathan had anticipated Darbin would offer encouragement or at least a clear plan of what to do next, but the investigator's words had contained more reprimand than optimism. Now, another day had dawned—one more day to be reminded of his father's mistakes, his concern for his sister's future, and his own inadequacies.

By now he should have had the ruby in his possession, but

he and Penelope would leave for Kettering Hall empty-handed. What a fool he had been to think that recovering the gem would be as simple as walking into a shop and taking it.

After Darbin took his leave, Jonathan had remained in his father's study instead of retiring to his chamber. He had never been one to require much sleep. Ever since he was a boy, he had enjoyed being awake in the midnight hours while the rest of the world slumbered. The darkness fueled his imagination, providing the perfect solitude to learn and contemplate. And his profession often required him to be awake at odd hours.

But tonight, thoughts of his father and their current situation cluttered every corner of his mind. He knew that even if he did retreat to the silence and solace of his chamber, sleep would elude him, for his thoughts, wild and uncontrollable, ran rampant.

And leading the pack were thoughts of Miss Camille Iverness.

He was not of a romantic bent, but never would Jonathan have anticipated that such a beautiful young woman was involved in a situation so daring as the one at present. True, Miss Iverness could be an innocent bystander, a victim of unfortunate circumstances. Or perhaps Darbin was right—perhaps she was intimately involved.

He had been struck by her bravery. Not many women would have been able to endure such an event with the fortitude she displayed—not the women he was acquainted with, by any means. But whether or not she would be willing to assist him was another matter entirely.

He should have asked her last night about the ruby, when all was quiet. This was his purpose, was it not? To recover a ruby that would eventually be sold to right his family's debts? But she had been so shaken that the timing of such a question would have seemed almost cruel.

He sat up straight and thumbed through a book on the desk. Surely this morning, at breakfast, he would have a moment to talk with Miss Iverness. He could find out what he needed to know.

He stood up and crossed the room to the window. Dawn's blue light squeezed its way through the tight row of townhouses and spilled over the roofs. Mist and smoke intermingled, and carts rumbled over the cobbled streets. Two boys dashed across an alleyway.

But it was something unusual that caught his attention.

A woman, unaccompanied and clad in a pale gown and shawl, passed beneath his window. She carried a bundle of cloth and wore no bonnet, revealing a mass of ebony tresses. He noticed that she wore no gloves either, a sight very unusual for Chire Street.

And then he noticed a bulge under her sleeve.

Miss Iverness.

Without pausing for another thought, he snatched his discarded coat from the chair and shoved his arms through the sleeves as he crossed the foyer.

What was she doing out at this hour?

His concern for her arm was valid, of course, but now his concern extended to much more than that, for she could very well hold the answers he sought regarding the Bevoy.

He reached the door, flung it open, and burst out into the cool, bleary dawn. All around him, the evidence of morning revealed itself—merchants setting up their wares, a lamplighter dousing the lamps, a sweeper bent at his work. Jonathan lunged around a cart just in time to see pale yellow fabric swish around the corner and out of sight.

"Miss Iverness!" He knew better than to shout at ladies across the street. But could it be helped? "Miss Iverness! Wait!"

At the sound of her name, the woman stopped and turned. She lifted her hand to brush away a thick lock of hair that had fallen over her face.

He jogged toward her, his footsteps splashing through puddles left by the previous night's rain. "What are you doing out here at this hour?"

Miss Iverness inched back as he approached. "Mr. Gilchrist. I—I hope I did not wake you as I was leaving."

"No, you did not. I was in the study and saw you pass beneath the window." He stopped a few feet from her. "But I am surprised to see you this early. I would imagine you would be resting."

She glanced over one shoulder and then the other as if looking for something. Or someone. "Oh, no. I am so accustomed to rising early. You and your sister were kind to come to my assistance last night, but now I really must return to my shop."

He nodded toward the bulging bandage under her sleeve. "But your arm. I would feel more comfortable about it if you would allow me to assess it once more before you depart."

"I thank you, but it isn't necessary."

How different she looked by daylight. His first interactions with her had been wound with anxiety. She had been in pain. Discomfort had affected her appearance. But today, black hair escaped her comb and curled around her face in gentle waves. Soft color highlighted her high cheekbones and accentuated the fullness of her lips. But what struck him most was her eyes. They were every bit as black as her hair, mysterious and sharp. And entrancing. For even though her voice was steady, her eyes shared another story—one of cautious strength. Of observant tenacity. And a little spark of something he could not name.

"Are you not concerned for your safety?" he asked. "After what happened last night, I would think you would prefer to wait until all is settled once again."

"Last night was horrifying, to be sure. But no, I am not frightened to return."

"You might not be frightened, Miss Iverness, but I must protest." Jonathan knew he was overstepping his bounds. This woman had never asked for his help, and he had no right to offer his opinion so freely. And yet, after their shared encounter the night before, the need to protect her welled within him. "I feel you would be safer to remain with us for at least a little while longer. We could send word of your safety to your father."

She jutted her chin out confidently, her eyes meeting his with a boldness that took him by surprise. "My father will be waiting for me, I am certain. He is likely beside himself with concern at my absence."

The knowledge that he should stand down and let her go about her business nagged him. But something within him prevented him from doing so. "Would you allow me to accompany you home, at the very least? Do you even know the way from here? I should like to know you arrived safely."

He thought she was going to deny his request. The debate in her mind played clearly across her face. But at length she nodded her consent. He fell into step beside her.

Heavy clouds lingered, blanketing the morning in shades

of pewter and stone. The walk would be a short one, and from what he had gathered, Miss Iverness was a fairly direct woman, so he elected to approach his subject without preamble. "I was hoping to speak with you about what happened last night at the shop."

She looked up, her words brisk. "I am sure I have as many questions—if not more—than you do, Mr. Gilchrist. I do not know what help I will be."

She quickened her pace. He adjusted his to match hers. "As I am sure you have realized, I was at the shop last night for a reason."

"Few people like you just happen upon Blinkett Street without intention."

He did not take the time to consider her response too closely. "The man who attacked you—do you know who he was?"

"I do not."

Her seeming indifference was maddening.

"I believe it was a man named McCready," he continued. "Does that name sound familiar to you?"

She shook her head, her pace not slowing, her eyes not wavering from the cobbled street before her.

"My colleague and I were following him, hoping to locate an item that had been stolen from my father."

She did not respond. In fact, any sense of warmth seemed to leave her expression. Had he upset her? Offended her?

He had to keep trying. "We received information that McCready was going to purchase the item in your father's shop last night, and that is what brought us to you."

At this her steps slowed.

"Are you at all familiar with the Bevoy?"

She stopped and turned toward him. Her dark eyebrows drew together, and she cocked her head to the side. "The Bevoy?"

His pulse quickened. Now they were getting somewhere. Over her shoulder, Jonathan spied a small cluster of men staring at them. He motioned for Miss Iverness to continue walking. "Yes. It's a large gemstone, an uncut ruby. Apparently my father purchased the stone from your father several years ago, and from what we have heard, it was to be sold again at your shop."

She stopped short and finally turned to him, looking at him so directly he felt she was seeing his very thoughts. "You must be mistaken, Mr. Gilchrist. I have never heard of such a ruby, either now or in the past. My father may be a little eccentric, but he is not a thief, and if you think that I—"

"And I am not insinuating that he stole the gem," Jonathan hurried to add, "but only that my stolen property might have reached him under the pretenses of an honest transaction. It happens quite frequently, from what I understand about this business."

She narrowed her eyes.

He immediately regretted his words.

Her icy tone seemed to rise above the street's commotion. "And what exactly do you know about this business?"

"Very little, I confess."

There. He had done the last thing he had wanted to do—he had offended her.

"I am afraid I cannot help you." Miss Iverness folded her arms. "I appreciate your assistance last night, but this is where I must leave you. Good day."

She started walking again. Jonathan stood and watched her go. But before he could conjure another reason to detain her, she stopped short of her own accord. Curious as to the reason, he followed her, weaving around a passing cart and sidestepping a stack of wooden crates.

Then his own steps slowed.

For by the light of day, the damage to the Iverness Curiosity Shop was clear. One window was shattered, and glass littered the dirt walk. The door was propped open.

Miss Iverness said nothing. She broke away and ran toward the door.

Chapter Thirteen ──────────────

*C*amille halted at the shop's open door, heart thudding out a rhythm like a runaway horse's hooves.

She could hear her father inside, shuffling amongst the clutter she knew all too well and spewing profanity with familiar coarseness.

She would never have expected him to return this early, for it was just past dawn. Normally his night excursions kept him away much longer—sometimes days.

Fear, as rich and as deep as any she had experienced the night before, rushed through her. Last night she had feared for her safety, but this morning, the fear was different.

She stepped over the broken glass and splintered wood, all thoughts of her conversation with Mr. Gilchrist surrendered to the back of her mind.

Before she could even step inside, her father spied her through the broken window. "Camille, where in blazes have you been?"

She clutched her little bundle of belongings closer to her. Her words refused to form, as if her father's anger had stolen her ability to speak. She pushed the door open, scooting littered bits of glass and stone as she did.

He did not wait until she was fully inside before he pounced like a tiger attacking its prey. "I asked you a question, girl. I demand an explanation, and you had better have one to give me."

She barely heard his words. The sights around her had captured her attention. The shop was in shambles, the damage worse than she had imagined. She knew the intruder, Mr. McCready, had dropped a vase, and she remembered knocking over several items. But what she saw now was unlike anything she had expected. The only possible explanation was that the store had been looted overnight.

She stammered as her eyes raked from the broken birdcages to the ripped canvases. "I-I—"

But her father would not wait for her to utter a single word. "You. I leave you to oversee the shop, and I come home to this— with you no place to be found?"

"I-I can explain. You don't understand."

"I understand that you let this happen," he hurled back, his green eyes narrowed in sharp scrutiny.

"I did not!" She jutted her chin and did her best to stand her ground. "A man forced his way into the shop last night. He had a knife. I had no choice; it wasn't safe here. I—"

"There is always a choice, girl," he hissed, reaching for a dram of brandy and slamming it down his throat. "I left you in charge, and this is how you betray me? Leave my store alone? Let it be ransacked?"

Suddenly his expression changed. His eyes focused on something behind her, and a shadow against the far wall shifted. She turned around.

Mr. Gilchrist stood on the threshold, his broad shoulders cutting a black silhouette against the street behind him. She blinked and stared at him for several moments, confused.

She thought he had remained at the corner as they approached Blinkett Street, but no doubt her father's profane shouts and cursing had attracted his attention. How could they not? She was not sure if she was irritated that he had followed her or relieved to have another person present.

Her father's voice grew quiet. "Who are you?"

Mr. Gilchrist stepped inside. "My name's Gilchrist."

"Ian Gilchrist's boy?" No warmth of recognition lit her father's hard face as he assessed the man in the doorway. "What do you want?"

Camille swallowed the lump of fear and disbelief forming in her throat. So her father was acquainted, at least on some level, with the Gilchrists. She stepped aside to allow Mr. Gilchrist to brush past her. His presence brought with it a strange sense of calm. Her confidence seemed to rise with every step he took into the shop.

Mr. Gilchrist's voice was strong when hers felt weak. "I am here to make certain Miss Iverness is well. I happened by the shop yesterday night while the robbery was taking place, and she was injured."

Mr. Gilchrist's explanation did little to diffuse the fire in her father's eyes. "You just happened by the shop, did you? Then I suppose you can answer for some of this mess as well."

Mr. Gilchrist stared her father directly in the eye, something not many people dared to do. James Iverness was king of this street, accustomed to having people bow to his will. Perhaps it was Mr. Gilchrist's ignorance, or perhaps this well-bred stranger had more courage than she had been willing to give him credit for.

Mr. Gilchrist's voice was unshaken. "No, I'll not answer for the damage. That was someone else's doing. And your daughter is hardly to blame. When I arrived, she was being held at knifepoint by a rogue twice her size. She was fortunate to escape with her life."

Camille's heartbeat jumped wildly to her throat. Her father would never stand for such a response. She wanted to blink but felt physically unable. Her father's face was deepening to a sinister shade of crimson, his cheeks starting to shake. He was a volatile man, and once provoked, he was a volcano, heaving forth hot and angry words with the force of a massive explosion.

James Iverness stepped up to the much younger, much taller man, his hand waving in the air. For what he lacked in stature, he made up in volume. "I'll not be told who to blame for this disaster or how to speak to my daughter in my own shop, especially not by the son of a thieving, lying . . ." Several choice descriptions of the elder Mr. Gilchrist followed.

Camille looked to Mr. Gilchrist, her breath suspended, waiting for a response of any kind. But none came.

Her father spun around, mere inches from his daughter. "Is this the type of person you prefer to keep company with? This sort of man who disrespects me in my own shop?"

Her need to diffuse the situation overcame her fear. And Mr. Gilchrist's bravery bolstered her own. "But he helped me, Papa."

"He helped you, did he? Ha! I bet he did. Helped you right out of your shop." He pointed a shaky finger to Mr. Gilchrist. "Very convenient, wasn't it, boy, for you and your kind to have the shop left unattended. I'll wager I can go to your father's study and find half o' what's missing here now."

He whirled back to Camille. "And as for you, only a common

trollop would come flouncing in here in the morning with a man she doesn't know."

The words flamed through the air. Camille could feel Mr. Gilchrist's gaze on her. She wanted to melt into the floor, to disappear completely. She had told herself she didn't care what the man thought. He had already seen her at her worst, and she'd thought her humiliation was complete. But she'd been wrong.

Camille shook her head vehemently, as if her exaggerated movement could convince her father more aptly. "If you would just listen, I—"

"I want you gone!" he shouted, each word notably louder than the last. "Leave. Now."

At first Camille didn't believe his order. Her father was brash, and where she was concerned, his bark was almost always worse than his bite. But then he grabbed her by the arm—her injured arm. She howled in pain, and her knees buckled beneath her. He either did not notice or did not care. He wrapped his fingers tighter and all but pushed her out the door.

She stumbled onto the cobblestoned street, falling to her knees. The sharp pebbles and shards of glass jabbed her through her dress, and cold moisture seeped through the fine silk. Pain accosted her from every point of her body, but she felt numb in spite of it.

Her father had treated her harshly before, but never had he done anything like this. Though the threat had been present, like a ghost lingering in the air, he had never actually laid a hand on her before today.

But now, apparently, she had crossed a line. Her actions had cost him the one thing he loved more than anything else—money.

It could not have been helped, she was certain. No matter

how many times she recounted the events in her head, she simply could not see how she could have acted differently.

But her father would never see it that way.

She drew a sharp breath, preparing to push through the pain and rise, when a hand touched her elbow.

Camille recoiled at the touch.

"Let me help you."

A fresh wave of humiliation swept through her. Not only had Mr. Gilchrist been privy to last night's events. He now bore witness to something much more personal.

Mortification sank dull teeth into her, dissolving her will to stand and face him. But he had already seen the full extent of her shame. She bit her lip to prevent any emotion from writing itself on her face and pulled her arm away. "You have done enough."

She gathered the items that had escaped from her improvised reticule when she fell. She moved slowly, not so much because of the pain, but because she was unsure of what she was going to say when she did straighten and face Mr. Gilchrist. She sniffed and blinked as she wrapped her belongings once more in the apron, waiting for the sting of embarrassment to subside.

Her father's cursing and mumblings could be heard from within. And she could not blame his erratic behavior on intoxication, for he had seemed quite lucid. No, this time he meant what he said.

She was no longer welcome at the shop that she called home.

Mr. Gilchrist stepped back to give her room as she got to her feet, but he did not leave. She wanted him to, but she had not expected it.

No, Mr. Gilchrist was a gentleman. She had seen his home, outfitted with the taste and comfort only a privileged man could afford. And he had treated her kindly and equally, not as if she were merely a shopgirl from Blinkett Street, but someone worthwhile. He would not have it in him to walk away from a woman in distress.

He remained quiet while she rose and shook out the folds of her skirt. Then there was no excuse for her to not look him in the eye.

She clenched her jaw as she raised her gaze to meet his. She waited for him to speak and expected him to say something about her arm, but he did not. Instead, his words were soft and low, yet sure and swift, spoken as if he had knowledge of every aspect of her life. "You need to be away from here."

Tears wanted to fall. She looked past him and tried to focus on something else. Anything else. "Papa is just upset. Things will settle down."

"No." The intensity of his blue eyes weakened her knees. "It is not safe for you here."

She gave a little laugh, but her attempt to make light of the situation fell flat. "Are you always so certain of everything?"

Mr. Gilchrist did not laugh with her. He did not even crack a smile. "I am when I see a lady being treated in such a fashion."

Her false smile faded. "I know my father. This will pass. The matter will be set to right by day's end."

But even as she spoke, her father's shouts could be heard above the sounds of the street.

Oh, she did not want to be here.

She wanted to be far, far away from Blinkett Street and every-thing it represented. Her cheeks flamed anew at the thought that Mr. Gilchrist had seen what happened. The previous evening had almost been easier to bear—all had been in darkness. But today she felt completely exposed. There could be no hiding or masking the truth about her life.

Mr. Gilchrist's eyes were pinned on her. She could feel them as certainly as she could feel the fabric against her skin or the breeze on her face.

She knew men like him. They came into the shop often. They were easy to identify—well dressed in coats of fine wool, with polished Hessian boots and intricately tied cravats. Clean-shaven, wealthy young men seeking adventure and diversion from their otherwise dull lives. While Mr. Gilchrist did not appear to fit that mold, she had interacted with men long enough to know that they were rarely as they seemed.

Lost in her musings, she did not resist as he ushered her away from the shop's entrance. "I know a place," he said in a low voice, "where you will be safe. Somewhere you can get away from this."

That got her attention. The idea that where she came from was not good enough was far beyond what she deemed appropriate. It was insulting. "I appreciate your concern, but I have no intention of leaving my home."

Camille quickened her steps not only to put physical distance between them but to halt the topic of conversation.

Her gait was no match for his longer one. "And what if Mr. McCready comes again? Or another man, for that matter? Or what if your father will not let you return? What will you do?"

She pressed her lips together, refusing to answer. Her steps grew quicker. Stronger.

But he persisted. "Just hear what I have to say. I have a friend, a good friend, who is the superintendent of a school in Fellsworth, Surrey. Our family has a home nearby, so I know him well. He is always looking for assistance. I could inquire about a position for you."

She almost laughed at that. "Are you suggesting I could be a teacher? Perhaps you have not noticed, but I am hardly the teacher sort."

His blond eyebrows drew together as if her brash dismissal of his idea had surprised him. "The school has need of many kinds of help, not just teaching. I am sure there would be something for you to do." He brightened. "Perhaps you could show the girls how to keep books and balance accounts. You know how to do that, do you not? More important, working there would get you away from London. My sister and I will be returning to Fellsworth tomorrow. You could accompany us."

She shot back her response. "You are assuming that I want to get away."

"I'm not—" He paused and rethought his words. "I only mean to be of assistance."

She eyed him. His concern seemed so genuine. And how she wished it was. How lovely it would be to have someone like him care about her.

But he wanted something.

He wanted that ruby.

No man was as he seemed.

"You can trust me, Miss Iverness. I only want to help."

"I trust nobody." Her voice was firm. "And I have no intention of leaving London."

Chapter Fourteen ──────────────

$\mathcal{M}$iss Iverness turned sharply and hurried away.

Jonathan watched as she wove her way through the crowds on Blinkett Street and around a carriage. She clutched her bundle to her chest and was almost running. She cast one glance over her shoulder at him, but before he could react she had turned again.

Though the rain had not returned, a canopy of clouds and smoke painted everything around them with its steely paintbrush, reinforcing the stark melancholy. He continued to study her retreating form, her yellow gown a bright spot in the dreary, hopeless gray.

Then she disappeared around the corner.

He stood without moving, stunned at what he had just witnessed. Never had he seen the like. Such violence was foreign to him. Of course, he and his brother had their bouts of boyish roughhousing, but this could not compare.

A man, a grown man, laying hands on his daughter and pushing her into the street?

Unbelievable.

He drew a deep breath, the scents of rotting garbage and smoke from the nearby forge reminding him of where he was.

He huffed angrily under his breath, ignoring the puddled

water that splashed onto his boots and legs with every step. His blood continued to boil at the injustice of Miss Iverness's plight.

But what could he do? She did not want his help. And why should she? She knew nothing of him, other than he was somehow connected to a stolen ruby that had probably been the cause of her injury.

He had no idea what had possessed him to suggest a position at the school. He had no authority to make such an offer, other than the fact that Mr. Langsby owed him a few favors and was an agreeable man.

And yet he wanted to help. His concern for Miss Iverness, this mysterious creature with black hair and startling eyes, would not leave him alone. He could not tell why, other than he recognized something in her—something restrained. Something suppressed to the point of pain.

Something deeply familiar.

For he too knew something about living in isolation—side by side with people with whom one should share love but somehow remained strangers.

He could leave the rough confines of Blinkett Street. Pretend he never met her. The thread that would bind an apothecary from Fellsworth to a London shopkeeper's daughter was nonexistent. The most prudent course of action would be to leave this moment behind him, reconnect with Darbin, and start a new search, then find his ruby as he originally planned, and return to quiet Fellsworth. He would likely never see Miss Iverness again.

He cast one final glance up the street, but she was gone. No yellow.

Only gray and smoke.

Camille could scarcely believe she had been able to hold back tears.

She rarely wept, and never in front of others. But now that she had turned off Blinkett Street and was in an alley, protected from prying eyes, she let a tear slip. And then another.

How vividly she could recall the stab in her chest, the sick feeling in her stomach after her mother departed for Portugal all those years ago. She had run to her chamber that day sobbing bitter tears. There had been no one to calm or soothe her. And the next morning, when she awoke, she had determined with all the stubbornness of youth never to allow another person to take her to such a state.

Until now, she'd been successful.

But now that ache was back. The sharp ache that reached into her heart and twisted, gripping it in a vise of anger and hopelessness until the tears just had to flow.

She didn't know which hurt more—her father's harsh rejection or the fact that Mr. Gilchrist had witnessed it.

She was not exactly clear why she cared so about Mr. Gilchrist's opinion. After all, he was surely using her as a means to an end, his concern no doubt self-serving. He did intervene on her behalf, but by doing so he had seen a part of her life rarely seen by others.

Camille allowed herself the luxury of one sob and two very slow, very controlled breaths. She pressed the back of her hand to her cheek and wiped it. She had to move forward.

The tears blurred everything before her into a misty mess of browns and grays. She peered through them at a group of young girls playing by a back stoop and then a cluster of women chatting with baskets over their arms and mobcaps on their heads.

Slowly reality dawned.

After a lifetime of living in one place, surrounded by the same people, she should have somewhere to go.

But there was no one for her to turn to.

Like it or not, her life was defined by the hours spent in the shop, her social connections limited to her patrons and the occasional merchant. Beyond that, she had little in common with the women who lived near her. She had been raised differently than most of them. Her speech was different due to the time spent on her grandfather's estate—less like the voice of a Blinkett Street native and more like a lady. She looked different as well, her black hair and dark eyes giving her the appearance of a foreigner.

And then there was her father, of course. James Iverness, a man whose doubtful reputation preceded him.

Mothers did not want their daughters associating with the daughter of such a man. Men did not want to court a woman whose father had such a volatile reputation. There was no other family that she knew of, except for her mother in a faraway country.

She was alone, literally cast out into the streets.

She walked for several hours among the shoddy shops and narrow houses, careful to avoid the straw and dung on the streets. She held her hand to her nose to block the putrid scents of dirty animals and human waste. The smoke from the forge burned her eyes, and the thick air made her lungs ache.

Her body cried, ironically, for the solace of her little chamber above the shop. The pain of her arm was making her sick to her stomach, and the desire for something familiar trumped the anger she felt toward her father.

She thought of Mr. Gilchrist. Those arresting blue eyes. The kindness in his expression. The manner in which he stood up to her father. And his outrageous suggestion—that she leave Blinkett Street and start fresh.

In truth, she left Blinkett Street nearly every night in her dreams, but it had never occurred to her actually to go away.

She had always believed it her duty to stay and help her father, to take care of him as her mother had instructed. She had told herself he was a good man in essence, that despite his brusque manner he loved her and she him.

But was it true?

Somehow, over the years, their relationship had cracked. She had continued striving to do as he bid, to please him. But her efforts were never enough, and now his harsh words and actions echoed painfully in her mind.

Another question nagged as well. Mr. Gilchrist had implied that her father could be involved in a theft? Surely not. She knew his methods were questionable. But she kept the books and had never seen any evidence of outright villainy.

What if he were stealing? Would she be implicated in the theft as well? Could she be hanged for her father's crimes?

She couldn't think anymore. Her aching body cried out for rest and her stomach rumbled with hunger. Her head felt both light and full at the same time, and her cut arm throbbed painfully. She looked down and saw it was bleeding again. The bright blood had seeped through the bandage to stain the fine fabric of her borrowed gown.

She could not wander the streets in this condition. She needed to go home. Perhaps she could slip up to her room without her father noticing.

She slowed her steps as she reached the gated entrance to the small bit of earth behind their home. She heard two voices—no, three. All were male. One of them was Papa's.

Considering the anger he had displayed a short while ago, the laughter she heard now surprised her. Words, when spoken, were muffled, the voices slurred.

She strained to make out the nuances of each voice, trying to determine their owners. As she listened to the cadence of the tones, apprehension tightened her nerves.

"Never suspected," one growled. "But then again, what's that for a little extra?" Another voice sounded, thick with a foreign accent. "How long?"

She had no idea what they were talking about. Summoning her courage, Camille picked her steps carefully to avoid the clutter of broken crates and debris in the alley, stepped closer to the gate, and peered through the wooden slats. She made out the back of Papa's graying head. The rough wool of another man's coat swayed in and out of her view.

An insect swirled around her, and she squinted in sunshine that had suddenly emerged from behind the cloud's silver curtain. She leaned closer to the fence and held her breath, attempting to hear more.

"But what about the girl?"

"You didn't have to hurt her." Papa's voice was unmistakable.

Camille bit her lip. They were talking about her.

"'Twas an accident, I told you. Besides, you said she was a tough sort, and that she was. Fought me like a cat, she did."

"And what of my shop?" Her father's voice again. "Looks like you let a pair of wild horses loose in there."

"Couldn't be helped. Like I said, fought me like a cat."

"And my window. How in blazes did that happen?"

There was a pause. "That man pushed me into it. Lost my balance."

Papa's voice was raspy. "Well, I suppose it was a small price to pay. Most of the goods have been taken to the warehouse anyway. At least the plan played out. We need her to be completely unaware. And we need to throw that boy off."

The blood pounded through her ears. Surely she had heard him wrong. Unaware of what? And who did he mean by boy? Mr. Gilchrist?

She bit back her breath and angled her body. Nothing made sense, but fear that Papa might some way be involved in a robbery sent shivers through her.

She could see the back of the man with whom Papa was speaking. He was tall. Broad. And what he wore was not a coat, but a long cape.

He turned, and as his profile came into view, she was certain it was him. The man Mr. Gilchrist had named as Mr. McCready—the man who had held her at knifepoint and then cut her—was laughing and talking with Papa. And Papa, who seemed to be completely aware of Mr. McCready's actions, was not angered in the least.

She kept watching as their laughter died down.

"Where's the girl now?"

"Don't know. Kicked her out. She shouldn't have left the shop like she did, so I needed to teach her a lesson. But she'll be back."

"Just make sure she doesn't cause problems."

"Camille? She won't." Papa's voice was ripe with confidence. "That was the whole purpose of your little sham of a robbery—to distract the girl. We don't need to concern ourselves with her."

"You so sure about that, Iverness?" asked the third man. "You know women."

"If anyone asks her what is going on, she will be convincing because she knows nothing about it. But even if she did suspect something, she'd not say a word. The girl knows better."

She knows better.

Camille had heard enough. She inched away from the gate.

Yes, she *did* know better.

She had blinded herself to what her father had become, ignored all the signs for far too long. She could do so no longer.

She had never been truly afraid of Papa, despite his rough ways, but seeing him there, laughing and plotting with her attacker, sent a wave of nausea washing over her. If he was in cahoots with the caped man, that meant he found his daughter's stabbing an acceptable price to pay for whatever scheme he was pursuing.

Camille recoiled backward as if the invisible thread tying her to her family had suddenly snapped. Her stomach flopped within her as she retraced her steps, treading lightly over the loose cobblestones. She had to get away. But where could she go?

Then Mr. Gilchrist's outlandish offer flashed in her mind.

It had been so long since she had been outside of London. Painting after painting had made its way through their shop— paintings of idyllic countrysides, tranquil streams, contented livestock, so reminiscent of her grandfather's estate. What would it be like to walk away from what she knew and start a new life in a place like that? Could she be so brave, so daring? Was she ready to break a tie that, once severed, could likely never be repaired?

She wasn't sure. But fear is a convincing advocate. Her world was crumbling around her, and with each passing moment, it seemed, another piece tumbled to the ground.

What choice did she have?

She thought of her worldly possessions, tucked away neatly in the small upstairs room. There was little there worth going after—not if it meant encountering her father.

She cast another glance through the fence. But as she did, the first thing her eyes landed on was Tevy. The big brown dog's tail started wagging when he saw her. He stood from where he was sitting and started walking toward the gate.

Camille shook her head and backed away.

Papa's voice sounded. "What do you see, Tevy?"

The men grew quiet.

Camille's breath lodged in her throat, refusing to move. Now was not the time to panic. If they discovered her, no doubt they would pull her into their world, involve her in their underhanded business.

She didn't want to be a part of that. Not ever again.

She backed away from her spot, careful to be silent. She attempted to place her feet exactly where she had on her approach, but her boot caught on a piece of a broken crate, and the wood cracked beneath her heel.

She froze. The men's hushed talking ceased.

"Hold fast," one of the gruff voices whispered. "Someone's there."

Camille cast a glance over her shoulder, identifying her path to the main street.

"Get on, Tevy," Papa's rough voice ordered. "Find who is there."

Camille needed no more incentive. Tevy would never hurt her, but he would find her and no doubt lead Papa to her. She could not face him. Not now. Not when she had heard what she did. And if he thought she had overheard their conversation, there was no telling what the next steps would be.

So she ran. She ran down the alleyway, ignoring the dirty rainwater from the previous night's storm as it splashed on her borrowed skirt. She ran down the street, past the storefronts and shops. For a while she heard shouts, and she heard Tevy bark. But it was easy to get lost amongst the carts and carriages, the horses and people. The ever-present cover of smoke hovered, creating a misty shroud of secrecy. But the familiar sea of faces around her seemed odd and terrifying, a reminder that even though she'd lived her entire life here, she was still a stranger.

Her pulse raced, urging her further and faster through the crowd toward the west end of Blinkett Street. The sun was warm now, trapping a yellow glow in the smoke hovering over the street.

Mr. Gilchrist had said that he and his sister would depart tomorrow.

Would that be soon enough?

For she was certain of one thing: she could not go back home. But it was not home, she told herself. It was a place of business, and it had been such ever since her mother left all those years ago.

Hurt blistered into anger. Her father had spoken as if she were dispensable.

She had given her all to helping him, and he took no notice of it. What would happen to his shop, his little empire, if she were not there to make sure the merchants were paid? That the books were kept?

Indignation pushed her feet faster. She brushed her way past a gathering of people, sidestepped a dog, and dodged a low-hanging sign. She retraced her steps back away from Blinkett Street and to the Gilchrist home. She rarely had a reason to be in such an elegant part of town, and no doubt she looked terribly out of place.

She tucked her arm beneath her bundle of belongings to disguise the blood as she neared the Gilchrists' door. Then her footsteps slowed until she was standing frozen before it.

She was poised between two evils. If she returned home, her fate would be sealed. She would forever be cemented into her father's world. But if she agreed to Mr. Gilchrist's suggestion, she could never return. And though Mr. Gilchrist had offered to help her, what if the country school he had mentioned had no positions for which she was suited?

Then I will find something else to do, she told herself. She might be a woman, but she was independent. Smart. She didn't need another living soul. Not her father. Not her mother. Nobody except, for the moment, the person who had offered to help her. And she would accept from him only what she truly needed.

Yellow light blinked from behind drawn curtains. Mr. Gilchrist might or might not be inside. But someone, at least, was home.

She stepped up to the door, but embarrassment choked her as she lifted her hand. Never in her life would she have thought she would be knocking on a stranger's door, as forward as the women who walked the street in front of the public houses across from their shop. She well remembered the rules of polite society and knew it was highly improper for her to arrive without invitation. Perhaps she should seek a servants' entrance.

But at this point, what did it matter? What had she to lose?

The opinion of a family she did not know and, if she were turned away, would never see again?

This was a chance she was willing to take.

A blinding flash of fear made her glance over her shoulder. What if her father was looking for her? He had seen her with Mr. Gilchrist and said he knew the man's father. What if he knew about this house? Or what if one of his cronies saw her and informed him of her whereabouts? She did not know what he was up to, but he was clearly involved in something shady.

She turned back to the door and bit her lip. It was now or never. She took the elegantly carved brass knocker in her work-worn hand and let it fall against the door.

Chapter Fifteen

$\mathcal{N}$ ewspaper in hand, Jonathan sat and watched his sister pace the narrow parlor.

The empty parlor.

Normally, whenever they were in London, a cluster of ladies would be assembled in this room, their hands busy with their needlework, laughing and exchanging the latest gossip with Penelope.

But no ladies had called during their last several visits to London.

Jonathan had not really noticed the change until now, when the silence was broken only by the clattering of carriages on the street outside, the voices of pedestrians as they passed, and his sister's worried footsteps.

The rumors of his father's financial issues had started circulating several months ago. Jonathan had managed to ignore most of the chatter, but Penelope had a much more difficult time of it. As the gossip increased, the number of people in her circle had decreased. Now she was often alone. Fortunately, her engagement had been announced before the latest set of rumors began to circulate, but even that prospect seemed to grow more uncertain with each passing day.

Penelope dropped to a chair, her normally pristine posture

sagging. Her cheeks were pale, and dark circles marked the space beneath her eyes. "I suppose I should have expected this."

Jonathan frowned at her statement. "Expected what?"

She rubbed the back of her neck as if to relieve tension gathering there. "I tried to tell you, Jonathan. People are starting to talk."

She had mentioned this the previous evening, when they were speaking of Miss Iverness. But now she was much calmer, her expression much more sober.

He cleared his throat. "What are they saying?"

"I'm not sure exactly, but I felt it last night at the Dowdens'."

It was not unusual for his sister to exaggerate. But there was a sadness in her voice, a genuine sorrow that tugged at him. "Are you sure you did not imagine it?"

"No, Jonathan." She shook her head with emphasis. "You weren't there. Miss Vallum barely said two words to me, and more than once I saw Miss Stathem and Miss Crenshaw looking my way and whispering to each other. It was mortifying. Miss Marbury had warned me it might be so, but nothing could have truly prepared me for the coldness I felt. Even Alfred was distant."

Normally, Jonathan paid little attention to his sister's social activities. But as the date for her wedding drew near, she was growing particularly sensitive to the whispers concerning their father and the possible implications for her marriage to Mr. Dowden.

Penelope leaned with her elbow on the arm's chair and rested her chin in her hand. "What if he changes his mind?"

"He won't." Jonathan knew his words of consolation were

hardly adequate. Alfred Dowden would not be the first man to call off a wedding due to a change in dowry expectations. It would be a scandal, of course, but the taint would eventually pass for Dowden, whose family was wealthy and well-connected. Penelope, on the other hand, might never recover from the slight.

"We'll find the ruby," he assured her. "Mr. Darbin knows what he is doing."

Penelope sighed. "So I have heard, yet my hope dwindles with every day that passes."

"Even if we do not recover the Bevoy, we will figure something out."

Her posture straightened, and her expression brightened. "You do have another option, you know."

He frowned. "What do you mean?"

"Miss Marbury asked about you again last night. She always does." The words seemed to tumble out of her. "You know, she is quite fond of you and doesn't seem to mind at all that you are an apothecary. And, after all, settling down isn't such a bad idea, is it? Her family is well respected, and if you would—"

"We have been through this before, Penelope. No."

"But if you would only—"

"I have no intentions of marrying," he interrupted. "Especially for money."

She slouched back in her chair, a pout darkening her face.

On this topic he would not negotiate. Jonathan had resigned himself to hearing his family speak of his profession as if it were a disease. But the very mention of his "improving his circumstances" through matrimony was enough to set him on edge.

His sister was not willing to let the topic drop. "Must you

be so stubborn? I simply do not understand your aversion to the idea. It is not at all unusual to marry for practical reasons—for the good of others. The love comes later."

"Is that so?" Jonathan sucked in a deep breath. "And did it ever come for Mother?"

She looked as if she had been struck. "How could you say such a thing?"

"Do you think Mother was happy, married to Father all those years?"

Before she could respond, a sharp knock echoed on the front door.

Penelope's face brightened, and she jumped from her chair and ran to the window. Her voice squeaked with disbelief as she leaned to look out the window. "It is she! She is here. I do not believe it."

"Miss Marbury?"

"No, Miss Iverness." Penelope whirled from the window, her blue eyes bright and wide, the drama of such an event covering her melancholy.

Jonathan snapped his head up. "Miss Iverness is here?"

"Indeed." Penelope quickly returned to the window, pressing herself against the wall to get a better view through the narrow panes. "The nerve that woman has, to disappear so suddenly, without so much as a word of gratitude, and then to return all these hours later—to the main entrance no less. I suppose we shouldn't be too shocked, however, considering where she comes from. She likely never learned proper manners."

Jonathan laid his paper aside. He had left Miss Iverness earlier that day on Blinkett Street, certain he had overstepped the bounds of propriety and would never see her again. Yet here she was, hours later, on his doorstep. His mind raced to consider the possibilities. Miss Iverness's presence here could mean one of two things: either she had information about the ruby or she had changed her mind about his suggestion.

The butler's heavy footsteps could be heard outside the parlor, followed by the creak of the opening door.

Penelope hurried to the mirror and patted her hair into place. "Perhaps she has news of the ruby. Wouldn't that be something?"

Penelope had been irked to wake up late that morning and find Miss Iverness gone. So Jonathan had told her about escorting Miss Iverness home, omitting from his tale the encounter with Miss Iverness's father or his own suggestion that Miss Iverness consider a position in Fellsworth.

Now he cleared his throat. "There is something I need to tell you, just in case it should come up in conversation."

"What did you say, Jonathan?" Penelope was far too interested in primping to listen to him.

But before he could repeat himself, a knock echoed on the paneled parlor door and Winston appeared. "Miss Iverness is in the main hall, sir. She has asked to speak with you."

Penelope shook her head. Jonathan knew what she was thinking. He himself was surprised that Miss Iverness had not asked for Penelope. A woman calling on a man was simply unheard of. The impropriety of the action was damning.

But she was here, and he could hardly send her away.

"Show her in."

Camille winced as the heavy front door fell closed behind her.

It was too late now. Too late to change her mind or formulate another plan. She was standing in the Gilchrists' hall.

She swallowed the lump of doubt in her throat and sank her teeth into her lip. She could do nothing about the fluttering in her stomach or the trembling of her arms. This was all too strange. Too uncomfortable. Every instinct screamed for her to turn and run as fast as she could.

The thought of admitting she needed assistance galled her. If there was one thing she had learned from her father it was self-reliance, depending on no one person or thing. And for years she had been successful at that.

How quickly her situation had changed. She had told herself she had nothing to lose. But in truth she had everything to lose. For if Mr. Gilchrist retracted his offer of assistance, where would she go? She could not—would not—return home.

The butler, an older man with white hair and long side-whiskers, reappeared. "Mr. and Miss Gilchrist will see you."

Camille pressed her hand to her stomach. How she wished the gown she wore was cleaner, her hair tidier. She had to swallow every bit of pride to follow him into the parlor.

Last night, she had only seen the parlor by firelight, but by day, the colors in the room were much more vibrant, the polished mahogany shinier, the murals richer, the exotic fabrics more plush and exquisite.

Mr. Gilchrist stood when she entered. His gaze locked with hers, the simple act rattling her senses and simultaneously infusing her with courage. "Miss Iverness. This is a surprise."

Camille's throat was dry, almost too dry for words to form.

Miss Gilchrist rushed forward, her golden tresses perfectly curled, her cream-colored gown of sateen glimmering with every motion. "Miss Iverness, are you all right? I was so concerned when I woke this morning to find you had left us without a word."

Camille heard the rebuke behind the expression of concern. "I do apologize for leaving without bidding you farewell." She offered a smile. "It was rude of me."

Miss Gilchrist waved a dismissive hand in the air. "Please, pay it no heed. Jonathan told me you were eager to return home, and I cannot blame you. One's own home is always preferable when one is injured or feeling ill."

Mr. Gilchrist stepped forward, his blue eyes locked on hers. "Welcome back to our home, Miss Iverness."

Camille was rarely at a loss for words. But now she could do nothing but nod.

"Please be seated." He ushered her to a chair with elegantly curved armrests—the very one in which he had sat the previous evening.

She sank into the fine upholstery, uncomfortably aware that the smells of Blinkett Street still clung to her clothing. She had to take a steadying breath before looking up at him. "Thank you."

He smiled, but then his gaze fell on the bit of red visible from beneath the bundle she carried. "Your arm."

At first she attempted to push it further beneath the items she was carrying, but then, realizing her secret had been noticed, she held it out.

From behind him, Miss Gilchrist gasped. "Mercy, Miss Iverness! Jonathan, look."

Mr. Gilchrist extended a hand toward her as if to ask permission. "May I?"

Camille set her bundle on the floor next to her and gingerly rolled back the bloodstained sleeve. She looked up at Miss Gilchrist. "I do apologize for the state of your gown. You see, I have—"

"That dressing needs to be changed," Mr. Gilchrist stated, "and my guess is that the wound has opened up again. I can take care of that."

Camille shook her head. "I hate to trouble you, Mr. Gilchrist. This is not why I am here."

"It is no trouble at all. And your reason for calling can wait until your arm has been tended to." He left the room and returned quickly with a box. Minutes later the butler followed with a basin of water, which he placed on a nearby footstool.

Mr. Gilchrist drew a chair up next to hers and sat. With gentle, practiced hands he soaked the soiled bandage and carefully removed it.

"I know the wound looks angry," he said, "but I believe it will heal cleanly. You will most likely have a scar, but I will make you a compound to help it heal smoothly."

"Thank you, Mr. Gilchrist," she said. "I fear I have been quite a burden to you."

"I am happy to be of service."

His smile was warm, but Camille could not help but notice his sister's cool gaze on the both of them. Despite her welcoming words, Miss Gilchrist's crossed arms and pinched expression conveyed her reservations about Camille's presence. Camille did not blame her. But she had come too far to turn back now. She would make her request despite Penelope Gilchrist's disapproval.

"I hope this is not too forward, Mr. Gilchrist, but I have been reconsidering your offer about the possibility of employment at Fellsworth School. I—I may have been too brash in my refusal."

This was clearly a surprise to Miss Gilchrist. Camille could feel the shock radiating from her. Though masked behind a pleasant expression, her displeasure pulsed through the air like lightning during a summer's storm. Clearly, her brother had not mentioned his offer to her.

Mr. Gilchrist must have sensed his sister's disapproval as well, but he looked only at Camille. "Am I to understand that you have changed your mind?"

Camille turned her arm to give Mr. Gilchrist better access to the wound. "It has been a long time since I have been in the country, and I should like to return. My father is quite capable of handling his own affairs, and I do not believe he needs my assistance."

The words hung stiff in the air as Mr. Gilchrist retrieved a glass vial from his box and began to clean the wound. He did not make eye contact with her. "As I mentioned, I cannot guarantee a position, but our family's relationship with the school is long-standing. I am certain a recommendation from us would secure you a position of some sort. Mr. Langsby is a kindly sort of fellow and always looking for people who have experience to share with his pupils."

"I would like to—"

"What is this plan you two have concocted?" Miss Gilchrist's nonchalant air concealed a sharp edge as she stepped closer to her brother. The previous evening Miss Gilchrist had seemed so amiable. But today her eyes narrowed in what could only be annoyance.

"After speaking with Miss Iverness this morning, I thought she might be able to find work at Fellsworth School." Mr. Gilchrist's quiet tone seemed designed to soothe his sister's pique. He reached for a long, clean strip of linen and looked at Camille as he wrapped the bandage. "I will post a letter and give notice to the superintendent, but we are planning on departing for Fellsworth in the morning, so we will likely reach home before a letter would."

"Jonathan, what are you talking—"

He looked up at his sister. "I have invited Miss Iverness to share our carriage when we return home tomorrow."

"I confess, I had hoped to do just that." Camille paused, disappointed that they were not leaving until the morrow. If allowed too much time to consider her options, she would certainly falter and change her mind. She drew a deep breath. They were doing her a service. She was hardly in a position to make demands.

"Mr. Gilchrist, it is pointless for me to try to hide the fact that the situation surrounding my home life is a bit . . . unusual. Circumstances are such that it would be best for me to leave London as soon as possible—at your convenience, of course."

Jonathan heard the pleading in Miss Iverness's voice, saw the desperation that marked her features. He cleared his throat and exchanged glances with Penelope, whose lips were pressed together in a tight line of frustration. He looked back to their guest. "Is your father comfortable with your taking this position?"

Miss Iverness rolled her sleeve back down over the bandage, her eyes steadfastly on him. "He does not know."

So she had left home. The idea did not bode well with Jonathan, though after seeing the interaction between her and her father he could hardly blame her. He did want more than ever to help her in some way. But had his hurried offer been ill considered?

His sister's clenched jaw told him that she thought so, and perhaps she was right. But if Miss Iverness were to accompany them to Fellsworth, he would at least know she was safe. And if he could earn her trust, perhaps she could assist him in finding the ruby.

Perhaps. But even if she could help him, there was a very strong chance that he could help her.

"Do you have anything to take with you?" he asked. "Your belongings?"

She looked to the bundle at her feet. "Just these things. And my dress, if your maid has been able to clean it."

"I see." He made up his mind swiftly. The sooner they departed for Fellsworth, the more confidence he had in their plan. "Penelope, do you think you could be ready to depart for Kettering Hall today?"

"Today?" His sister gasped, obviously flustered by the request. "Jonathan, I don't think I—"

"We would need to leave within the next couple of hours if we are to have the day's light." He met her eyes and held her gaze.

Penelope folded her arms across her chest, looking more like a spoiled child than a woman of twenty-three. Finally she blew out a sigh. "Very well. I shall ask Meeks to finish packing right away."

Jonathan waited for Penelope to leave before turning back to Miss Iverness. He lowered his voice. "After this morning, I can understand your need for urgency. You can stay at Kettering Hall, our family home, tonight, and then tomorrow we can visit the school, which is not far away."

Miss Iverness's shoulders seemed to relax at the words, and for the first time, he noticed her lips curve into the slightest hint of a smile.

Jonathan had not planned for them to leave for the country until the following day. But why should they not? He had been unsuccessful in retrieving the ruby and would need to develop a new plan. And getting home earlier meant he could get back to his work that much more quickly.

Leaving Miss Iverness to rest in the parlor, Jonathan headed for the stairs but stopped when he encountered Winston in the vestibule.

"We have changed our plans and will be leaving for Kettering Hall later today. Miss Iverness will accompany us. Please make the appropriate arrangements."

Winston bowed in compliance, but not before Jonathan noted the fleeting expression on his face. The butler had been part of their London home for as long as Jonathan's memory would stretch. But whereas he felt he could trust Abbott at Kettering Hall, it was no secret that Winston's loyalty skewed toward Ian Gilchrist, not Jonathan. He no doubt had firm opinions about what he had observed in the house yesterday and today—including

Miss Iverness's condition when Jonathan first brought her to the house—though he would never express them in earshot of the family.

Jonathan chose to ignore the manner in which the old man looked down his long nose, his bushy eyebrows furrowed in disapproval. How Jonathan hated this game of innuendo and judgment. Of perceived rights versus perceived wrongs, propriety and impropriety, who belonged in society and who did not. Did not the Almighty judge mankind on a different scale?

Once satisfied that the butler understood his directions, Jonathan started up the stairs to gather his own belongings. Penelope met him halfway.

"This has gone too far, Jonathan." She hissed the words through clenched teeth, her blue eyes wide with indignation.

Jonathan continued up the stairs, his hand gripping the thick oak railing. He did not respond—partly because his decision had already been made, and partly because he knew well his sister's tendencies. She relished a good argument.

He would not give her one.

Penelope followed him closely—so closely, in fact, that he felt the swish of her skirt on the back of his boots. "Have you lost your senses? Hasn't our family had enough of scandal and gossip? It is clear that this woman is in some sort of trouble. Did you see how fidgety she is? She is involved with the wrong sorts of people, and possibly up to her neck in criminal activity. Spending the night here was one thing, but inviting her to Fellsworth and Kettering Hall is another matter entirely."

Jonathan paused on the landing and turned to her, employing every ounce of self-control to remain calm. "Camille Iverness is the closest link we have to the ruby at the moment. So I would prefer to keep her close. Do you not agree?"

"I think you are overestimating her knowledge of the ruby," she sniffed. "I do not think she knows a thing about it."

"Perhaps she does. Perhaps she does not. But you know this as well as I: either we get that ruby back or Father loses everything. Which means you have no dowry, as you yourself mentioned not twenty minutes ago. If taking the woman with us to Kettering Hall gives us even half a chance of learning more about the ruby, then I am eager to do so. And if we can help her escape an untenable situation by doing it, all the better."

"Mark my words, Jonathan, you are inviting trouble." A flush rushed to her cheeks as the words tumbled from her mouth. "And what of Mr. Darbin? Surely he would not agree."

"Keep your voice down. I will send word and apprise Darbin of these developments. But I could not care less if he agrees or not. Kettering Hall is not so far should he desire to visit and discuss the matter. And he is certainly welcome to continue searching for the stone without my direct help."

Penelope grabbed his arm to stop him when he turned to leave. "So you do not care what this will do to our reputation?"

"On the contrary. My intention is to prevent further damage to our reputation. But if I may say so, you care far too much for such things."

"Well, someone in our family needs to, and if I am the only one who will pay heed, then so be it."

Jonathan expelled his breath. "There is nothing improper in what we are doing."

"Nothing improper!" she cried. "You bring an injured woman

to our house—a stranger, I might add. You implore her to stay the night, escort her home in the wee hours of the morning, and then invite her to accompany us to Kettering Hall? No, there is no scandal in that at all."

"My mind is made up." He shrugged matter-of-factly and resumed climbing the stairs.

"Father will be furious," she shot back, following on his heels.

He stopped short. "The only thing that will infuriate Father is if we—if I—fail to recover the ruby—to cover debts he foolishly secured with *your* dowry money."

Penelope threw up her hands in mock surrender. "Well, dear brother, you surely know what is best. I will just sit back and keep my mouth closed." She pointed a finger toward his face. "I just want you to know right now that I claim no responsibility in this whatsoever."

"You must trust me. Miss Iverness is hardly a threat to any of us. And even if she knows nothing about the ruby, we will surely be doing her a service. Do we not have an obligation to help one who is injured and in danger?"

"Tsk. You and your sentimental ideals. You will adopt any stray kitten, any sad child—anyone. Perhaps it is time that you concern yourself with your family and leave the rest to fate."

He pressed his lips together. Arguing with her would get him nowhere. "We leave for Kettering Hall shortly. See to it that you are ready."

With determined steps he continued to his bedchamber. Behind him he heard Penelope's exasperated huff, then her retreating footsteps.

Penelope's opposition to the prospect of taking Miss Iverness with them did not surprise him. In fact, his sister was probably right. Taking responsibility for a penniless young woman with unsavory connections was surely the last thing his family needed.

But no matter how hard he tried, he could not free his mind from the image of Miss Iverness, frightened and embarrassed yet unconquered, determined to make her own way in the world. Nor could he forget the cruel tone of James Iverness's voice.

No one deserved to be treated in such a fashion, and it seemed unacceptable to stand by and offer no help.

Chapter Sixteen

Camille had thought it would be easier to leave London.

Ever since she made the decision earlier in the day, she had tried to imagine what it would feel like to leave behind the city and everything it represented for a new beginning.

But as she sat in the carriage and watched the recognizable scenery jostle into a strange mosaic of twisted streets and unfamiliar buildings, an unwelcome lump formed in her throat.

Memories rushed her, like fingers reaching out, attempting to hold her in place. Memories of playing in the street and alleys on warm summer days. Memories of rare excursions to parks or markets or the river. Memories of long afternoons in the shop with Tevy and Link for company.

But overshadowing them all was the memory of her father's harsh words this morning.

Miss Gilchrist's lady's maid, Meeks, who was traveling in the carriage with them, had given her a cloak to wear on the journey. Camille clutched the soft wool fabric more tightly around her and drew a deep, steadying breath. Meeks had also been able to clean her gown and mend the sleeve, so Camille enjoyed the small comfort in being dressed in her own garment of modest linen. The rain had returned, dousing the short-lived warmth from the sun, and the damp spring air seeped in around the carriage's doors and windows.

Miss Gilchrist sat across from her, next to Meeks. She truly was a beautiful woman. Her hair was the same pale gold of Mr. Gilchrist's, but her eyes were a deeper shade of blue, almost violet, and her chin was delicately pointed. Her traveling ensemble consisted of a deep plum spencer with velvet-covered buttons and a lighter lavender gown beneath. Her smooth, rosy complexion reminded Camille of the porcelain that would come through the shop from time to time.

Camille looked down at her own ungloved hands. Their soft tawny hue bore testament to her mother's Portuguese heritage. One finger was still stained with ink from working on the books. Could that have been only yesterday? She tucked that hand to her side.

Outside the window, she could see Mr. Gilchrist riding his dappled horse with the dark gray mane. He sat tall and straight, his broad shoulders cutting a handsome figure against the flashing landscape. Camille watched as he urged the animal to a canter and rode out ahead of the carriage, his coat catching the wind and billowing out behind him with each of the horse's footfalls. Before long he was out of sight.

How different the two siblings seemed to be—Miss Gilchrist, sharp and highly strung, a stark contrast to her brother, whose gentleness and seemingly genuine concern made Camille feel welcome.

The carriage rumbled further away from London, the road now lined on both sides with lush greenery. Camille's head ached and the jerking movements upset her injury, but the discomfort couldn't dampen her curiosity about what her new life would be like.

She spoke to break the silence. The Gilchrists would be the

only people she knew in her new town. It would not hurt to attempt to develop a cordial relationship. "I do appreciate your altering your plans to include me."

Miss Gilchrist tossed her head, her gaze not leaving the scenery outside the window. "My brother was quite insistent about it."

The words hung icy in the air. Miss Gilchrist had made little effort to hide her displeasure at her brother's decision, and she made even less of an effort now to show any warmth to Camille. In fact, she could not be more different than the woman who had shown such kindness just the night before.

Camille looked over to the lady's maid, seeking reassurance or assistance, but the somber woman sat stone-faced, her brown eyes staring straight ahead.

Suddenly, Miss Gilchrist pinned Camille with her gaze. "I trust my brother shared with you what brought us to London."

Camille stammered, unsure of what to say. "He mentioned he was looking for something that had been stolen, but I—"

"It is a ruby called the Bevoy, Miss Iverness," Miss Gilchrist interrupted sharply.

The carriage hit a rut and joggled Camille against the carriage wall. "Yes, Mr. Gilchrist told me of such. I believe you mentioned it as well."

"Even though this particular visit was unsuccessful, he and I hope you will be able to assist us in our search."

Camille adjusted the cloak around her shoulders. She had known this question was coming. "I do wish to be of help, but as I shared with Mr. Gilchrist, I am afraid my knowledge of such things is limited. I only worked at the counter in my father's shop. I know very little about his business dealings."

"Be that as it may, you can surely understand how much we would appreciate your assistance, little or great, in making sure the jewel is returned to my father, its rightful owner. From what I understand, your knowledge of such things could prove invaluable. For you know all sorts of people, do you not? Your connections could well prove helpful in our recovery efforts."

Camille pressed her lips together. So this was the reason they had been so kind. They needed her help. "If I can be of assistance in returning a piece of jewelry to its rightful owner, then I will be happy to do so, but please do not overestimate my abilities in this regard."

Miss Gilchrist's eyes widened. "Oh it is not merely a piece of jewelry as you say, Miss Iverness. It is rumored to possess mystical powers—to bring blessings or curses on those who possess it. Of course, those are just silly legends, but as I am sure you are aware, such folklore attached to any artifact makes it all the more valuable. To be honest, I am a bit surprised that someone in your position has not heard of it. I understand from Mr. Darbin that my father originally purchased the ruby from your father."

Camille could not help but bristle at the hidden jab. "Who, may I ask, is Mr. Darbin?"

"Do you not know Mr. Henry Darbin? He is the man my brother hired to track down the villain who stole the ruby. He was a very good friend of my late brother, Thomas."

A sinking feeling rolled through Camille. It seemed she had underestimated the lengths to which the Gilchrists were willing to go to recover this trinket.

Miss Gilchrist's voice grew sharper. "I hope I do not offend you with what I am about to say, but I thought we should have a discussion about what will be said when we arrive at Kettering Hall."

Camille frowned. "A discussion?"

"Of course. My brother told me all about what happened, you poor creature." Her voice was rich with condescension. "But you don't want to start off on the wrong foot with the good people in Fellsworth, do you?"

"I am not certain I follow you." Camille fussed with the tassels on her cape.

Miss Gilchrist shook her blond head, her bouncy curls twisting to and fro. "Come now. People will ask how you are acquainted with our family. Surely you are not going to share all the details of our . . . connection, are you? We want you to be embraced, and your story could cause some to, well, misconstrue your situation."

Camille's face began to burn as Miss Gilchrist's true meaning became clear. Until she met this family, she had never been ashamed of who she was or where she came from. True, her home was not nearly as elegant as the Gilchrists'. Her clothing was not as fashionable or expensive. But she was the granddaughter of a gentleman. She knew proper manners. Why did Miss Gilchrist, with her perfect complexion and elegant posture and thinly veiled insults, make her feel like such a ragamuffin?

"Let's just tell them you are a friend of mine from London." A forced smile lit Miss Gilchrist's face. "It is indeed fortunate that your speech sounds like that of a lady, not like most people from your part of London. But there is a lilt to your diction, Miss Iverness. I can't quite place my finger on it. Where is it you are from? Surely not from London."

Camille bristled. Her refined manner of speaking had been an asset in the shop as she worked with wealthy patrons, but a liability when she tried to make friends with those around her. "I was born on my grandfather's estate in Somerset. I lived there until he died. Then I moved with my parents to London."

At the mention of an estate, Miss Gilchrist's eyes sparkled. "There, then, that's the truth, isn't it? You are a lady, a friend from London, and we can just omit the bit about the robbery and your father's shop. I think that is best, do you not agree?"

Camille received the message behind the innocent expression, the hopeful tone. Practically speaking, Miss Gilchrist's advice was probably sound, though not given with true kindness.

But did Camille want to start out her new life on a bed of lies?

She looked from Miss Gilchrist's guileless face to the stern visage of the lady maid's. Then, with a sigh, she peered out the window at the passing countryside—the countryside she had never thought she would see again.

She was indebted to this family, and she knew it. "Very well. I shall keep that information to myself if you wish."

"I think it is for the best. You know how the servants can talk. Of course, Meeks here can be trusted completely. I only suggest this for your sake."

Camille swallowed. Tears pricked her eyes. She did not know why Miss Gilchrist's suggestion should affect her so. She was certainly no stranger to unkind speech, even outright abuse. Perhaps she could blame her feelings on the extreme events of the past day. But she had so rarely been exposed to the world outside her father's shop. At the moment, that world seemed like an unbearably harsh and judgmental place.

She could not help but wonder if Mr. Gilchrist shared his sister's sentiment.

Camille looked out the window, hoping to catch another glimpse of Mr. Gilchrist, but she saw only rain-shrouded woods. She had formed a quick opinion of the man—something she rarely did. A lifetime of broken promises and subtle deception had made her hesitant, but he had been so kind from the beginning—seemingly so genuine.

Perhaps he was. But Camille knew too well that nothing comes free. Nothing was without a price.

She straightened her posture, refusing to give in to melancholy. Now, more than ever, she needed to be away from London. If her father was willing to risk her safety for whatever deal he was working, then any situation would be preferable to living with him—even if it meant remaining under the scrutinizing eye of the Gilchrist family.

She wasn't sure how much time passed before the carriage slowed and then turned. Dusk was falling, but through the dimness she caught a glimpse of a massive brick structure looming against the darkening sky. The horses pulled to a stop, and the sudden silence, the absence of movement left Camille feeling strangely numb.

Then Mr. Gilchrist opened the carriage door.

And the next thing Camille noticed was the air.

It was smooth and clean, and her lungs responded as the freshness swirled into the carriage. Aromas of earth and trees rode the slight breeze, inviting her to explore.

Each breath filled her deeper than the last, thrusting energy into every limb, reviving her spirit.

This was a place she had never been. Yet the clean air, the majestic trees, the spacious vistas felt familiar and reminiscent of a happier time.

Deep inside, she knew she was closer to finding home.

Chapter Seventeen ⸻

The ride from London had not been a particularly long or difficult one, though rain had plagued most of their journey.

Jonathan didn't mind. He was just grateful not to be in the carriage. He would much rather battle the elements than spend hours in an enclosed space with the women.

He had been pleased, albeit surprised, when Miss Iverness asked to accompany them, though his sister's antagonism had tempered his enthusiasm. He suspected Miss Iverness was more than a match for his strong-willed sister, and he could not help but wonder what the conversation in the carriage was like. But the day's developments had happened so quickly and with such intensity that he needed the solitude of the ride to sort them out.

He'd ridden ahead of the carriage to give the staff advance notice that they were arriving early and that there was to be a guest. The overcast sky was just beginning to dim as he turned into the long drive that led to Kettering Hall.

The place really was impressive. A hipped roof capped its three stories, with shuttered dormer windows symmetrically spaced along the roofline. Trees and shrubbery flanked the structure, and a brick wall enclosing one of the many rose gardens met up against the side of the building.

One day, if all continued as planned, he would be master—a title he had never expected and a responsibility he did not relish.

In the meantime, he had to answer to his father.

That reality did not settle well at all.

He did not look forward to informing Ian Gilchrist of what had happened in London. The man did not accept failure. And not bringing the Bevoy home, in his eyes, would be failure.

The house was relatively dark as he approached. Clearly, they were not expected. His horse's hooves thudded against the muddy drive.

He pulled to a stop in front of the hall. A footman appeared and steadied his horse. "Welcome back, Mr. Gilchrist."

Jonathan dismounted, tossed the reins to the footman, and strode toward the door.

At his arrival, the house, already wrapped in the sleepy silence, began to revive. Candles appeared in windows. A torch was brought out to light the entryway. And his father, already dressed to retire in a robe of red and green brocade, hobbled down the main steps, leaning heavily on his cane.

"You're home earlier than I expected." His father's welcome was more of a growl.

Jonathan stepped up to meet the old man. "Yes."

"Well?" he barked. "Did you get it?"

Jonathan shook his head, looked down, and pulled the glove from his hand finger by finger. "No."

His father scowled, his jaw trembling. "Why not?"

"It could not be helped."

"I told you not to come back without it."

"We cannot stay in London forever, Father. Besides, Darbin is still working on it. Ah, here's the carriage."

Sarah E. Ladd

The coach and four rumbled up the drive and pulled to a stop. Jonathan, grateful for the diversion, walked over to help the women step down.

First, his sister. Judging by the tightness of her expression, he guessed the conversation on the way had not gone well.

Penelope raced to their father, placed her hands on his shoulders, and kissed his withered cheek before scurrying inside. Meeks followed close behind, already calling out orders, their guest apparently forgotten.

He then turned to Miss Iverness. He half wondered if she would allow him to help her from the carriage, so stubborn and independent she was. But she cast him a grateful look and laid her slender hand in his.

"How was your journey, Miss Iverness?" he asked.

But before she could respond, before she even had both feet on the ground, his father barked, "Who in blazes is that?"

Jonathan felt the muscles in Miss Iverness's hand tighten as she whirled around in surprise at the sudden shout.

Jonathan nodded toward her. "Father, allow me to present Miss Camille Iverness."

The older man flinched. He narrowed his eyes on her again, looking at her more closely. "Iverness?"

"Yes, sir. Let's go inside for introductions. I fear the rain will return."

Jonathan led the way through the door. Warmth immediately rushed them, a welcome relief from the damp, cool evening. The marble-floored entryway opened to a grand hall marked by dark paneled walls and heavy molding at the ceiling and corners. A wide fireplace graced the opposite wall, encircled by a

130

wine-colored sofa and two high-backed chairs. Paintings much taller than Jonathan lined the dark walls.

The hall never changed. It looked exactly the same as it had ever since he was a boy, but tonight, somehow, it felt different.

Perhaps it was he who was different, not the hall.

Jonathan handed his wet cloak to Abbott and assisted Miss Iverness with her cloak before completing his introductions. "Miss Iverness, may I present my father, Mr. Gilchrist."

She curtsied as elegantly, he noted, as any gentlewoman he'd met. He was struck by how graceful her movements were—so unexpected for a woman from Blinkett Street.

The older Mr. Gilchrist did not bow in response. He did not even nod. He only leaned heavily on his cane and fixed his steely gaze on her, his words more an observation than a greeting. "James Iverness's daughter."

Camille straightened and jutted her chin out in a gesture that was rapidly becoming familiar to Jonathan. "Yes, sir. I am."

The old man approached her, making no attempt to hide his assessment. He lifted a monocle to his eye and examined her from the top of her head to her boots. "What is wrong with your arm?"

She shifted, but she did not respond quickly enough.

"I asked you a question, girl!" he thundered, causing her to jump. "What happened to your arm?"

"It is a knife wound, sir."

"Knife. Hmph."

"Yes, sir."

Jonathan stepped forward. "Miss Iverness will be staying at Kettering Hall for the night."

His father whirled as quickly as his aging form would allow. "And I am expected to put that man's daughter up for the night? Absolutely not."

Miss Iverness's eyebrows lifted, but otherwise she made no response.

Jonathan ignored his father's protest and motioned for one of the footmen. "See that one of the rooms close to Miss Gilchrist's is prepared for Miss Iverness and that she has everything she needs for a comfortable night's stay. But before you do, will you show Miss Iverness to the parlor and send for tea? I should like to speak with my father privately for a moment."

The staff snapped to action. Jonathan waited for the parlor door to close behind Miss Iverness before turning to his father.

Ian Gilchrist paced the main hall, his cane rapping sharply against the wooden floor. Jonathan recognized the signs of his father's annoyance—the trembling jowls, the furrowed brow. But Jonathan was annoyed as well and growing more so with each passing moment. He crossed his arms over his chest and planted his feet firmly on the floor, prepared for the lashing that was sure to follow. "You might as well speak your mind. I know you have an opinion. There must be some explanation for your rudeness toward Miss Iverness."

His father's quiet, gritty words sliced through the silence, the softness of which would rival the intensity of any shout. "You travel to London to get the ruby. I trust you with a task that I am unable to do myself. But not only do you fail in your task; you also bring home a girl. And not just any girl, but the daughter of a criminal who may well be behind the theft of my ruby. And you ask me my opinion?"

The familiar awareness tugged at Jonathan—the sinking knowledge that he had yet again disappointed his father. And yet he knew the truth of what had happened. If his father had been present, surely he would understand.

But there could be no understanding tonight. Once his father's opinions formed, he was steadfast. Unwavering.

"We cannot be certain who was behind the theft," Jonathan ventured.

"It matters not if we are certain. James Iverness is a suspect. That should have been enough for you to leave that sprig of a woman alone." He fairly spit out the words, and the force behind them incited a series of coughs that racked his body. Ian Gilchrist lowered himself into one of the chairs flanking the fireplace.

Jonathan expelled his breath, searching for the delicate balance of respecting his father and respecting himself. "We made our best attempt to locate the ruby and will not cease. Darbin remains in London, and—"

"I knew I should have gone myself," interrupted his father, rubbing a finger over his whiskered cheek.

Jonathan shook his head, taking the seat opposite his father. "You are hardly in a condition to travel."

"Apparently I am the only one who realizes the severity of this situation." The old man rose from the chair as quickly as his gout would allow. "I sent you to London with one responsibility, and this is the result. Your brother would have known what to do."

"No doubt," huffed Jonathan, the inflection of his voice divulging much more than he intended.

"How dare you take that tone when speaking of your brother,

God rest his soul. You are set to inherit. *You,* Jonathan. Need I remind you of that detail? Apparently I must, because from your actions one would think that you care very little for this estate."

"To the contrary, the present situation concerns me immensely. But I am not going to get myself killed or risk the life of another to see that happen."

"Spineless boy," his father hissed.

The words stung far more strongly than Jonathan would ever admit. They were the audible reminder of the chronic dissatisfaction that choked the relationship between father and son. Years of such exchanges had pressed down and compressed it until it was dry, hard, and unmoving.

"But what of this girl?" his father continued. "Why is she here?"

Jonathan looked up. In the face of his father's criticism he'd almost forgotten about Miss Iverness. "Darbin had information which led us to Iverness's shop. When we arrived there was a burglary in progress. She was injured. And then her brute of a father threw her out. What would you have me do? Leave her there?"

The sarcasm in his father's laugh chaffed his taut nerves. "Weak men are influenced by women. You let your guard down, allowed her to influence you."

"She can help us find the ruby," Jonathan argued.

"Do you think that, boy? Then you have much to learn of the ways of men outside of Fellsworth."

His father swept his arm as if to display the room in a grand gesture. "Kettering Hall has been part of our family's legacy for generation upon generation and will remain so if we will fight for it. But you are too much like your mother, not enough like your brother. He understood the importance of doing what must be done."

Jonathan bit his tongue and nodded to his father. Then he got to his feet and walked away.

He could not compete with a dead man. He would not even try.

Chapter Eighteen

Camille stood motionless in Kettering Hall's sumptuous parlor as the footman lit the candles, then relaxed as he exited. This moment of solitude was what her soul desperately needed. But the shouts and bitter tones coming from the other room gave her reason to pause.

She could not make out the words. She was not sure she wanted to.

She drew close to the fire, hoping the warmth would dry the bits of moisture clinging to her clothing and hair, and turned to survey her surroundings. The room was large—much larger than the parlor in the London house. And all around her were signs that she was in the home of a collector.

From the paintings on the walls and the decorations in the main hall she had sensed that such was the case, but now there could be no question. For every nook and cranny in this room was filled with unique and interesting items, the kind of items she had sold in her father's shop.

Though weariness pulled at her limbs, curiosity won over her exhaustion. She strolled about the room.

Many times she had wished that her family was in a different business. But a lifetime of learning about rare and unique foreign pieces had left its mark. In this room she was in her element. Her entire existence had prepared her for this house.

A boar's head was mounted above the chimneypiece, flanked by two sizable ivory elephant statues. A Chinese tapestry hung on the far wall next to an intricately carved table of Indian teak. She took her time, studying each piece in the candlelight.

There was no denying Mr. Ian Gilchrist's eye. His pieces were rare and costly, and it was a treat to see items displayed as they should be instead of piled in a back room or stuffed on rickety shelves as her father kept them.

She was not sure how much time had passed. Ten minutes. Perhaps twenty. She stepped forward to admire a full suit of armor next to the door. She had reached out to run her hand over the rivets on the curved metal, when a voice sounded behind her.

"What do you think of it?"

She snatched her hand back and laced her fingers behind her back. The elder Mr. Gilchrist stood in the doorway. "Forgive me, sir. I did not know you were there."

He hobbled closer, taking several moments to look at the armor she had been studying. His eyes were like his son's—startlingly blue and unnervingly direct. "I asked you what you thought of it."

She turned back to the piece, assessing the red plume atop the helmet and the jewel-encrusted sheath. "It is exquisite. A Scottish piece, is it not?"

"Very astute. Yes. Bought it at an auction in Glasgow more than a decade ago now. I'd bet you are curious about how much I paid for it."

She could feel her cheeks growing warm. The thought had crossed her mind, and she had a number in her head of what she thought the piece would sell for. But she would never offer such an opinion so freely. "That is your business, sir."

"You are right. It is my business, and I am glad you recognize that. But I will tell you that I parted with way too much for it—not that that should surprise you. But you know how it is. I saw a piece I needed for the collection. Once I saw it, I was not to be deterred."

Camille did understand. She had known buyers to spend months, even years, tracking down very specific pieces for very definitive reasons. And once they found what they wanted, they would pay any price for it.

She released her fingers from her back. "A piece is worth what someone is willing to pay for it. That is what my papa always said." The words slipped out of her mouth before she really thought about them. Then came the rush of hurt as she remembered her father talking to the men in the alley.

If Mr. Gilchrist was surprised by the reference to James Iverness, he gave no indication of such. He shuffled over to a painting near the armor and studied it for several moments before speaking. "Your father and I do not see eye to eye, Miss Iverness. I do not trust him. Not anymore."

She stood still, unsure of how to respond. Her normal reaction would be to jump to her father's defense, regardless if the accusation held any merit. But tonight she was confused on that matter. For had she not, just that morning, witnessed a betrayal of her own? She had been unaware of any relationship between the two men—indeed, she had never heard of Ian Gilchrist. But now what the younger Mr. Gilchrist had suggested was being verified.

"My son tells me you are going to try for a position at the school."

"Yes, sir."

"Have you ever spent time in a school, Miss Iverness?"

"No, sir. I have not."

"And to what position do you aspire? Will you be a teacher?"

"Your son said that not all the positions involve teaching. If they are seeking a teacher, perhaps I could instruct others in the practical skills I learned in my father's shop. But I do not think myself above any work. I would be grateful for any position the opportunity afforded."

She continued to study the armor, grateful to have something to look at instead of Mr. Gilchrist and particularly relieved at the shift of conversation. She had never been a shy person. But the directness of the man's questions, combined with her unfamiliarity with her surroundings, had slowed her response.

"My family is well connected with the school. We have been patrons for a very long time." He continued to walk around the room.

At this point, Camille was not sure if he was there to speak with her or to peruse his collection. He paused several times to pick up an urn or a statue or the like, and for a moment she would think he was absorbed in his own thoughts. Then he would speak again.

"Did that son of mine tell you why he was in London?"

Not knowing what else to do, she answered directly. "He was looking for a ruby. The Bevoy."

He raised his bushy eyebrow in her direction. "And do you know anything about its whereabouts?"

"No, sir, I do not."

He returned the statue to the table. "I bought it from your father. He sourced it for me. Did my son tell you that?"

She gave a little shrug. "I wish I could be of more help. But I think you know my father. He can be quite secretive about such things. And when he is working with a private buyer such as yourself, he rarely shares the secrets with me."

Mr. Gilchrist stared at her for several moments, the intensity of his deep-set eyes unsettling. But then, as quickly and suddenly as he had appeared, he made his way to the door.

"You are welcome at Kettering Hall for the night, Miss Iverness."

Later that evening, a meal of cold meat and vegetables was served to the weary travelers.

The older Mr. Gilchrist, having already eaten, retired to his chambers at an early hour, but the younger Mr. Gilchrist and his sister sat with Camille in Kettering Hall's dining chamber.

The meal passed in relative silence, and Camille was glad of it. She was grateful for the warmth and nourishment.

The extravagance of the room, with its blue-striped wallpaper, abundance of candlelight, and row of poker-straight footmen lining the wall, could have set her nerves on edge. She was accustomed to taking meals alone and without ceremony. But fortunately her time at her grandfather's estate had taught her how to behave in such an environment, even though her table manners were a bit rusty. By following the lead of her hosts, she was able to eat without embarrassing herself and to immerse herself in her own thoughts.

When she arrived at Kettering Hall, her first impression of the elder Mr. Gilchrist had been fiercely negative. But her apprehension had lessened after spending a few moments alone with him in the privacy of the parlor, in a world they both under-stood. He was a gruff man, to be sure, hard around the edges. But something about his mannerisms, his presence, reminded her of her father, and that slim bit of familiarity in a strange place comforted her.

Mr. Gilchrist broke the silence, interrupting her quiet stream of thoughts. "I trust your food is satisfactory. Is there anything else you would care for?"

Camille tapped her napkin to her lips before speaking. "The food is wonderful, thank you. I am quite content."

Miss Gilchrist balanced her fork in her fingers. "Normally our dinner would be much more elaborate, but Father rarely eats a formal meal when we are not present. He much prefers to eat in his chamber, and the cook was not expecting us until tomorrow."

Camille raised an eyebrow. Miss Gilchrist's statement seemed an odd one, as if it had only been spoken to prove that their early return was a major source of inconvenience or that their wealth far surpassed what the current repast suggested. But Mr. Gilchrist ignored his sister completely.

He took a sip of wine and turned to Camille. "I am sure you are eager to feel settled, Miss Iverness. Tomorrow I will go to the superintendent and see about arranging a position for you. His name is Mr. Langsby, and I think you will find him a kind employer."

"And if there is no position available?"

"Do not fret." Mr. Gilchrist's smile was kind. Reassuring. "The tie between the school and our family is a long one. My own mother taught there in the days before she married my father, and I myself visit the school several times a week as part of my rounds. I am sure that Mr. Langsby will be able to find a place for you."

Miss Gilchrist returned her fork to the table. "You forgot to say that our family has given large sums of money to the school. In fact, Father completely funded their library years ago. That alone should make a case for employing you at our request."

Mr. Gilchrist shot a warning glance at his sister. "As I was saying, I am certain he will be able to find a position for you. And if not, well, I will not rest until I find you a suitable arrangement. After all, it was on my recommendation that you left your home. Rest assured—we will not abandon you."

Camille stiffened. Did he think that she was counting on him to rescue her, like the knight who'd worn the armor in the parlor? Was he planning to take her out of a bad situation and make it all better? She could feel Miss Gilchrist's condescending gaze on her. Heat crept up her neck.

"I fear I must clarify something." Camille sat back from her plate, her stomach suddenly sour. "While I am wholeheartedly grateful to you for your kindness and your interest in my welfare, I do not wish to overstep my bounds. Without your assistance it is very unlikely that I would have been able to leave London and have found safety, so I thank you for that. But now that I have a little distance and have had a chance to find a little clarity, I think it is time that I take responsibility for my own situation."

Mr. Gilchrist frowned. "Do you not wish to apply for a position at the school?"

"Oh, I do think it would be the ideal situation for me. But I think it is best if I inquire after a position on my own."

A shadow of concern darkened Mr. Gilchrist's countenance. "Are you certain you have thought that through, Miss Iverness?

The superintendent is a kind man, as I mentioned, but he is also quite attentive to rules and traditions, and I know he is a stickler for propriety. I do not think he would consider an unsolicited candidate. I am not even sure if there is a position. But I know that if I—"

"I do not fear representing myself. And I cannot in good faith allow you to do something for me that I am quite capable of doing myself. If I am to obtain a position at the school, it should be on my merit."

Miss Gilchrist's mouth dropped open. "But Miss Iverness, it is just not done that way! Consider. My brother has a very good friendship with Mr. Langsby. Our family has a long-standing relationship with that school. Pray do not let your pride stand in the way of letting us help you."

"It is not pride. And I do understand what you are willing to do for me."

"But I will be at the school to check on the students," he continued. "I will be there anyway."

Why did they not see? How could they not understand why this was so very important to her? And then it struck her—she herself had not realized how important it was until this very moment.

For as long as she had remembered, she had worked hard. In her own way, she had been quite successful. Even though she lived with her father, it had been she who built the business on Blinkett Street. Without her skills with inventory and accounts, her carefully developed eye for what would sell, the shop would have succumbed long ago.

She suppressed the sharp words that simmered in her mind and wanted to come out. She had to remember that the Gilchrists were trying to help her. At least it *seemed* that they were trying to help her. The line between suspicion and gratitude was growing impossibly thin, and more so by the passing moment.

Mr. Gilchrist's expression softened. His eyes focused on her, and she found it difficult to look away. Their blueness seemed to cast a spell over her, drawing her into a trance. His voice, soothing and low, was quite unlike any she had heard. It lacked the rough accents of Londoners or the broken qualities of foreigners—the kinds of people she encountered most often. Instead it was smooth and melodic, quiet and slow.

"I believe I understand. Were I in your situation, I should want to proceed in the same manner. But at least allow me the opportunity to drive you there and introduce you. Surely you cannot object to that."

Camille wavered. She still wanted to do this her way. But here she was in an unfamiliar world, with people who were not at all like her. And despite the war waging within her, in this moment she wanted to believe he had her best interests at heart. "I-I suppose not."

"Good." He put his napkin on the table next to his plate and pushed away. "I will leave you now. But I will be by in the morning, and we can all go to Fellsworth together."

"Leave?" The words were out of Camille's mouth before she could stop them. "Where are you going?"

"Home."

"You do not live here?"

"No, I live in the village, in the apothecary's cottage."

Camille was unsure why that should surprise her so. He had told her he was an apothecary. Indeed she had been a beneficiary of his skills. But he was also the heir to an estate and had walked around Kettering Hall with such a sense of authority that she had just assumed he was a permanent fixture. The very thought of his leaving for the night sent an unsettling tremor through her.

She didn't want to feel this way. For years she had needed nobody. Wanted nobody, except perhaps the company of Tevy and Link.

But over the course of the last few days this man had rescued her. Protected her. Provided for her. Shown her kindness. Even tended her wounds.

Much as she hated to admit it, she was starting to depend on him.

Chapter Nineteen ─────────────

A borrowed shift. A borrowed room. A borrowed wrapper. Camille sat in silence on the floor next to the fire, its vibrant warmth attempting to soothe the aching chill within her. Her freshly washed hair, still damp from her bath, fell untethered down her back, the extra coolness sending a fresh shiver through her.

It was not cold in the great house. Quite the opposite. But Camille felt as if the surrounding pastures and meadows must surely be covered with a blanket of snow.

Someone had started the evening fire for her, just as someone had drawn her bath, turned down her bed, and brought her a tray of tea to end her evening. The idea of other people doing such things for her, things she was entirely capable of doing on her own, seemed every bit as foreign as the world she now found herself in.

Her gaze lingered on the leaping flames, their brightness and movement animating the faces on the carvings that flanked the chimneypiece. She had tried to ignore the memory of the events of the past two days, but now they screamed so loudly that she doubted she could focus on anything else. They blurred in and out of her consciousness, the memory of each leg of her journey a mixture of the unbelievable and the painfully real.

Most of the day she had been able to avoid directly confronting the realities of her circumstances. She had been preoccupied with leaving London. Preoccupied with the tasks at hand. But now she was completely alone, in silence, with nothing to listen to but the voices whispering in her heart.

How she wished she had not borne witness to Papa's words. But there could be no denying it. She had heard every bitter syllable, each one burned into the recesses of her brain. But as difficult as they had been to hear, somehow they had not been a surprise.

She had always wanted to blame his behavior on her mother's leaving. But the truth was, he had always been a harsh man. Perhaps that was the reason Mother had left.

As I am leaving.

She drew her knees up beneath her chin, just as she used to do when she was a child, sitting at her mother's feet for a story. She had gathered her few belongings around her from her apron. Her mother's letter. Her brooch watch. The shop scissors and coins. The little parcel, its linen wrapping somewhat worse for wear.

They were all just things. Paper. Metal. Cloth. But they seemed to be breathing the same air she was, whispering to her just as any person would.

She picked up the parcel her father had given her. She hadn't time to get it to the courier prior to her attack. She could feel its hard edges through the wrapping. On impulse she pulled away the linen to reveal a miniature puzzle box, the kind she had loved to play with as a young girl. Intricately carved from shining wood, it fit neatly into the palm of her hand.

Was it valuable? Her father had treated every item that came into their shop as if it were priceless, leaving Camille to determine its real worth—a skill she had honed over years of practice. She carefully assessed the box, turning it in her hands. The fine carvings boasted images of elephants and palm trees. An appealing piece, but by no means an extravagant one.

She shook the box to see if anything was inside, but no sound came forth. She tried to twist the top. It did not move. She pushed the corners, hoping it would pop open like other puzzle boxes she had seen. No movement. She sighed and placed it on the floor next to her.

It was exactly what she had thought it to be—a silly trinket intended to make her mother love her father again. Only a fool would keep up such a pursuit after nine years. And in the meantime, the man had pushed away the one person who had remained loyal to him all that time.

But no longer.

She set the box aside and picked up the letter from her mother. Even when she closed her eyes, she could see her mother's handwriting. Elegant. Sophisticated. Everything her mother had wanted her to be and tried to instill in her during her early years. Yet the woman had not stayed long enough to complete the lessons.

Yes, she had sent letters. But a letter was no substitute for a mother's love.

At first Camille had received a letter like this every couple of months. Each had offered chatty descriptions of her mother's new life in Portugal and the painful news that she would not be returning soon.

After two years, Camille had stopped reading them.

Her tears of longing and loneliness had ceased. She had grown numb to the letters. Numb to the memory.

At least, that is what she had wanted to do.

Eventually the frequency with which she received the letters had tapered to the point where she was lucky to receive two or three a year.

Camille flipped the letter over. The wax seal bore her maternal family's initial. How simple it would be to break the seal and read the letter. But to do so would open a portal to thoughts and emotions long suppressed. It would leave her vulnerable, and she could ill afford to be vulnerable now. Those feelings were best left sealed in the letter.

She might obtain a position at the school, or she might not. But if her father passed along one attribute, it was resolve. She was resolved to build a new life for herself, a different life, far from the filth of Blinkett Street. She was trading darkness for light, family for freedom. And she was almost there.

She touched her injured arm thoughtfully. No, she would never go back.

She tossed the letter by the box and stood, leaving both discarded on the floor as she crawled into the bed. Tomorrow she would wake up a new person. And her heart was at peace with that.

Camille awoke the next morning to glorious sunshine spilling through the windows, its golden brightness spreading over the coverlet.

Finally, after days of feeling chill and discomfort, she felt blessedly warm.

She took in a deep breath. No hint of a coal fire met her

nostrils—strange after years of waking to the foundry smells. Instead, the aroma of the lavender soap that she had used the previous night mixed with a hint of woodsmoke from the fireplace.

Stillness blanketed everything. Normally, the sounds of carts and the sounds of merchants peddling their wares would rouse her from sleep. But now complete silence met her ears.

She sat up, stretched her fingers above her head, and looked down at her nightdress. Miss Gilchrist might not be pleased over Camille's presence, but she had certainly been generous. Camille had departed London with no clothing of her own other than what she had worn the night she was attacked. But now she slept in a gown of linen edged with pink trimming.

By the light of morning, she was getting her first real glance at the bedchamber. Last night, by the time she'd been shown to the room, she had been too weary to take much notice of the extravagance surrounding her. But now she saw that her chamber was every bit as eclectic as the parlor had been. Floral, painted wallpaper in hues of pink, red, and green adorned all four walls. A large mirror framed in leaves of gold was situated above a white marble chimneypiece. Statues of Athena flanked the chimneypiece, as if standing guard over the simmering flames. Red velvet curtains hung from moldings at the ceiling to the gleaming wooden floor.

Curiosity coerced her from bed. She crossed to the window, the boards cool beneath her bare feet. The sight of a bright blue sky pulled a smile from her, but what solicited a sigh was the broad expanse of green that met her eyes.

Neatly partitioned fields and flowering orchards patch-worked the land, bordered by dense forest land that seemed to stretch to the soft green horizon. Closer in were gardens with stone paths and a riot of late-spring blooms. The colors were so bright, so clear, that the scene almost did not seem real. Camille felt her chest tighten. She was not looking at a painting, a mere likeness created by a painter's stroke. No, she was looking at the countryside, the real countryside, created by God's hand.

She drew a shaky breath, wanting to run downstairs and out into the picture. Instead she stayed by the window, pondering her old life and her new. By now her father would surely have noticed her absence. She imagined him in the dark, dingy shop, surrounded by the stale scents of soot and vapors and old things, and the very thought threatened to suffocate her. She never wanted to go back, especially now. Whatever position she could find had to be better than what she had left. She would work as a kitchen maid if she had to.

She turned back to her room. Someone had been in while she slept, for the fire had not yet burned out. On the small table was a comb and a little box of tooth powder, and water was in the basin.

There was a knock at the door, and a young woman entered with a bundle in her arms. "Good morning, Miss Iverness."

Camille smiled. "Good morning."

"I am Mary," said the girl. "I am here to help you dress, if that is agreeable to you."

"Of course. I was just admiring the scenery."

Mary placed the bundle she was carrying in a trunk at the foot of the bed and straightened, her gaze following Camille's out the window. "Lovely, isn't it? When the autumn comes, all those trees turn yellow and gold. Looks like they are on fire. It is a sight to behold."

"Sounds beautiful." A thrill shot through Camille. She

could hardly imagine a sight more stunning than the one she was seeing now. But then again, it had been many years since she had seen a forest in the fall.

How she hoped to still be here to see it. Not in this room, of course. But somewhere in this lovely countryside.

Mary could not be much younger than she was herself. She was a pretty girl with warm hazel eyes and a smattering of freckles across her fair nose and cheeks. Her copper hair was pulled into a simple chignon at the base of her neck.

"Miss Gilchrist told me your trunk was lost on the journey here. Toppled right off the top of the carriage! 'Tis no wonder, the way those drivers handle the horses—like the devil himself was at their heels."

Camille stiffened. Apparently Miss Gilchrist had already put her plan into action and was spreading her own version of the truth.

Mary shook out one of the gowns she had brought with her. "Miss Gilchrist had me bring these gowns. One should fit you, I should think. Then she would like you to join her in the breakfast room. I can show you where."

Camille fought the pang of resistance. Her spirits were high this morning, and she didn't want them dampened by an unpleasant interaction. But she supposed she had no choice, since Miss Gilchrist was her hostess.

Mary helped Camille with her stays and petticoat. Then she tried on two different gowns. The first, a summer gown of pale green muslin, was a bit too big. But the second, with blue stripes and white cotton trim, fit her very well.

"Now," the maid announced, "we will do your hair."

Camille sat at the room's small dressing table, thinking how strange it was to have someone else do something she did for herself nearly every day. But soon, with a few quick plaits, Mary had dressed Camille's hair in a fashion she would never have imagined was possible. Her black tresses were swept back away from her face, gathered in loose twists on the crown of her head, and held in place with two ivory combs.

Camille studied her reflection in the mirror, a little shocked at the transformation. Only yesterday she had worn a dress of tan linen and a simple apron, her hair falling about her face in an unbecoming fashion. Often, in fact, she wore it down over her shoulder. But today, in her refined dress and her hair arranged so fashionably, she almost looked like she fit in the Gilchrists' world.

A flutter danced within her. Today, she would visit the school. In a final act of preparation, she pinned her grandfather's watch to her bodice, careful not to damage the fine fabric.

Today might mark a new beginning for her. But first, she was expected for breakfast.

Camille fully expected to see Miss Gilchrist in the room waiting for her. But after Mary showed her to the breakfast room, she was a little surprised to find the elder Mr. Gilchrist sitting alone, his graying head bent over his newspaper as he ate.

A little wave of panic rattled her. She had not looked forward to breakfast with Miss Gilchrist, but she had not expected to be alone again with Miss Gilchrist's father either. Considering her last interactions with both, however, she found herself preferring the old man's company to his daughter's.

The likeness between father and children was strong, especially that between father and son. Evidence that Ian Gilchrist's gray hair had once been blond was still visible on the crown of his head and in the shadow of beard on his face. His build, though stooped, resembled that of his son as well, with broad shoulders, a strong jaw, and strong eyebrows over deep-set blue eyes.

He did not look up at her when she entered.

She glanced right and left, taking in her surroundings. Heavy blue curtains were pulled back from two windows, and the morning sun glittered from the silver service. At home she usually ate a bite or two of cold bread and cheese before the shop opened for the day. But here a long table of dark cherry spanned the length of the room, and a matching sideboard boasted more rolls, jams, and fruit than anyone could possibly eat. She glanced to her left. A footman, tall and straight, stepped forward and handed her a plate.

She nodded. The intoxicating scents of ham, bacon, and fresh bread wafted to her from the platters of food on the table. Her stomach rumbled, reminding her how long it had been since their dinner the previous evening.

Once her plate was full, she hesitated again. Should she address Mr. Gilchrist or simply take a seat? But as she pondered, he looked up, fixing his piercing blue eyes on her. "Well, are you going to just stand there?"

His abrupt manner brought a rush of blood to her face, heating it from temple to chin. "N-no, sir. Thank you."

She was not of a timid bent, not normally. But the austere silence of the room had rattled her. She selected a chair and sat.

The old man made no other attempt to speak, so she applied

herself to her plate, assessing him from the corner of her eye. He was probably about the age of her own father. But the fine cut of his tailcoat, his emerald waistcoat, and the stark brightness of his neckcloth made it clear that he was a gentleman. She could not help but notice that his hands shook as he held his paper.

He was the sort of man she was used to dealing with on a daily basis.

All around her were more signs of his collection. Antlers were mounted above the chimneypieces. Medieval tapestries depicting battles in muted shades were showcased on the wall opposite the window, and three carved tigers were perched amidst the platters on the sideboard. A vase of blue and red glass caught her eye.

Eager to dispel the awkward silence, she finally spoke. "That is a very interesting vase on the mantle. Japanese, is it not?"

At this he lifted his eyes and stared at her. She froze, thinking she had overstepped her bounds. But after several moments of staring, he lowered his paper. "Yes, it is. I purchased it in Italy, of all places, many years ago."

He fixed his pale eyes on her, his eyebrows raised in amusement. "I daresay, Miss Iverness, not many ladies I know would be able to correctly identify such a piece."

She cocked her head to the side. "Do not forget who my father is."

"That will not happen, I assure you." His tone was icy and he turned his head as if dismissing her. But then after several seconds he turned back. "Tell me, have you ever been to the ports at Plymouth?"

She wiped her mouth on her napkin. She did not want

to admit that Fellsworth was the farthest she had been from London in many years. "I have not, sir."

He settled back in his chair and laced his fingers over his belly. "That is where I first met your father. I shall never forget the day."

She dropped her head and stared at her plate. The reference to her father had slipped from her lips quite by accident. Now, apparently, the old man was intent upon continuing the conversation. "Yes, it was a blasted cold winter day—January, I think—and I was there to collect a shipment from India. The fog was so thick you could barely see a hand in front of you. Your father was working on the dock. He'd just returned from the East Indies, or some such place. He was with another man named Handley."

"Yes, I am acquainted with Mr. Handley."

"I daresay you are. You and every other collector from here to Scotland." He adjusted himself in his chair, grimacing as he did. "I was there with my son—my elder son, God rest his soul—when he was just a boy." He stared up at her again. "At one time, I would have considered your father a trusted colleague. A friend, even. Used to visit your shop often, in fact, though I doubt you remember."

With a start, Camille realized that she did remember. She could remember a much younger version of the man coming in periodically and staying to talk curiosities with her father. But those visits had grown quite infrequent, and try as she might, she could not recall the last time he came into the establishment.

"But time changes all." His curt words slammed the conversation to a halt, and he forked a piece of ham into his mouth.

Then, minutes later: "Do you enjoy your family's business, Miss Iverness?"

She lowered her teacup. "I suppose. In truth, it is all I have known for quite a few years. But all that will change for me soon. Today, I hope. I lived in the country as a young child and would dearly love to do so again."

"That is right," he stated, his expression brightening as if recalling an important fact. "You and your mother lived with old Mr. George Iverness while your father was gallivanting about in foreign lands. The estate was in Somerset, was it?"

Camille nodded.

He jumped back to his previous thread of conversation. "I do not think you will be satisfied in a different profession. Collecting gets in your soul and flows through your veins as surely as blood. My older son shared my passion. Shared it to his dying day."

"Mr. Thomas Gilchrist?" she confirmed.

"Aye. He was a good man. Smart and clever and a brave one too. But he died two years ago now."

The exclusion of his remaining son was glaring. "And Mr. Jonathan Gilchrist? Is he interested in such things?"

"Bah." The father's expression had hardened at the mention of his younger son. He straightened in his chair. "Jonathan has never shown interest in anything much beyond his bottles and jars and life in the village. Hard to believe he's my son, what with how different he is."

He abruptly stood from the table, leaving his breakfast half eaten. "Come with me, Miss Iverness. I wish to show you something."

She jerked her head up from her own breakfast. She was not

about to deny him. She followed him from the room and down a wide corridor to a set of closed doors off the main parlor.

"'Tis something I rarely share—because most people do not understand. But I think you'll appreciate it."

The old man pulled a key from the welt pocket in his waist-coat with his shaking, wrinkled hand and bent to unlock the door. It swung open with great ceremony. Stale air rushed from the room, carrying with it the perfume of tobacco smoke and musty books. She stepped inside and drew a breath.

The room was a treasure trove.

As much as she wanted to leave her old self behind, wanted to forget how she had spent the last years of her life, she could not deny the excitement that chamber stirred in her. She had always wondered what the collections of others looked like. And this was exactly as she had imagined. She wanted to dive in and examine every rare and unusual item in every dusty, dirty corner.

"Why, this is incredible!" she exclaimed, resisting the urge to run her finger over the marble bust of Zeus.

The old man did not respond. He simply hobbled to a table in the far corner of the cluttered room, pulled a key from the box on top, and unlocked the drawer of the desk. She followed, leaning over his shoulder to see what he had retrieved.

He turned to her. In his hands was a small pendant boasting a clear green stone and ivory carvings. "Do you know what this is?"

She shook her head.

"This is the first piece I ever bought from your father—paid cash for it that day on the docks. It is an emerald from the great continent of Africa. The gem itself is called the Vesper, and I paid far too much for it. But this is what started those many years of doing business with your father. That is until this issue with the Bevoy."

The enchantment she felt with the eclectic room began to fade. "I assure you, Mr. Gilchrist, I know nothing about the Bevoy."

"I believe you. As you yourself mentioned, your father was not the type to share information about his business dealings." Annoyance tinged the man's words with sharpness as he propped his hands on his hips and looked about the room.

Camille was looking too. "May I?" She pointed to a book on a nearby shelf.

He nodded in agreement, so she lifted the book in her hands and held it to the light. As she had so many times over the years, she examined the book, assessing the value. The hand-inscribed pages were written in a foreign language, but the penmanship was pure art. Painted pictures within the volume were highlighted in bits of gold.

She closed the book again and ran her fingertips over the smooth, aged leather. "Magnificent," she breathed.

For the first time, a smile cracked the old man's lips. "I am glad you think so."

Chapter Twenty

*J*onathan sat on a long wooden bench in the foyer of the Fellsworth School, right outside the superintendent's study. It was a Wednesday morning. On Wednesdays he normally visited the school to check on any students who had fallen ill. The habit had been instituted by his Uncle Martin, with whom he had apprenticed, and Jonathan had continued it after his uncle's death.

Next to him sat Miss Iverness, dressed in a gown of blue and white. As promised, he and Penelope had driven her to the school. Penelope had remained outside in the carriage. Miss Iverness had accompanied him inside and sat beside him now.

And her presence unnerved him.

In truth, she had unnerved him long before this moment.

He cast a sideways glance toward her. Her black hair was dressed neatly and properly, braided and curled atop her head, with a ribbon woven through the ebony locks. But his mind's eye still recalled her wild tresses, freed from the confines of a comb or whatever it was that ladies used to keep their hair pinned.

Neither of them would willingly reveal what had happened in the curiosity shop that night to a single soul in Fellsworth. Indeed, neither of them knew all the particulars. But he had witnessed a side of her that night, a vulnerable side, that awoke a strong sense of protection within him. The intensity of their situation had bound them together in an inexplicable way—or at least he had thought.

Today, however, she seemed proper and reserved, more like one of his sister's companions than the stubborn shopkeeper from Blinkett Street. She sat serenely, her hands folded neatly in her lap, the slight bulge of bandage beneath her sleeve the only indication of the trauma she had endured. If she had any qualms about meeting with the superintendent, she gave no indication.

She must have noticed him staring, for she tilted her chin toward him and smiled.

He'd been caught staring like a schoolboy.

Jonathan cleared his throat and got to his feet. He walked over to the window and watched the students crossing the grounds.

He tugged on his neckcloth. The room felt unseasonably warm, or perhaps it was just the strange sensation nagging him.

He stole another glance in her direction. Everything about her presence boasted confidence—her calm expression, her straight posture. And he was as fidgety as a child.

Had he made a promise he could not keep? It had been upon his suggestion that Miss Iverness left everything she knew for a position at a school that might or might not have a place for her. That would quickly become known when Mr. Langsby was ready to speak with them. But whatever the outcome, Jonathan was willing to wager that Miss Iverness would somehow prevail. The woman kept surprising him.

Even this morning, when he arrived at Kettering Hall to escort the women to the school, he had found Miss Iverness in his father's study—the very place to which he had been denied admittance for so long. Miss Iverness and his father had been laughing together. Talking.

He shook his head in disbelief and turned from the window. "I still cannot believe that my father invited you into his study."

A smile curved her lips as she straightened her glove. "I must confess I was intimidated when I first met the man. He seemed so surly. I thought that he was going to throw me from Kettering Hall when he realized who my father was. But under all that gruffness he is really quite interesting."

"Interesting?" Jonathan raked his fingers through his hair. "You may not know, Miss Iverness, that my father will not allow me in that chamber—nor my sister, for that matter. So you must understand why we find your being there so unusual."

She smoothed her skirt. "Your father and I share a common interest, Mr. Gilchrist. He is proud of his collection, and he has every right to be. It really is impressive."

"It ought to be," snorted Jonathan. "It consumes enough of his time and money."

"You sound as if you disapprove."

"It is not that—not exactly. As far as I am concerned, my father can do whatever he chooses. He always has done, at any rate. I confess, however, that I have never seen the beauty in those old things as he does."

"Old things tell a story, Mr. Gilchrist, just as the lives of people do." Miss Iverness's dark eyes were fixed intently on him. "They preserve the past and remind us of how far we have come."

"Ah." Jonathan could not help but smile. "Now I understand why my father was so keen on showing you the room. You are one of *them*. A collector, I mean."

She shrugged and tilted her head to the side. "I suppose I am—although I do not have the same urge to possess rare items.

But one cannot grow up as I did and not at least appreciate their appeal."

"Well, at least my father has taken a fancy to you, and that is a rare thing these days."

Their conversation was interrupted when two teachers clad in black exited the superintendent's study, closing the door behind them. Jonathan walked back to sit beside Miss Iverness. "Are you certain you would not rather I speak to Mr. Langsby on your behalf?"

She shook her head. "No, sir. I am quite certain. It is a conversation I should like to conduct myself."

She lifted her head at the sound of the door opening again, and Jonathan turned around to see Mr. Langsby standing on the threshold.

"Ah, Mr. Gilchrist. Is it Wednesday again already?" Mr. Langsby propped his hands on his hips, his tall frame nearly brushing the top of the door frame.

"That it is," Jonathan replied, standing.

Miss Iverness rose next to him. The movement drew the superintendent's attention. "And who do we have here?"

Jonathan stepped forward. "Allow me to present Miss Iverness. Miss Iverness, this is Mr. Langsby, the superintendent of Fellsworth School." The two exchanged their greetings, then Jonathan continued the introduction. "Miss Iverness is a friend of the family. She is visiting us from London."

"Well, then, if you are a friend of the Gilchrist family, you are more than welcome in the halls of Fellsworth School."

A genuine smile accompanied her response. "I thank you."

Mr. Langsby turned his attention back to Jonathan. "You

are later than usual. The students will be seeing to their stud-ies now. I hope that all is well and you have not been detained unpleasantly."

"No, not at all." Jonathan stepped aside to allow a line of little girls to cross the foyer. "We returned from London last night and I had a few matters to attend to this morning."

"Ah yes," Mr. Langsby exclaimed. "I thought I heard that you had gone to London. Business or pleasure?"

Jonathan scratched the back of his head and cast a glance at Miss Iverness. Definitely not pleasure. "A bit of a family matter. Nothing significant."

The words "nothing significant" tasted bitter in his mouth. But even if he were to share the real reason that had taken him to London, Mr. Langsby would likely not believe him. Ian Gilchrist was rumored to be one of the richest men in the county. But Jonathan knew what very few knew—that the excessive spend-ing and giving was a facade.

His father had always been a prideful man, not a generous one. He hated to part with money in any manner that was not to his benefit, but was always willing to share his wealth if doing so elevated him in the opinion of the community. Even now that his fortune had turned, he refused to curb his generosity, fearing that others might discover the situation and think less of him. He certainly would not want anyone to know that Jonathan had traveled to London to meet with a hired investigator as a last-ditch effort to save the family fortune. Such news would certainly raise a local eyebrow or two.

"And how is your father?" Mr. Langsby's question pulled him back to the present. "And Miss Gilchrist?"

"Father is well, thank you, though his gout is giving him

trouble these days. My sister is well as always. How are the children? Any bumps or bruises that I need to tend to today?"

Mr. Langsby bobbed his head. "They are as well as can be expected. One of the boys fell and sprained his ankle. It has been tended to, but it would be good for you to look at it. Robert Wright and Reginald Rutherford have both complained of stomachaches. And a teacher just informed me that one of our young ladies, Jane Sonten, has been confined to bed this morning with chills."

Jonathan searched his memory, but the girl's name did not register. "I do not think I am acquainted with Jane Sonten."

"Likely not. She is a relatively new addition. Furthermore, she has just returned from an unexpected and lengthy visit home. Her mother died, and her father has just now decided that she should return here. I think the poor child is simply overcome with grief, but I would like you to look at her just the same."

"I see. I will check in on her then."

"Very good."

The finality in Mr. Langsby's tone suggested he was finished with their conversation. But Jonathan turned to Miss Iverness, who had been standing silently. Their eyes met, and her expression brightened. He resisted the urge to speak on her behalf, which he would have undoubtedly done for most of the women he knew. But Miss Iverness was different.

"I will go about my business," he said. "But before I leave, Miss Iverness was hoping that you would grant her a moment or two of your time."

"Oh?" The superintendent was understandably surprised at the notion. He folded his arms across his chest. "Miss Iverness, I would be happy to give you any amount of time you wish."

Chapter Twenty-One

Camille's stomach flipped as she was introduced to Mr. Langsby.

Mr. Langsby was so calm and assured—his collected demeanor such a contrast to the anxiety swirling within her. He was a tall man, straight and slim as a huntsman's arrow, with a long, hooked nose dominating his narrow face. But his expression was kind.

She listened as the two men talked without hearing any of it, for her mind had already leaped into a rehearsal of what she would say and how she would convince the superintendent that she would be suitable for a position. Any position.

At length she heard Mr. Gilchrist suggest that she would like to speak with Mr. Langsby. And then the superintendent was speaking to her. "Miss Iverness, would you care to join me in my study?"

She had known this conversation was coming ever since that moment she decided to accompany the Gilchrists to Fellsworth. But until this moment it had never before seemed real. It was merely something they discussed, an idea that merited consideration. But now the moment was here. Camille's confidence plummeted, taking with it her breath and her ability to concentrate.

She caught the eye of Mr. Gilchrist. His gaze was direct. Compassionate. Somehow bracing. And it occurred to her to wonder why a glance from him should impact her so.

Perhaps it was that her defenses had fallen. Perhaps it was that each moment she seemed to learn something new about him and his family. Perhaps it was just the fact that when he looked at her, he actually seemed to *see* her.

He smiled. And that smile completely disarmed her—just as he nodded and walked away.

"Please, Miss Iverness, be seated wherever you will be most comfortable," Mr. Langsby offered as he led the way into the expansive study. Camille was struck by the sheer size of the room. In London, everything was cramped, and the ever present mist of clouds and smoke made everything seem dark. Buildings sat atop buildings. Rooms were narrow and confined. The very heavens seemed to press down upon the earth, suppressing and binding everything beneath them.

But here in Surrey everything was open and free. The rooms, even the most modest and unassuming, were spacious and airy. Clear, white light filtered through broad windows. She filled her lungs with air, expanding them to their full extent and then blowing it out.

"Miss Iverness?" Mr. Langsby's voice brought her back to the present. It all came down to this moment.

"You must think it odd that I should ask to see you." Camille took a high-backed chair next to the fireplace, hoping that the gentle warmth it radiated would soothe her nerves.

"Not at all, Miss Iverness. Now, tell me. How is it that I may assist you?"

She summoned every ounce of her courage. She had faced

much more frightening men and situations in recent days. This slim, kind-faced man could hardly pose an immediate threat.

She looked down at her hands, worn and rough from working in the shop. Her father would never welcome her back there, not now. And after what she had overheard in the alley, she did not want to go back.

Her hurt fueled her resolve. She sat taller and began. "I know you must be very busy, so I will be direct. I am seeking employment, and Mr. Gilchrist suggested that you might be able to use me here at Fellsworth School."

Mr. Langsby raised his bushy eyebrows. "A position? Are you a teacher, then, Miss Iverness?"

Panic bubbled. No, she was not a teacher. But somehow, she had to convince him of her abilities. "No, sir. Not exactly. But I have worked in a London shop nearly my entire life, and as such I have extensive experience in keeping accounts and running a business. Mr. Gilchrist mentioned that might be something you would like to offer your young ladies as they prepare to enter the world, so I hoped to offer my assistance in that regard. Or if you have no opening for such lessons, I am young and strong and able to work in a variety of other capacities."

Her words had come out in a rush, so much so that she wondered if Mr. Langsby had understood them. But after several seconds he shifted in his chair and folded his long arms across his chest, crinkling his plain black jacket at the elbows. "I see. And Mr. Gilchrist recommended this to you?"

"He did."

"And why is it that he did not speak to me about this?"

"I told him I preferred to speak for myself."

Mr. Langsby stood from behind the desk and crossed the

room to the window. His next words shifted their discussion in a different direction, jarring her. "London is quite a distance from our quiet Fellsworth. Have you always lived there?"

"No, sir. I spent the first several years of my life in Somerset. London has been my home for the past eleven years, however."

"I see. And as you have spent so much time in London, why would you wish to leave it?"

Camille decided to respond with a question of her own. "I trust you have been to London, Mr. Langsby?"

He sat down in the chair opposite her. "Of course. Several times."

"Then you must know that, with all of its attractions and opportunities, it can be quite overwhelming. Dirty and crowded. I am seeking a fresh beginning in a quieter—dare I say greener? —part of England."

Mr. Langsby stared at her, as if assessing her. His dark eyes fixed on her with such intensity that she fancied he could see into her very soul. She shifted, growing uneasy under his understated scrutiny. "And your family, Miss Iverness—what do they think of your presence here in Fellsworth? Surely they must miss you a great deal."

His questions were leading her down a path she did not wish to tread. Camille had not anticipated that anyone, especially a potential employer, would ask about her family. But as she was quickly learning, customs here in the country were vastly different than they were in London.

Heat crept up from her borrowed bodice. She pushed the words from her lips, forcing them to sound though they fought to stay silent. "My mother is in Portugal and has been there for several years. My father owns the shop where I have worked these many years, but his current pursuits are of such a nature that he no longer needs my assistance."

The words were just true enough. Camille bit her lower lip and met his eyes directly with her own, waiting for his response.

But he did not respond, merely settled back in his chair. Desperation began to settle over her like a cloak. She had wanted a quick response, and his every word seemed painfully slow. This trip had been exhausting, and with every passing hour her situation became that much more tenuous. She could not return to Blinkett Street. Not now. And every fiber within her tensed in fear at the thought of having no means to support herself.

At length he spoke. "At present, Miss Iverness, we do not have an opening for the kind of work you describe. But I must say I am intrigued with Mr. Gilchrist's suggestion that we might educate our young ladies in the practical art of bookkeeping. The school has a very long-standing relationship with the Gilchrists, and I take their counsel to heart. If Mr. Gilchrist is of the opinion that this would be a beneficial addition to our school, then it is one I should like to consider.

"It is not uncommon for us to take on junior teachers—that is, teachers who act as assistants to our more experienced teachers. We usually reserve these spots for our own students so that they might gain experience as they prepare to enter the world, but we might be able to make an exception in this instance."

The blood began to pound in her ears, and she willed it, unsuccessfully, to subside. She wanted to jump up from the chair and extract an answer, but her manners, such as they were, prevailed. She sensed the man's desire to comply with the request, though more to satisfy the request of the Gilchrist heir than out of respect for her abilities. At this moment, she decided that it didn't matter.

Mr. Langsby's thoughts played out on his face, his lips pressing together in contemplation. "I will consider this, Miss Iverness. I must say that I am impressed by your willingness to approach me personally with such a request. You have shown the very confidence and self-awareness we hope to instill in our young ladies. But you must understand that I make my decisions based on what is best for the school as a whole."

She nodded in agreement, both her actions and her words fighting the emotions in her heart. "Of course."

"You are a guest at Kettering Hall, I trust?"

"I am."

"Then please allow me time to consider this and speak with my staff."

She drew a deep breath. At least he had not denied her outright. "I am grateful for your consideration."

She stood and prepared to take her leave, then stopped and turned back to him.

"I want you to know, Mr. Langsby, that I do not shrink from hard work. It is in my blood. I am convinced I can be an asset here at Fellsworth School."

Chapter Twenty-Two

*J*onathan hesitated before ascending the stairs to Fellsworth School's upper levels, his thoughts still on Miss Iverness and her conversation with Mr. Langsby.

In truth, he found himself baffled by the way she had changed in the short time they had known each other. At their first meeting she had seemed so vulnerable and in need of protection. But with each passing event, she had grown more confident, more self-assured. She had even shown that she could stand up to their father—a feat neither he nor his sister had fully mastered.

Meanwhile, however, he had a patient to see. He adjusted the apothecary's box in his arms. The entrance to the sickroom was a separate entrance off the kitchen, so he headed out into the morning's air and around to the back of the school.

The small sickroom was situated on the far side of the building, above the back kitchen and separated from the general sleeping and teaching quarters. Four beds, evenly spaced, occupied the narrow room, and a table with three chairs stood next to the window. At present the curtains had been drawn, but a sliver of light sliced through the still air and landed across the farthest bed.

On the nearest bed, under a wool blanket, was a tiny lump. His patient, no doubt.

At the sight, his focus shifted. This was what he did well—

caring for the sick and helping them heal, not searching for rubies or arranging positions for young women running from their fathers.

A black-clad woman sat next to the bed. He recognized her as one of the teachers, Miss Redburn. When Jonathan entered, she rose from her seat and approached him.

"Good day, Mr. Gilchrist," she whispered.

"Good day. And how is the patient?"

"She is resting. Finally."

He stepped toward the child, careful to keep his boots from clicking too loudly on the rough wooden floors. The child's eyes were closed, and a tangle of light-brown hair framed her flushed cheeks. Judging by her size, he guessed she could be no more than seven or eight years of age.

"Has she been asleep long?"

"She was awake most of the night, but she has been sleeping for an hour or so."

Jonathan sat down on the chair the teacher vacated. At the motion the little girl stirred. Her eyelids fluttered before finally opening, and golden-brown eyes focused on him.

He smiled. "Hello there, my dear."

The little girl shifted in the bed, her wide eyes frantic as she searched for her guardian.

"Do not be frightened, Jane," he said. "I know we have not met before, but I am here to help you feel better. My name is Mr. Gilchrist."

The girl's expression did not change, though her chapped lips trembled.

"It is all right, dearest," urged the teacher. "Mr. Gilchrist is a nice man."

The little girl attempted to sit up, but Jonathan gently held her down. "Just be still." He kept his voice as quiet as possible. "I am going to take a look at you. Tell me, what hurts the most?"

She cut her eyes toward her guardian before pointing to her neck.

"Your throat, is it?" He removed a cloth from her forehead and placed his hand there. Moist skin, hot and clammy, met his own cool hand. "You have quite a fever, do you not?"

She did not respond, just stared at him with round, golden eyes.

He placed his finger on her chin and tilted it toward him. At first he thought she was merely flushed, but a closer glance revealed that tiny red bumps dotted her forehead, cheeks, and chin. He rubbed his finger on her cheek. It felt rough, and when he applied pressure to the rosy skin, it blanched.

He lifted her hand from the top of the coverlet to feel her pulse. "How long has she been feeling this way?"

"'Bout a day, sir."

He lifted the edge of her sleeve. At his touch, the small muscles in her arm tightened and flinched. Tiny red bumps covered her arm, but the rash was not nearly as intense there as on the child's face.

Jonathan lowered her sleeve, patted her hand, and smiled to mask the concern growing within him. "Tell me, Miss Jane. Do you like kittens?"

The little girl nodded.

"A cat in my father's stable had a large litter of kittens several weeks ago. Seven of them. Now they are quite big and are the fattest, furriest things you ever did see."

At this a little smile tugged at the corner of the child's mouth. Her muscles relaxed.

"Would you like to see them? Perhaps someday I will bring one. That is, if I can catch it."

She smiled broadly enough to show a missing tooth.

"What a pretty smile. Can you open your mouth for me?"

She complied, and what he saw confirmed his fear. A whitish film coated her tongue.

He turned toward Miss Redburn. "Has she been coughing much?"

"Not at all."

"I would like for you to leave these heavy blankets off of her."

"Yes, sir."

He looked down at the girl. "Jane, will you do something for me? I want you to stay right here in this bed and not move from it. Do you think you can do that?"

She nodded her response.

"And I am going to have some broth brought up for you, and I know your throat hurts, but you need to drink it. Do you think you can do that?"

She did not blink, only nodded.

He stood and spoke to Mrs. Redburn. "I do not want her moved. Leave her here and keep the other children away from her. Keep the door closed, and open the window. I will prepare something that should help her and will be back later today."

The teacher agreed.

He looked back to his patient. "Jane, can you remember to do what I said? Stay in bed and drink your broth. I will be back to see you soon."

Jonathan's heart was heavy as he gathered his things together and prepared to leave. He recognized Miss Sonten's symptoms, and the knowledge sent a chill through him. He'd battled it before. And he had witnessed firsthand the devastation it could cause.

Poor Jane would be fortunate indeed if she escaped the ravages of what was to come.

Camille could not help but smile as she made her way back to the carriage where Miss Gilchrist was waiting. She lifted her skirts to avoid soiling her borrowed gown on the dirt drive as the footman handed her in.

"Thank goodness you are finally here." Miss Gilchrist set aside the book she had been reading, her lips arranged in her pretty pout. "I thought they must have put you to work already."

"Not today." Camille settled against the tufted seat with a happy sigh. Not even a slight or backhanded comment by Miss Gilchrist could dampen her spirits.

"And how did you find Mr. Langsby?" Miss Gilchrist asked.

"He was quite agreeable. And while he does not have a position open at the moment, he will consider establishing one. He said he would send word to Kettering Hall shortly."

"Did you speak with him yourself, as you planned?"

"Oh, yes."

Miss Gilchrist shook her head. "I declare, Miss Iverness, I still cannot believe that you did not have Jonathan speak to him on your behalf. I never could have done what you did."

Camille did not want to jump to brash conclusions, but from

the way Miss Gilchrist spoke, she was beginning to believe that ladies of her elevated station were rarely expected to do much for themselves. The idea was foreign to Camille, for she had cared for herself and been her own advocate for as long as she could remember.

"I do not care to rely on others if I can help it, Miss Gilchrist."

"Yes, I can see that quite plainly. Now, shall we be off?"

"Should we wait for Mr. Gilchrist?"

"Oh, no. Jonathan will likely be here for a while. Besides, he can find his way home. Do not worry."

With her visit to Mr. Langsby behind her, Camille had nothing to do but wait. She might as well accompany Miss Gilchrist on her errands, though in truth she would rather stay and explore the school. She peered out the carriage window at the manicured grounds. She had liked the place the minute she saw it. Gardens and trees surrounded the building, and somehow she felt safe in the small fortress of gray stone and wooded land.

The carriage lurched forward. Very soon they would be in the actual village of Fellsworth. The prospect piqued Camille's curiosity.

"I do thank you for accompanying me, my dear. These weekly visits can so wear on one's spirits, and a bit of company is welcome. Normally Meeks accompanies me, but it will be nice to have you with me for a change. Plus, it will give you the opportunity to see a bit more of our village. It's quite charming, I think."

Charming indeed. Never would Camille have imagined that a place like Fellsworth really existed. Tidy shops with their doors open to the morning air. Women with baskets over their arms and children playing on the green. Farm wagons passing them on the wide road. Houses and gardens not stained with soot. Two young men eyeing the wares in the haberdashery through a clean window. An ancient graveyard circling the stone church.

Once again, Camille felt as if she had stepped into a painting. She closed her eyes and allowed the soft morning breeze to kiss her cheeks. Half fearing she would open her eyes to find herself back on Blinkett Street, she pressed her lashes together for another second. But when she opened her eyes again, the colors seemed even more vibrant.

Presently the carriage turned off the main road through town and jostled over a bridge. Trees shadowed the road, blocking the sun. After several more moments, the carriage rumbled to a stop. Miss Gilchrist fussed with her fichu and adjusted the satin ribbons on her bonnet.

"We have arrived."

Camille looked out the window, and for the first time since arriving in Fellsworth, what she saw reminded her of Blinkett Street. A row of stone houses lined the road, their shutters hanging askew and their thatched roofs in noticeable need of repair. Misty smoke rose from crooked chimneys, intermingling with the low-hanging clouds, and tattered bits of cloth peeked through the crooked shutters.

Miss Gilchrist looked from the window, her pretty blue eyes taking in the scene before her. A weary sigh passed her parted lips. "Oh Miss Iverness, I do not mind telling you that I grow ever so fatigued with this work."

The words surprised Camille, for Miss Gilchrist seemed to be doing very little work. Nonetheless, she followed Miss Gilchrist wordlessly from the carriage. Already the footmen were unloading baskets of fresh vegetables and baked goods and setting them on the ground.

"No, not there, James!" barked Miss Gilchrist, her sharp instructions flustering the young footman to the point of frustration. "The carrots will spill all over the ground."

Miss Gilchrist turned to her. "You would think I was asking him to paint the ceiling of the Sistine Chapel instead of transporting vegetables for the poor."

Camille assessed the baskets of food. An abundance of green vegetables, bright apples, and glossy breads topped the bundles. "This is so very generous. I am certain the recipients will be very grateful."

"One does what one can." Miss Gilchrist tossed her blond head and adjusted her sleeve, her attentions now much more focused on her wardrobe than on the footman. "Father insists upon it. He is quite determined that we, as the wealthiest family in the area, do our part to help those less fortunate. And of course I agree. It is our duty, do you not think?"

Camille laced her fingers behind her back. The Gilchrists did seem like a charitable lot. Having been welcomed into their home and showered with support, she could not shake the suspicion that she was one of their pet projects. But whereas the younger Mr. Gilchrist seemed genuinely concerned about her welfare, Miss Gilchrist's efforts seemed much more focused on appearances.

Either way, Camille knew that without their help she would still be back on Blinkett Street. "What can I do to help?"

"Not much. James will do the carrying. You and I will simply go down this row of houses and pass out the goods." Miss Gilchrist pointed down the rutted street. "This is where the poorest of the poor live here in Fellsworth—where our help is most needed."

Camille looked at the nearest house. The nonchalance with which Miss Gilchrist spoke unnerved her slightly. And then something caught her eye. A small face, smudged with dirt or soot, stared at her through one of the windows. She would have missed the child except for the bright yellow ribbon that gathered her hair. Camille smiled, and the little face quickly disappeared.

Had Miss Gilchrist even seen the child? Camille sensed that the woman had little connection to the people she was helping. That did not discredit her service, for surely the goods were sorely needed. But it was one thing to bring people food every week. It was quite another to *know* them, to recognize their common humanity. Mr. Gilchrist seemed to appreciate the similarity that connected him with others, regardless of their position. But that attitude seemed lost on his sister.

Camille bent to pick up a basket, but Miss Gilchrist stopped her. "No, no, my dear. James will carry that."

"But I am perfectly capable of—"

"No, it is quite out of the question." Miss Gilchrist's gaze narrowed on her, and her voice grew direct. "You are a guest in the Gilchrist home. Miss Iverness—a *lady*, after all, unaccustomed to such tasks, I am sure." She reached out and adjusted the bonnet ribbon under Camille's chin. "There is no need for you to carry a thing."

Camille had to stifle a smirk. She wondered what Miss Gilchrist would think if she visited Blinkett Street. If only she could see Camille prying the tops from wooden crates, hefting swords and statues, arranging boxes of silks or silverware. She liked to think that such work had made her quite strong, and the idea that a simple basket of bread was too much for her to carry struck her as amusing.

But Miss Gilchrist was right that Camille was a guest in their home. If being a lady meant that she would not heft a single thing, then, if just for today, she would comply.

She lifted the hem of her gown to step over a puddle of mud and paused as a duck scurried across their path. Miss Gilchrist drew a deep breath of annoyance and shooed the squawking animal away. Then she stepped purposely to the first house, where she lifted a delicate, gloved hand and knocked.

Within seconds a young woman opened the door a few inches. She could not have been much older than Camille. Her brown eyes flashed from Camille to Miss Gilchrist and then back again. From inside, the sounds of children's chatter echoed, and an infant wailed. The shadows beneath the young woman's eyes and the tangles in her waist-length hair told a story without a single word.

The woman did not smile, but after several moments she opened the door the rest of the way and curtsied as best she could with a baby at her hip. Behind her, two small children wrestled on the floor, another pounded with a spoon on a pot, and a fourth galloped through the room as if riding a horse.

The mother ignored them all. "Miss Gilchrist. Welcome to our home."

Miss Gilchrist's expression immediately altered. Suddenly her voice was enthusiastic, her expression warm. "My dear Mrs. Whitborn! How are you today?"

The hollow, haunting light in Mrs. Whitborn's eyes struck Camille. She was not sure what the emotion was that she saw there, but it touched her. Moved her.

Mrs. Gilchrist turned to Camille. "Miss Iverness, may I present Mrs. Whitborn. Mrs. Whitborn's husband is currently stationed on the continent. Mrs. Whitborn, this is my dear friend Miss Iverness. She is visiting us from London."

The woman assessed Camille with tired eyes, an expression Camille recognized from the neighbors on Blinkett Street. She wanted to say something encouraging, something to break down the invisible shield Mrs. Whitborn had raised, but with the children's voices and the constant motion within the house, her thoughts ran still.

Miss Gilchrist pointed to the footman. "James, please take those things and put them wherever Mrs. Whitborn directs, will you?"

Mrs. Whitborn stepped aside to allow the footman to pass. Her eyes lingered on the baskets, but her expression did not change. "You have our gratitude, Miss Gilchrist. Please pass along our thanks to your father."

At this Miss Gilchrist brightened, and what seemed to be her first genuine smile of the day curved her lips. "Why, I shall tell him."

Camille watched the interaction with interest. The women chatted for a few moments as if oblivious to her presence. No doubt the food being carried into the home would help sustain Mrs. Whitborn's family, and they were grateful, just as Camille was for the Gilchrist assistance. But the interaction seemed forced, lacking in genuine interest, just as she felt her own interactions with Miss Gilchrist were.

Was this what it felt like to rely on the donations of others? On the whims of those who did their duty but with little charitable thought or feeling?

But then her thoughts turned to Mr. Jonathan Gilchrist.

And her heart warmed.

Chapter Twenty-Three

$\mathcal{J}$onathan packed his apothecary's box and rolled down his sleeves. The afternoon had been a long one, even to one used to odd hours and sleepless nights.

After tending to the boys, whose ailments were much less severe than young Jane's, he had checked back in on her. The fever had intensified, and she seemed much more restless. The red rash had spread significantly on her arms and legs.

He left the child and paid another visit to the superintendent's study. Upon finding the door already ajar, he knocked to signal his arrival and stepped inside.

Mr. Langsby looked up from his desk, his quill poised over the paper, spectacles balanced on his nose. "Ah, Mr. Gilchrist, I trust you found everything in order. How are our patients?"

Without waiting for an invitation, Jonathan moved to the chair opposite the desk and gripped the back of it, leaning his weight against it. The afternoon sun slanted through the windows, far too cheery for the situation. "The boys will be fine; they are a hardy lot. But it is little Jane who concerns me."

Mr. Langsby lowered the quill. "Oh?"

"Yes. I fear she may have scarlet fever."

A shadow crossed the superintendent's face, just as Jonathan had expected. For Mr. Langsby knew as well as Jonathan that scarlet fever had the potential to be deadly, especially around children.

"Are you sure?" the superintendent asked.

"I am certain."

Mr. Langsby returned the quill to its holder, shaking his head. "This is unwelcome news, Mr. Gilchrist."

Jonathan nodded. "You must keep her separated from the others. I also advise removing her bed linens and anything else she might have come into contact with from the chamber she shared with the other young ladies."

"We will see to that immediately."

"And we will want to ask if any members of your staff have had scarlet fever. Young Jane will require constant tending, and it is much preferable that someone who has already survived the disease stay with her. They are much less likely to succumb themselves."

"Of course," the superintendent said. "I will find out right away."

"Where did you say she came from?"

"London, I believe, but I would have to confirm this with the school registrar. One of the teachers might know more readily."

"At any rate, we must keep her away from the other children. And if any of them start showing any symptoms, please send word to me immediately—any time, day or night. This is a very unpleasant and dangerous sickness, but if we catch it early we may be able to lessen its severity."

Mr. Langsby sighed like a man faced with an impossible task and removed his spectacles from his face. "This is a grim matter indeed. Is Jane's a serious case?"

"Any case can be serious, as you well know, but hers does

not look to be far advanced. I am going to return to my shop now for something to ease her, but in the meantime, I have given the woman caring for her instructions."

"Very good. Thank you for coming."

"I am at your service."

"Yes, I know you are, Mr. Gilchrist. You never fail to come to our rescue, and for that I am most grateful. Now, if you can spare me a minute, there is another matter I would like to discuss with you."

"Of course." Jonathan circled the chair he had been leaning on and seated himself in it.

"I had a lovely chat with Miss Iverness."

Jonathan leaned forward and rested his elbows on his knees. "I hope I did not take you by surprise with such an introduction."

"Do not give it another thought. I found her to be quite charming."

"I trust she spoke to you about a position?"

"She did indeed." Mr. Langsby paced the narrow space between his desk and the window. "Are you well acquainted with Miss Iverness?"

"Our acquaintance is a recent one, but our fathers have known each other for quite some time." It was not a lie. Not exactly.

"Can you speak to her moral character?"

The events of the past several days ran rampant through his mind. He shifted uncomfortably in the chair. "As I mentioned, I have not known her long myself, but I can say that I have been very impressed with the manner in which she handles herself."

"Oh? Can you elaborate?"

Jonathan considered his answer carefully. "I can say that I have seen her handle a very difficult situation with grace and dignity."

His answer apparently did not suit Mr. Langsby, for the man crossed his arms over his chest. "You are reluctant to give me details."

"Her story is not mine to tell. I am sure she would be more than happy to answer any further questions you have of her."

Mr. Langsby tilted his head to the side like a man in possession of a secret. "So like your mother you are."

Jonathan allowed himself a smile. It was something that Mr. Langsby always did—called out the similarity between himself and his mother while very pointedly leaving out a similarity to his father.

His host continued. "So you recommend Miss Iverness, then?"

Jonathan drew a deep breath. "Yes."

"She is not a teacher, by her own admission, yet I am intrigued by her eagerness to share her experience as a shopkeeper. Especially as we do train our charges to go out into the world and make their way. Learning such skills could surely be beneficial."

Mr. Langsby tapped his finger against his lip before going to his desk and retrieving a piece of paper. He sat down, reached for his quill, and began penning a letter.

Jonathan waited in silence, a glimmer of hope beginning to burn. Securing a position at the school would give Miss Iverness a safe haven from her father's ill treatment as well as a chance to better herself. And she would remain close at hand—a distinct advantage. He sensed she was warming to him, and her assistance with recovering the ruby could be invaluable.

That, at least, is what he told himself as he stood waiting for Mr. Langsby to finish his task. He strove to confine his thoughts about her to those that concerned her welfare and that of his family.

But how quickly and how frequently she distracted him from such an objective by simply being present.

Chapter Twenty-Four

*W*hat a day this has been! Truly, I am exhausted. I can hardly wait to be home."

Camille understood Miss Gilchrist's sentiment. Her own legs were beginning to ache. But she could not deny that she felt more alive than she had in ever so long. The air was warm and scented with grass. Ivory clouds, wispy and fresh, adorned an azure sky. A skylark's soft call met her ears, so different than the harsh shopkeepers' cries and the sounds of noisy carriages she had grown so accustomed to. She lifted her face to the sky, the light filtering through brilliant leaves and dappling her face.

She and Miss Gilchrist had elected to walk home from the village and had sent the carriage on to the school to collect Mr. Gilchrist when his rounds were complete. Camille had suggested the outing, feeling certain Miss Gilchrist would decline the offer. But to her surprise, Miss Gilchrist had expressed an interest in taking some fresh air after so much time in the carriage.

Whatever the reasoning, and despite her weariness, Camille was grateful for the opportunity to enjoy the countryside. They passed over a bridge leading to the edge of the village, and her gaze lit on a cluster of black-faced sheep on the far side of a hedge. "I don't know when I have ever been somewhere so lovely."

"Really?" Miss Gilchrist shot her a look of disbelief, and then looked around her. "I suppose it is pretty enough. But a lifetime of living here will make one quite accustomed to it, I suppose. Charming and pastoral are one thing, but I have always preferred to be somewhere more exciting."

"Such as?"

"Town, of course," Miss Gilchrist exclaimed with a wave of her gloved hand. "London, Bath, anywhere there is a fashionable set. It gets terribly lonely out here. There is no one within an hour's drive who is truly a suitable companion for me."

Camille frowned, confused. "The town is hardly deserted."

"True. But most are below my station."

The words rang familiar, but it took Camille a few moments to place them. And then it struck her.

Mama.

Her mother had spoken similar words to her father after Grandfather's death. Mama had been furious with Papa for selling her grandfather's estate and moving them to London to open the shop. Camille had been young at the time, and even though distance blurred her mother's exact words, not even time could erase the harshness of the tones.

She had thought the shop was beneath her station. Was that the real reason she had left?

"Oh, look." Miss Gilchrist's sudden stop jerked Camille to the present. "There is Jonathan. He must have decided to walk home."

Camille followed the woman's gaze. There, coming around a corner, was Mr. Gilchrist. Her heart lurched within her chest. How handsome he appeared with the sun filtering through the fluttering leaves, speckling his golden hair and broad shoulders. His expression was distant; he clearly was not aware of them.

Camille allowed her gaze to linger on him longer than she knew she should.

She found it amazing that the man still looked so crisp and put together after hours of tending sick children. His dark-gray coat was neatly fitted, with a black high collar and a snowy cravat that met his chin. His tan buckskin breeches were tucked into tall black boots. Under his arm he carried his box and in his other hand a satchel. He was looking out over the field of hay as he walked.

Miss Gilchrist interrupted her thoughts. "I would call him to us, but I know he has many people yet to visit before he can retire for the day."

"Whom does he visit?" Camille asked, her curiosity about the man growing with each passing encounter.

"Oh, he calls on so many people. He is the only apothecary for this village and the one to the south of us, so he is rarely in his shop."

"You both seem to be quite involved in your community."

"We are indeed. My mother used to refer to it as 'doing God's work.' But my father, to this day, is furious about Jonathan working as an apothecary."

"But why?"

"I do not think it is unkind of me to say that Father judges success in monetary terms. He does not understand why Jonathan should spend his time as he does when there are other ways to make more money. Especially now that Jonathan stands to inherit the estate."

"But from what I understand, he would have started learning the ways of an apothecary at a very young age. Correct?"

"Yes. My uncle Martin, who was my mother's brother, was the apothecary here in Fellsworth for many years. When we were young, it was my older brother Thomas who was set to inherit Kettering Hall. And cruel as it sounds, my father was never fond of Jonathan. He put all of his efforts into educating Thomas and paid little thought to Jonathan."

Miss Gilchrist paused her speech to adjust the ties of her bonnet. "But all changed abruptly when Thomas died and Jonathan became the heir. Father has tried everything to get him to learn the business of the estate, but Jonathan balks. I suppose he is just too set in his ways—a family trait, I'd say. He makes very little money as an apothecary, but I suppose he has some satisfaction in it—otherwise he would not continue the work. Still, it irks my father to no end."

"It speaks volumes of your brother's character, does it not— to help those without much to give in return?"

"How kind of you to see the good in his actions. And yes, it would appear that his character must be that of pure gold— that, or he is the most stubborn man to ever walk the paths of Surrey. And much as I love my brother, I must admit the latter is possible. That is the quandary, Miss Iverness. Either Jonathan really is as selfless and giving as he would lead us to believe, or he is so bent on defying our father that he continues down this path simply to spite him."

The words, spoken so candidly, resonated—they splintered through the afternoon air like the piercing crow call. "To spite your father? Do you really think he would do that?"

"My dear, if you are around Kettering Hall long enough, you will soon learn that my father and my brother are often at odds. They have quite different views on the world—more specifically, on the estate and how it should be handled."

"Did your brother always want to be an apothecary?"

Miss Gilchrist gave a little laugh. "No, not at all. Jonathan wanted to be a physician or a surgeon, like my uncle. When his own son, my cousin, died, he and my mother decided Jonathan should go learn the trade. Father was not happy about his son's learning such a lowly profession. But with my older brother set to inherit and with other factors pressing on him, Father consented. And Jonathan did not argue. He knew he would need some way to support himself."

"He seems quite dedicated to his work now."

"He does. Although I agree with Father that it's time he gave it up. Now that Thomas is dead, Jonathan needs to start acting more like a gentleman."

"Perhaps he finds satisfaction in being able to help people."

"Perhaps. Or perhaps, as I suggested, he continues down this path to agitate our father. Do you see my logic now?"

"There is greatness in bringing healing and comfort to others, Miss Gilchrist."

"I am sure you are right. But I do not wish to weary you with the petty details of our lives. Every family has such stories, to be sure. What is your family like? I know your father owns a shop, but what of your mother?"

It had been so long since Camille had spoken the words aloud that they almost wouldn't form. They were a bitter confirmation of the pain she tried to forget on a daily basis.

"My mother is in Portugal."

"Portugal! How interesting. Is she there on holiday?"

It was not interesting in the least, at least not to Camille. "She was born in Portugal and returned there when I was much younger to care for her own mother, who was gravely ill. She has not returned."

"Oh my. That is quite a long time. And your grandmother?"

"My grandmother recovered, but . . . my mother decided to stay."

Awkward silence muted the sounds of the breeze through the trees—or perhaps the discussion was only awkward because of the sentiments Camille harbored on the subject.

"And your siblings?" continued Miss Gilchrist. "Do you have any brothers or sisters?"

"No. I am my parents' only child."

"Ah, what a shame. You must miss your family very much."

Camille did not respond, for she would have to conquer her anger at her parents before she could admit to missing them.

The conversation dropped, and they continued their walk to Kettering Hall.

※ ※

The walk had been a bit longer than Camille expected, but more beautiful and more refreshing than she ever thought possible.

Miss Gilchrist, on the other hand, had grown quite red in the face with the exertion. Once on the estate's grounds, she headed toward the main entrance. But Camille was not quite ready to return.

Camille stopped as they reached the front drive. "Do you mind if I walk around a bit before joining you in the house?"

"Of course I do not mind." Miss Gilchrist fanned her face with her hand. "But are you not warm after all that walking?"

Camille lifted her hand to shield her eyes from the low-hanging sun. "I confess to being a little weary. But the gardens are so lovely. I should like to enjoy them for a few moments."

"Then you will have to forgive me, for I must go inside and lie down for a bit before dinner. I find that walks on hot days always take their toll. You can find your way back inside and to your chamber, I trust?"

Camille nodded.

"Very well, then, I shall leave you to your solitude."

Once Miss Gilchrist had entered the house, Camille made her way to the back of Kettering Hall, where a lavish formal garden—an intricate maze of boxwoods accented with lavender—stood surrounded by birches and elms. She made her way to the garden's far right, where a line of closely planted willow trees formed a protective canopy over a brick path.

She walked in silence, each step taking her further and further away from Kettering Hall. She fixed her attention beyond the line of trees, where grazing land gave way to a forest, dark and deep, and a creek flowed peacefully at the forest's edge.

A bench tucked beneath the bough of an ash tree caught her eye, and she made her way to the wooden seat. From here she could see a small pond beyond the break in the forest. She watched as a pair of swans crossed the water. They bent their elegant necks as they swam, the very embodiment of grace and simplicity.

How often had she dreamed of such a place, longed for this kind of beauty and tranquil serenity? She wanted to forget everything about her life in London. Was it possible to shed the skins of past experiences and begin anew?

She was not as refined as Miss Gilchrist nor as adept with the social graces. How could she be? She had been taught manners when she was young. Both her mother and her governess had been unfailingly strict about propriety and etiquette. But once she moved to London and her mother left for Portugal, there had been little need for such disciplined behavior. In fact, it had been almost a liability.

The knowledge of such things was within her, however. She just needed practice. No doubt the school would not be as elegant as this home. But if it were half as calm, half as peaceful, perhaps her mind would be free enough to strive for something different.

Camille drew a breath, long and satisfying, slow, steady, relaxed. Then she gasped, suddenly alert to movement that drew her attention to the garden behind her. Life on Blinkett Street, where danger could lurk in every alley and alcove, had made her wary. She froze in place and held the breath that seconds ago had flown so freely.

Then Mr. Gilchrist appeared, and her tight shoulders lowered.

That, in and of itself, alarmed her. Few men in her life had proved themselves trustworthy, with the exception of her grandfather. Did she dare relax her guard so easily?

"Miss Iverness!" His expression was one of genuine surprise. "Whatever are you doing out here in this part of the garden? I thought you would be with Penelope."

"Mr. Gilchrist." She nodded her greeting. "Your sister and I just returned from the village. She was ready to retire, but I found myself wanting to explore."

He propped his hands on his hips and surveyed the pond.

"This is one of my favorite places on the property." He spoke the words almost more to himself than to her. He then motioned to the bench where she sat. "May I join you?"

She slid to the edge of the bench to give him plenty of space. For the second time in the day she sat next to him. She had grown more comfortable in his company and yet, the more she was with him, the more aware of him she grew. Aware of not only his mannerisms and the things he would say, but also of the impact he was having on her.

"And how did you find Fellsworth?" he asked.

She looked down to the long grass by her boots. "It is quite a lovely village, quite different from London."

He smiled and cast his gaze out over the pond as if searching for something. "And how do you like it? Do you miss the busyness of Blinkett Street?"

"Not at all. I had always hoped one day to visit the country. In fact, several years ago a painting of a green meadow came into the shop. I took it up to my room, always imagining that one day I would walk through such a place again. But I never expected those idle fancies to become a reality."

"I am glad to hear that being here pleases you. My sister does not agree, but I much prefer the quietness of the countryside to London."

For several moments they sat in silence. Mr. Gilchrist seemed quite content to be there in the moment, watching the swans swim about. She summoned her courage and watched him from the corner of her eye. He was a handsome man. A strong, straight nose. Blond eyebrows framed blue eyes so pale they were almost startling. His side-whiskers highlighted the square cut of his jaw, and his light hair fell against his forehead with rakish charm.

She inhaled. "I am glad to have a moment alone with you, Mr. Gilchrist, for I never thanked you for your services that night in the shop. What you did was very gallant. I am not sure what would have happened had you not come by."

He turned and studied her for several moments. He had a quiet way about him, a habit of slow contemplation that brought a flush to her cheeks. He then smiled. "It was my pleasure."

She swallowed. "I do wish I was able to offer more assistance concerning the ruby." As the words came out of her mouth, she realized the truth in them. "And it pains me to think your efforts on my behalf may have hindered your ability to recover it."

"I admit that I threw quite a knot into our investigator's plan with my actions, but I would not act differently if I had the chance. The Bevoy is merely a thing. A trinket. Hardly worth the safety of a person. Besides, I am confident we will find it in time."

She knew better. Once gone, once in the underground markets and out of respectable hands, such a rarity was unlikely to reappear.

"I fear your father may not share your sentiment that the ruby is merely a trinket."

He smiled. "My father does not share a great number of my sentiments, Miss Iverness."

She looked down at her interlaced fingers in her lap, recalling what Miss Gilchrist had shared about the relationship between father and son. Reluctant to pry into such a personal matter, she shifted the conversation.

"What are the next steps to find the ruby?"

He stretched out his booted foot. "Our investigator claims

that he is still on the search. If anyone is able to locate the ruby, it will be him. Or so my father tells me."

Camille shifted on the seat, unable to shake the horrid memory of Papa laughing and talking to the man in the long cape in the alley behind the shop. She was coming to suspect that her father was involved in the disappearance of the Bevoy, as much as she didn't want that to be the case. At one point she had considered him a sharp but honest businessman. But now, considering his behavior over the past several years and the odd exchange she had witnessed in the alley, she wasn't sure.

But she could not admit it aloud. Not yet, and certainly not to Mr. Gilchrist. For as much as she wanted to trust him, a small voice in her mind whispered caution. She barely knew the man, after all. How could she be certain about his character or his intentions?

"I have something for you."

Mr. Gilchrist's words pulled her from her reverie. "For me?"

He did not respond, only reached into his coat and retrieved a letter. He pressed it between his forefinger and middle finger and held it in the air.

"What is that?"

"A letter, of course." He extended it toward her. "It is for you."

Panic settled over her. Who would be sending her a letter? She wanted anonymity. She wanted separation from her previous life. Did someone know where she was?

She drew a deep breath, then took the letter in her hands. Her name was scrawled across the front. But the writing was not that of her mother or father or anyone else whose hand she recognized. Unable to remain still, she stood as she broke open the letter's seal. She unfolded it, trying to mask the trembling in her hands.

Miss Iverness,

I am pleased to offer you the position of junior teacher at Fellsworth School. Based on your experience and your recommendation by the Gilchrist family, I feel confident that you would do well. If you do indeed accept this position, please visit the school tomorrow afternoon and we will make the necessary arrangements.

Until then,

Mr. Edward Langsby

Camille's hand flew to her mouth. Could it be? Could her future really fall into place so quickly, so seamlessly?

"Good news, I hope?" Mr. Gilchrist's voice was kind. Steady. Earnest.

"Indeed!" She lowered the letter, unable to prevent a smile from turning up the corners of her mouth. "It is from Mr. Langsby. It appears that there will be a position for me at the school after all."

"There—I am glad to hear it."

She sat back down and read the letter again. Warmed by Mr. Gilchrist's kind smile, she allowed herself to relax into the moment, enjoying the rare pleasure of sharing good news with another.

"Well, then, I would call this day a success." He stood. "Tomorrow afternoon you will go to the school. I cannot deny that I am relieved. After all, it was I who convinced you to accompany us to Surrey, making a promise that, in truth, I had no right to make."

"Let us be perfectly clear on the matter, Mr. Gilchrist. You forced me to do nothing, nor did you deceive me. I came of my own free will, knowing full well that this opportunity might not come to fruition. But I am resourceful, sir. I felt confident all would be well."

"You are a remarkable woman, Miss Iverness." He rested his palm on his knee and rotated to look at her. "And I confess I find your outlook quite refreshing. I daresay that few women I know would approach such a situation with such optimism."

They walked back to Kettering Hall together as the sun began its descent over the pond. And for the first time in a very long while, Camille felt happy.

Chapter Twenty-Five ———————

he next morning a steady drizzle kept Camille and Miss Gilchrist indoors. The humid morning and the misty rain made everything feel dewy—a sensation Miss Gilchrist lamented, claiming the weather gave her quite the headache. But nothing could dampen Camille's spirits on this morning, not even the tenderness of the wound on her arm. Not when a new future was so within her reach.

In light of her host's ailment, Camille borrowed a book from Kettering Hall's library and, after a quiet breakfast, retreated to the parlor with it. Reading had always been a luxury for her. Despite the number of dusty and exotic tomes that passed through their shop, she had rarely had time to read for pleasure.

She settled in a comfortable chair with a sense of pleasant anticipation and opened the little volume of verse. Within minutes, however, she found herself distracted. Her nerves tightened in anticipation of her afternoon visit to the school, and though the words were masterfully woven together, she could not bring herself to concentrate on them.

Laying the book aside, she went up to her chamber to retrieve her small bundle of possessions, including the letter from her mother. Perhaps it was the uncertainty of what lay ahead, but a strange stirring within her had inflamed a sense of finality. Was now the time finally to read what Mama had written?

Torn between the need to read the letter or discard it, she hurried back to the silence of the parlor. She untied the bundle and laid out her meager possessions on the sofa next to her.

She considered reading the letter from her mother but decided against it. Instead, she held up the scissors and looked at them. What a strange keepsake they had turned out to be, considering she left her home with only the items in her apron pockets.

The metal scissors put her in mind of the shop, where she had used them daily. She could not stop herself from wondering if Papa was angry about her disappearance. Was he worried at all? Had he even noticed she was gone?

She pushed aside the coins, brooch, and the box from her father and retrieved the letter again, but the echo of hoofbeats drew her attention to the drive in front. Curious, she rose and looked out the window to see a tall man with a cloak, slick from the weather, dismount a dark bay horse. A little thrill surged through her at the sight. But then the man pivoted to hand his reins to a stableboy, and she noticed the hair under his hat was dark.

Her shoulders sank ever so slightly.

It was not Mr. Gilchrist.

With a sigh she returned to the sofa and prepared to gather her things.

But then, suddenly, the parlor door flew open. The dark-haired man appeared in the doorway, his clothes wet and his boots muddy. Startled, Camille jumped to her feet. The two stared at each other for several seconds.

At length the stranger gave a sharp bow, and then he spoke. "Please accept my apologies. I was not aware you were here."

She clasped her hands behind her, feeling as awkward as a child who had been discovered doing something naughty. Having no desire to introduce herself or to explain why she was at Kettering Hall, she gave him a brief nod and turned to gather her things.

Then he spoke. "Miss Iverness."

She froze, her breath suspended. The man's face was shadowed, but to her knowledge she had never seen him before. Why did he know her name?

She assessed him more carefully, searching her memory for hints as to who he might be. He was a very tall, thin man, his hair blackened by the rain and hanging in clumps about his face. He stepped further into the room, and the fire's glow fell on a vaguely familiar face—one she could not precisely recall, but one that drew a recollection from the recesses of her mind.

They stood in silence for a few moments, each staring at the other, he with a smile on his face and she trying to recall who he was and where she had known him. Was he a customer?

"Forgive me," she said once she found her voice. "You know who I am?"

"Of course. You are Miss Iverness, James Iverness's daughter. Or have I gotten it wrong?"

She bit her lower lip, hesitant to look at the man yet compelled to discern his identity. "No, sir, you are quite correct."

"You needn't look so alarmed." The stranger smiled a good-natured smile, the simple act relieving the room's mounting tension.

Camille gave a nervous laugh and blew out the breath she had been holding. "I am merely surprised to encounter someone here at Kettering Hall who knows who I am."

The man stepped further into the room until he was quite close to her. "I am harmless, I assure you. I am here to call on Mr. Gilchrist. But, I must say, your company is more charming by far."

She was not normally susceptible to words of flattery, but a strange flutter affected her heart as she met his chocolate eyes with her own. She was relieved when the butler appeared in the threshold, looking slightly alarmed that the new guest had gotten away from him and entered the parlor independently. Clearly this man had been a guest here before, for he seemed to know the layout of the house.

The butler, having heard the man's declaration that he was calling on Mr. Gilchrist, cleared his throat. "Would you prefer to speak with Mr. Ian Gilchrist or Mr. Jonathan Gilchrist?"

"Either." His gaze did not leave Camille.

"And who may I say is calling?"

"You may tell him that Henry Darbin is here to see him. He will know what it is about."

Henry Darbin. The investigator. The man who was with Mr. Gilchrist the night I was attacked.

Camille looked back to the door behind her, the other parlor exit. Growing uncomfortable, she again reached to gather her belongings. "I will go tell Miss Gilchrist that you are here, Mr. Darbin. She has spoken very highly of you, and I am sure she would like to speak with you."

"That is a lovely watch. Is it Swiss?"

She realized he was assessing her brooch. "I-I do not think so. I believe it is English. It was a gift from my grandfather many years ago."

"And what an interesting little box."

She followed his gaze, struck silent by the sudden change of topic. "Oh, I should not have these things down here." She stuffed them quickly into her apron pocket and rerolled them into the apron.

"I am actually glad that I have found you," he said. "I suppose it is fate that has given me this opportunity to say something to you that I have been thinking of since that night at the shop."

His statement seemed odd, but now that he had started speaking, it would be impolite of her to leave now. She turned and rubbed her hand over her forearm. "Oh?"

"Yes. I was quite concerned for you after you disappeared. I received news from Gilchrist that you were well, but I am happy to see for myself that is indeed the case." She remained silent, unable to shake the sense that something was not as it should be. For he was too kind. Too polite. Too handsome.

"I did return afterward," he continued. "I wanted to make certain you were safe. But when I returned, no one was there. In fact, the building appeared to be in shambles."

She found her voice. "I am very grateful for the assistance you and Mr. Gilchrist offered. I was quite shaken by the night's events, and the Gilchrists were kind enough to open their home to me and allow me to pass the night with them."

"I understand from Jonathan Gilchrist that you sustained an injury."

"Only a cut to my arm."

He gave a little laugh. "You say that as if it is a justifiable occurrence. I assure you, it is not."

She looked down at the bandage peeking out from the hem of her sleeve.

"I have been following the blackguards who did this for quite some time now. I wanted to assure you that now, more than ever, I am resolved to bring to justice those who were responsible."

Camille turned away. For the millionth time, her father and the awkward conversation with the man in the cape flashed into her mind.

He must have interpreted her change of countenance. "Have I upset you?"

"No, not at all." She turned around. "Do you know who he is?"

"Who?"

"The man who attacked me." She eyed him, waiting for his response. Every bit of information she could collect was a clue. She knew her father had secrets he kept from her. As bookkeeper, she knew most of the names in the shop ledger. But as the years passed she had become increasingly aware of Papa's other trans-actions—the ones of which he never spoke. She had chosen to turn a blind eye, trusting that he would protect her.

Considering what she had witnessed, that was simply not true.

"Unfortunately, I cannot tell you the perpetrator's name—not out of cruelty or unnecessary secrecy, but for your own peace of mind. I beg you, leave this business to me."

He stepped forward. A little too close. She resisted the urge to shrink away, but the directness of his gaze, the steadiness of his voice, shook her.

She held her breath. He was a man who was paid to solve crimes, was he not? And he had been charged with recovering the Bevoy, so surely he would ask her questions about the ruby and Papa and the shop.

She waited, but no question came.

"You look as if you have seen a ghost," he said.

"Do I?" She gave a nervous laugh. "I suppose the events of the past several days are catching up with me." She sighed her relief when the butler returned to escort Mr. Darbin to the library, where Mr. Ian Gilchrist was reading.

Mr. Darbin bowed in parting, his dark eyes lingering on her for a bit too long. Camille watched him retreat, then clutched her book to her chest, quitted the parlor, and hurried to her chamber.

It was late morning when Henry Darbin arrived at the Fellsworth apothecary shop. Jonathan glanced up as the door opened and the investigator entered, looking every bit the gentleman. For Darbin's tastes were extravagant. His bright crimson waistcoat and intricately tied cravat seemed ridiculously flamboyant in the quiet village of Fellsworth.

"Well, look who it is." Jonathan straightened on his workbench and rested his fists on the top of his thighs.

"So this is the inside of an apothecary shop?" Darbin's gaze swept the shop from the low ceiling to the rough floor.

Jonathan looked around at the vials and jars of herbs and treatments, most of which had been made by his own hand.

"It is. It was my uncle's before me." Jonathan was not interested in idle chitchat. "When did you arrive from London?"

"Just this morning." Darbin picked up a glass jar, held it up to the light to examine the contents, then set it down on the other side of the bench. "I left London with dawn's light. I've just come from Kettering Hall."

"Oh?" Jonathan moved the jar back to its place in front of him.

"Yes. I spoke with your father. And Miss Iverness."

Jonathan tensed. He was not sure why, but he did not like the idea of Mr. Darbin speaking with Miss Iverness. He did not like it at all. Jonathan sealed the jar, then placed it on the shelf above his workbench.

Darbin reached for another jar, opened and sniffed it, then returned it to the shelf. "She is a very pretty thing, isn't she? Much prettier than one would expect, knowing what her father looks like. But they say her mother was Portuguese. Very exotic."

Jonathan stood abruptly and removed his leather apron. "What news do you have for me?"

Darbin found a chair in the corner, drew it closer, and then sat down, crossing one long leg over the other. "Nothing. The lead has dried up. McCready has apparently fled—no sign of him at all."

"And James Iverness?"

"He is angry as blazes about the state of his shop, but I have heard of no firm plans for retaliation."

"Is he capable of retaliating?" questioned Jonathan.

"Yes, he's capable. He knows I was involved."

The thought of Miss Iverness, with her soft, quiet ways, being alone with her brute of a father unsettled him. "Do you know if he realizes his daughter has quitted London?"

"Oh I am certain he does. Without her, who is there to run his shop?" Darbin narrowed his gaze on Jonathan. "Has she told you anything about the Bevoy?"

Jonathan drew a deep breath before he responded. He had known this question was coming, and for some reason, it seemed like a difficult one. He almost felt as if he were betraying Miss Iverness by speaking behind her back. "She says she has never heard of it."

"Bah." Darbin burst a quick laugh. "You do not believe her, do you?"

Jonathan did not like to think Miss Iverness capable of lying. True, he had not known her long and was not acquainted with her ways—or the ways of those involved in her line of business. Still, something about her compelled his trust. "I do believe her."

"Then you are a fool!" Darbin laughed again as if enjoying his own joke. "Perhaps your brother was right. The two of you are as different as night and day. He never would have let the woman stay at Kettering Hall without finding the truth."

Darbin leaned forward, all trace of laughter gone. "Of course she knows about the Bevoy, Gilchrist. It was her and her father in that little shop. Do you think she would be unaware of what was happening there? There are ways of getting women to talk, and as a man, I should hope you know what I am talking about. It should not be very difficult. After all, put her in a proper gown, and the little waif isn't half bad."

Jonathan winced at his guest's tone. "What she looks like is not what matters at the moment."

"Maybe not to you, but a pretty little thing like that makes the job a little more pleasant, dare I say?"

An image floated through his mind—how Miss Iverness had sat the previous evening, her hair bound in restrained formality, but with one long strand that had pulled loose.

Darbin's tone grew more serious. "There is one thing you need to understand about Miss Iverness. She is not like the ladies to which you are accustomed. She comes from a very different background—quite a contrast to your fair sister, who was raised with every manner of care. In fact, Miss Iverness is nothing like the other ladies you will encounter in this charming village you call home. Camille Iverness spent the last decade of her life on the streets of London. To take it a step further, she associates with people who are one step above criminals and may very well be criminals."

"I think you are judging Miss Iverness a bit harshly."

"Do you? Well, that is very noble of you. But consider, I have been tracking her father for months—nay, years. I would caution you to look beyond her fluttering eyelashes and attractive figure, for she is part of a world you do not know." A challenge infused the man's tone, weaving its way through each word uttered. "Your brother, now, he would have known how to handle her."

"Be that as it may, she is still a guest in our home."

Darbin held his hands out defensively. "Have it your way. But if that is the case, then I feel obliged to inform you on what I know of her father."

Jonathan sniffed. "And that is?"

"As I said, I have been following him for months. Several high-profile items have been stolen from the Wenton auction house. They hired me to investigate. And Iverness is right in the thick of it. I do not believe him to be the thief per se. But I do think he is collaborating with whoever is taking the items and is helping to sell them."

"It seems you have everything figured out."

Darbin shook his head, looking injured. "I do wish you would not be so cynical. Need I remind you that you and your father have hired me as well? It is not my normal policy to share details of another case with clients, but in light of the persons involved, I feel you have a right to know."

"Very well," Jonathan said. "Continue."

"As I said, I believe the thieves are working with James

Iverness to sell stolen items out of the country, making them harder to trace once they leave England's shores."

Jonathan pressed his lips together. Deep down, part of him knew there was a sliver of truth to what Darbin said.

But just how much truth was the question—and how deeply Camille Iverness was involved.

Chapter Twenty-Six

*C*amille arrived at Fellsworth School with little more than she had carried when she arrived at Kettering Hall. Everything fit into her borrowed valise. But at least now she had two new gowns, courtesy of Miss Gilchrist, her own linen gown that Meeks had cleaned, and the necessary underthings and personal items.

She arrived alone. Miss Gilchrist's headache had not subsided, and Mr. Jonathan Gilchrist had not been present at Kettering Hall at the time of her departure. Only a few days earlier, Camille would have preferred the solitude. But she'd grown accustomed to Mr. and Miss Gilchrist's company over the past few days. They had been so kind in opening their home to her when, in all honesty, most people in their position would have turned her away. Still, she told herself, she had little right to expect anything further, especially in the way of friendship.

The footman jumped from the carriage, handed her down, and picked up her valise.

"It is all right, Andrew. I can get it from here."

"Are you certain, Miss? 'Tis no trouble at all."

"I am certain. You have been most kind."

He gave a bow in her direction and returned to the carriage. It rumbled away behind her, leaving her standing alone in front of the school. To her left, a line of children hurried past her, their hands folded behind them. One of them looked in her direction and caught her eye.

Camille pressed her lips together. She didn't know anything about children. Not a single thing. She had grown up surrounded by adults. On her grandfather's estate she had been the only child, and she had rarely played with the other children on Blinkett Street. She had worked.

She bit her lower lip. She had come this far. If blazing a new path for herself meant immersing herself in yet another new world, she would do it. She took in a deep breath as if to remind herself that she was away from London's harsh streets and smoky air. That was one dream that had come true. And perhaps it was the start of many more.

She picked up her valise, lifted the hem of her gown, and started up the stairs. There was no one to greet her, no one to welcome her. She stepped inside and looked to the right, then to the left.

But then, an older woman appeared in the foyer. Her light hair was pulled back in a chignon, and a white cap sat atop her head. Her dark eyes were small, but her smile was kind. "Are you Miss Iverness?"

Camille smiled and shifted her valise from one hand to the other. "I am."

"I am Mrs. Langsby. I believe you have already met my husband. Come in, my dear. Come in." She took the valise from Camille. "Mr. Langsby told me you would be coming today. And you are most welcome."

Camille smiled. "It is lovely to meet you."

"Come with me. Mr. Langsby would like to see you, to go

over the terms of your employment here. After that, we will go upstairs to get you settled."

Mr. Langsby sat behind the desk in his spacious study. "Oh, there you are, Miss Iverness."

"I was most grateful to receive your letter, Mr. Langsby."

"And we are grateful to have you here. Now tell me, how much do you know about our school?"

"Not much, I confess."

"We have a rich and diverse history, but it is most important that you understand our goal and purpose here at Fellsworth School. Our school actually started in London several decades ago as a foundling home. And while caring for abandoned children is a noble pursuit, it soon became clear to my predecessors that it was not enough. For you see, these young children were growing up without the education they would need to make their way in the world. Gradually, then, the focus of the institution changed. This building was purchased, and our school was born.

"Our main priority, Miss Iverness, is to care for a child's spiritual needs. We oversee every aspect of our pupils' education, from religious to academic to the very practical. Our purpose is to give these children faithful hearts and sound morals, but we also strive to make sure their education is sufficient enough to see them through. Many of them, especially the boys, will go on to apprentice in a business. The girls also are given employable skills such as dressmaking and teaching.

"Now, our children do not come from well-off families, as you might expect. Quite the opposite. Some of the children pay tuition to come, but we do not turn away a child because of their inability to pay. That is taken care of by the kindness of the church and men like Mr. Gilchrist."

"I didn't realize that boys and girls attend school together." Camille frowned at the odd arrangement. "Is that not unusual?"

"It is indeed a forward-thinking idea. But we have found there is need to care for the minds and hearts of both young men and young women. But everything here, you will find, is very proper. The two sexes will rarely interact. The young ladies have their own wing, their own schoolroom, their own dining room, and even their own play areas. I will leave my wife to share with you the rest of the details and to make the necessary introductions. But I hope you will be happy with us here, Miss Iverness."

"I am sure I will be."

After a brief discussion of salary and terms, Mrs. Langsby stepped forward. "Come along, Miss Iverness. I will show you to your quarters and get you settled."

Camille curtsied to Mr. Langsby and followed the older woman from the study.

The building seemed remarkably quiet for a school. She had imagined that children would be running all about as she had seen them on the streets of London, but they were all out of sight.

"This is the girls' wing. The young boys are in a different wing entirely. I will show you the outbuildings at another time, but this should get you started.

"The girls' dining room is behind those doors there." Mrs. Langsby pointed down the hall. "And the kitchen is behind it. Food for both the boys and the girls is prepared in that kitchen, but it is transported to the boys' wing. Keeping the sexes separate is crucial, Miss Iverness. You will find it is one of our strictest rules."

Camille nodded, soaking in every bit of information.

"There are two levels above us. The floor directly above us is where you will find the schoolrooms, and the floor above that houses the sleeping quarters. Of course, now the girls are in their classes, so we will not disturb them, but I will show you to where you will be sleeping and where to put your things."

As they climbed the oak stairs, Camille could hear young voices reciting the alphabet. From another direction, she heard an adult female voice speaking a foreign language. Excitement began to build. This was so out of the ordinary, so different than her life in the shop. And she was ready to become acclimated to her new life.

They climbed the second set of stairs to a large, square landing that opened to three hallways. Mrs. Langsby pointed to the middle hall. "With the exception of Mrs. Wheddle, the housekeeper, all the female staff have their quarters in this hallway. I have placed you in a room with one other junior teacher, Miss McKinney. She is a very bright girl, and I think she will help you find your way around Fellsworth. Miss Brathay oversees the educational instruction in the girls' school, and she will give you more specific instructions concerning your duties here. But I thought you would like to put your things down first and see where you will be staying."

Mrs. Langsby took a key that hung around her neck and unlocked the third door on the left.

Eager to see her new surroundings, Camille followed the plump woman through the doorway, hugging her valise to her chest. The room was small, and there was but one bed. Camille eyed it with trepidation. It was certainly big enough for two people, but she had always had the luxury of sleeping alone.

"I asked Miss McKinney to clear a drawer in the bureau for you. You can put your things there."

Mrs. Langsby stepped to the bed and picked up a black gown. "Here is the dress you will wear while you are here. If you should continue on, we will have a second gown made for you, but in the meantime, this one can be taken in for you. Are you handy with a needle, Miss Iverness?"

Camille swallowed. She could not sew a stitch. But she nodded. "I can manage."

"Well, if you require assistance, Miss McKinney has quite a talent, and she has offered to help you."

Camille took the gown from Mrs. Langsby. She rubbed her finger over the coarse linen. The fabric was rough and the weave uneven, not nearly as fine as the gowns she had borrowed from Miss Gilchrist. In truth, it suited her much better than Miss Gilchrist's fashionable frocks. But as her fingers grazed the fabric, an unsettled feeling began to push against her positive intentions. Her new life was going to be different, very different, from anything she had experienced before.

"This is perfect. Thank you." Camille cast a final glance around the room, taking in the wooden floors, the painfully bare white plaster walls, and the faded pink coverlet on the bed. No paintings adorned the walls. But a glance out the window revealed the countryside spread before her like a beautiful quilt. Green. Rolling. Just as she had imagined.

She was one step closer to the life she had dreamed of. And she would not stop until she arrived.

Later that night the sun began its descent over the meadows and vale. The light outside had faded from golden yellow to a more solemn purple.

Camille's first evening had been quiet. Her dress was not ready yet, and Mrs. Langsby had not wanted her interacting with students until she was dressed properly. Since the staff normally ate in the same room as the students, she had taken her meal in her room.

Now she stood in the center of the room, arms outstretched, as her new roommate, Miss McKinney, pinned the side seam.

"'Tis a shame the woman who wore this before you wasn't a mite smaller," she exclaimed, stepping back to check her work. "I don't think we'll have to adjust the length at all. But these side seams are going to give me a bit of trouble, I think."

"I appreciate your help, Miss McKinney."

"Oh please," the girl exclaimed, adjusting one of the pins. "Call me Molly. Everyone does. Just don't let Mrs. Langsby hear you—or Miss Brathay, for that matter. They're pretty strict, they are."

"Very well, Molly. And please call me Camille."

"I cannot tell you how pleased I am that you are here. It can get so lonely with the same people around all the time. Of course, I adore the others who work here, but I am happy to have a new person to get to know." Hands full, she gestured with an elbow toward the bed, where the dress Camille had worn that day had been laid. "It will be a shame to trade in that pretty gown you were wearing for this plain black one."

"That gown is borrowed from Miss Gilchrist. Nothing of my own was that elegant, I assure you."

"Yes, I heard from one of the girls in the kitchen that your trunk took a spill."

Camille winced as she heard the lie. My, word did travel fast, even falsehoods. "Well, I can say I found myself in need of a gown, and Miss Gilchrist was kind enough to share."

Molly let the topic go and motioned for Camille to turn. "You are from London, no?"

Camille nodded.

"But you don't sound like you are from London."

"No. My youth was spent in Somerset. But how could you tell?"

Molly smiled. "Your speech."

"Is it that noticeable?"

"No cause for alarm. Here it doesn't matter how you sound as long as you speak properly. You will hear accents from every part of the country, even one from Scotland. The children come here from far and wide. In fact, some travel so far they don't make it home but once or twice in all their years at school."

Camille sobered as the severity of that comment soaked in. They lived their youth here?

Molly continued. "There was even a little one that didn't know a bit of English when she started here. Didn't take her long to catch on, though, and now you would never be able to pick out which girl it is."

Molly moved to the sleeve of Camille's gown, and as she did, she noticed the bandage. "Mercy, Camille, what happened to your arm?"

Camille cringed at the question. She had kept a bandage over the wound and had left Kettering Hall with enough supplies to keep it properly dressed for a while. But what she did not have was a good explanation—one, at least, that she was willing to share.

"It was an accident," she lied. "My fault completely."

Thankfully, the answer seemed to satisfy Molly. "Here," she said. "Let's take that dress off. Now that it's pinned I will take it in if you want. I'm fast with a needle, faster than most."

Camille let Molly help her with the gown, careful not to pull out the carefully placed pins. "I would appreciate that. I do not have much experience sewing. I am afraid I am all thumbs with a needle."

"How odd," exclaimed Molly, "for a woman not to have much experience sewing."

"I was raised by my father, and he ran a shop. I am afraid there was not a lot of time for sewing."

"And what about your clothes? Surely there was mending to tend to?"

"There was a woman a few doors down who would take on odd jobs."

The answer seemed to satisfy Molly, for she sat down in the room's only chair and reached in a basket for thread and a needle.

"I gather you are acquainted with the Gilchrists."

When Camille hesitated, Molly dropped her hand and lifted her face. "Oh, I apologize if I am interfering again. You'll get used to me, I promise."

"The Gilchrists are friends of mine." The words slipped out of her mouth without her thinking of their significance. But as she said them, the truth of them struck her. She was beginning to think of the Gilchrists as friends—even Miss Gilchrist with her haughty ways.

The realization both shocked her and pleased her.

But it was the question, and the tone in which Molly asked it, that made her leery. "And you? Are you acquainted with them?"

"No one here is acquainted with them—other than Mr. Langsby, I mean. They live up there on the hill with their servants and money, but they rarely bother with those of us here. Except for the younger Mr. Gilchrist, of course."

"What do you mean?"

"Mr. Gilchrist? Well, he lives in town, quite humbly, in a cottage, and he's here a couple times a week tending the little ones and such. But he doesn't interact much with the staff, although I daresay he has turned a head or two here."

Camille raised an eyebrow in question.

"Do you not know what I mean? Mr. Gilchrist is ever so handsome, and lots of the girls here have taken a fancy to him. Don't be surprised if some of them ask you about him. Rumor has it that he is connected to one of the fancy ladies in London. Can't say as I blame him, with him set to inherit a place like Kettering Hall. But a girl can dream, can't she?"

It would be an outright lie if Camille were to say she hadn't noticed how handsome Mr. Gilchrist was. But even if she did allow her mind to entertain the idea of Mr. Gilchrist as a suitor, reality would quickly shut down that fantasy. For he knew too much about her. And that in itself made him dangerous.

Chapter Twenty-Seven ────────────

*B*reakfast gave Camille her first opportunity to see her prospective pupils. The dining hall held about eighty girls ranging from children of five or six to young women who could not be much younger than she was herself.

Each of them was dressed plainly in a simple-cut gown of charcoal gray with black stockings and boots. All wore their hair in a single plait down their backs and a white cap atop their heads. They ate in silence at narrow wooden tables that ran the length of the expansive room. Sunshine filtered in through a row of windows that looked out over the school's main drive and front grounds.

The teachers sat at a table opposite the room's main entrance. The breakfast of oatmeal and bread seemed much too heavy for Camille's nervous stomach, but not wishing to appear ungrateful, she spooned a bite into her mouth.

She lifted her gaze and unintentionally locked eyes with one of the students near the front of the room—a younger girl with rosy cheeks and dark eyes. The girl did not smile. Camille's heart thudded within her. Doubts manifested in her mind.

To her left sat Molly, who leaned over as if sensing her discomfort. "You are not nervous now, are you? These children are quite harmless, I assure you."

Camille drew a deep breath. "There are so many of them."

Molly giggled. "Well, we are at a school. Did you attend school, or were you educated at home?"

Camille fussed with her napkin in her lap. The question was difficult to answer, for during her early years her parents had employed a governess, but after that the majority of her education had come through observing and reading. "I was educated at home."

"Have you ever taught in a school like this before?"

Camille shook her head. "I have not."

"Well, then you are in for a treat. I think this is a wonderful school. But I admit to a certain partiality. You see, I was a student here myself for several years."

Camille did not know why that bit of information should surprise her. "You were?"

"Indeed. I have been here since I was six years of age. Both my parents died while I was still a student, so I guess this is my home now."

Camille looked out over the children. They were so still and well behaved. How different it would have been to be raised in such a place, among so many other children. "My father oversaw most of my education. He was—is—a shopkeeper, and I grew up in his shop."

"What kind of shop?"

Camille took a bite to buy herself time. She did not want to share information about her past. Yet if she wanted to become friends with these women, she could not conceal everything about herself. "A curiosity shop. He was involved with importers. In the past few years he himself dealt mostly with the traders while I kept the accounts and ran the shop."

"I heard you had experience like that. That is just what our young ladies will need. As you know, we are not a school like the regular ones."

"Mrs. Langsby mentioned that."

"Our children are not privileged children, Miss Iverness. They do not come from wealthy families, and many cannot afford tuition. Most likely all will work, even these girls. And they are not pampered. They work while they are here. The boys mostly work for the local farmers, in the school's woodshop, or something along those lines. But the girls have chores, too, as you will soon see. Some assist in the kitchen and gardens. The older ones do the mending and sewing. In fact, your gown was most likely sewn by one of them.

"The world is changing, Miss Iverness, and we are preparing our young charges to change with it. Just because they were not born into money does not mean that they cannot flourish."

The words resonated with Camille. Change. There was no escaping it.

From where she was seated, she could see the main hall that led to Mr. Langsby's study. A constant stream of people passed through it. She absently watched the girls as she ate, but then something—someone—caught her eye in the hallway.

Mr. Gilchrist.

She saw him for but an instant, but his blond hair and tall, straight frame made him immediately recognizable.

She had not expected to see him so soon. How her heart soared to spot a kind, familiar face in a sea of unknowns. She resisted the improper urge to go speak with him. Instead, she watched him. His hair curled, windblown and wild, over his collar. He was talking with someone whom she could not see, but he laughed, his smile dimpling his cheek.

Her heart felt uncomfortably full at the sight of him. Perhaps it was because he knew so much truth about her, or perhaps it was merely because of his ability to make her feel at ease, but she found herself sincerely wishing to be by his side.

He moved slightly, swaying in and out of her line of vision. She found herself holding her breath, anticipating the next moment she might catch a glimpse. Her heart began to race within her chest, and she had to remind herself to breathe. As she watched him, Molly's words wove into her thoughts. He was indeed pleasant to behold. Side-whiskers outlined his strong jaw, and his teeth flashed white when he smiled. He laughed again at something said, but then he turned and he noticed her.

At first she looked away, embarrassed to be caught watching him so brazenly. She tucked a loose lock behind her ear and looked up again. He was looking at her. A smile curved his lip, and he bowed.

Never had such a simple gesture affected her so.

She nodded and smiled.

But then as quickly as he had noticed her, he returned to the conversation he had been engaged in. It felt as if someone had doused a candle or the sun had retreated behind a cloud.

At the conclusion of breakfast, the teachers gathered in a small room off the girls' dining room, adjacent to Mr. Langsby's study. There were eight women in total, three of whom were experienced teachers. The other five, including Camille, were the junior teachers. They were all dressed alike in their gowns of rough black linen with high necks and buttons on the front of the bodice. Camille could not help but feel like they looked to be in mourning instead of preparing to teach.

Miss Brathay, the head teacher for the girls' school, stood

before them. She was a severe-looking woman with faded hair and skin, but her eyes hinted at hidden warmth.

"Ladies, before we start the day, I wanted to share with you a bit of news." Miss Brathay clasped her hands before her. "We have a new junior teacher who will be joining us. Help me welcome Miss Iverness. I am sure you will all make her feel very welcome."

Camille smiled at the women surrounding her, but her smile faded when she was met with curious expressions.

Miss Brathay continued. "Now, I'm sure you know that young Jane Sonten has been unwell with scarlet fever. Miss Redburn has been helping care for her, as she has already been exposed to the illness. Do not worry, ladies. Mr. Gilchrist has shared that Miss Sonten is doing as well as can be expected, but it will be our main duty to prevent this illness from spreading among our charges."

Camille rubbed her arms, growing alarmed. She had not heard the news that such a sickness had befallen the school. But she had witnessed firsthand what havoc an illness like scarlet fever could induce.

Miss Brathay continued. "Scarlet fever is of course contagious and very dangerous, but once it has been contracted, it is unlikely that a person will suffer the symptoms twice. You were not all present at our brief meeting, so I wanted to check with you all again. Therefore I must ask, have any of you had the illness before? We need someone to care for the child and do not want to risk spreading the illness."

Camille looked around at the other teachers. A short, round woman with dark hair and eyes slipped her hand in the air.

Camille had contracted the fever when she was young, when an epidemic swept through the countryside surrounding her grandfather's estate. She raised her hand as well.

"Ah, Miss Smith, Miss Iverness. I hope you do not mind if we call upon you to assist if necessary during this time. I will speak to Mr. Gilchrist about the best way to handle this situation."

⁂

Camille stood in front of the room filled with students.

Fifteen sets of eyes watched her.

Silently.

Intently.

Camille felt faint. She actually felt faint.

How many times had she faced much more intimidating people—brawny, rough, angry men? And she could handle them without batting an eye. But these young women, with their sweet faces and quiet mannerisms, terrified her.

She swallowed. She'd been given a fairly easy task. All she needed to do on her first day was introduce herself to the older girls and explain her approach to keeping books. It was simple. It was a topic she knew like the back of her hand. And yet, as the eyes bore into her, her mind went blank.

This was her moment to prove herself. Her moment to prove her worth.

Her work had always come so easily to her before. Her tasks in the shop were second nature. She had a knack for dealing with the rough customers tactfully. She excelled at bookkeeping and tracking and acquiring merchandise.

But feelings of inadequacy bubbled within her, rising from deep within and choking her confidence. She had thought this would be easy, that she would be able to slip seamlessly from the identity of shopkeeper to that of schoolteacher. But as the young eyes assessed her, she faltered.

She glanced up at Molly, who normally taught this group of young ladies at this time of day and was now sitting in the back of the room. Molly nodded toward Camille eagerly.

Somehow Camille managed to make it through her introduction and share a bit about her experience, but as the children left the schoolroom, she blew out her air. This was not going to be as easy as she had expected.

After the morning classes and midday meal had concluded, the older students settled in for time for quiet study. As was the custom, the teachers were available to assist as needed. As Camille walked around the room supervising, a fair-haired student raised her hand in the air. Summoning her courage, Camille walked over to the girl. It would be the first time she helped a student, one on one. She breathed a deep breath.

"And what is your name?" Camille asked.

"Abigail Barnes, Miss Iverness."

"It is a pleasure to make your acquaintance, Miss Barnes. Now, what can I help you with?"

The young teenager showed her an arithmetic problem, and Camille breathed a sigh of relief. Arithmetic she could handle. But as she looked at the girl's slate, she could not help but notice the girl's hand was blotchy. It almost seemed to be trembling. Watching the girl's face as she worked her sums, Camille assessed the girl's complexion. It was waxy and pale, and her eyes were pink around the rims.

"Forgive me for asking, Miss Barnes, but do you feel all right?"

The girl turned to look at her fully for the first time. It was then that Camille could see the full extent of Abigail's watery eyes.

"I am well, Miss."

"But I do not think you are—look, your hand is trembling." Camille straightened. "I think you should come with me. Let's go find Miss McKinney. I would feel much better if someone looked at your symptoms. And if it is nothing, then the fault for disrupting your day will be mine."

Abigail stood and followed Camille to Miss McKinney. But as they went through the motions, a queer sensation pricked Camille, for she had seen those signs before. The blotchy, dotted skin. The raspy voice and waxy, feverish complexion.

Scarlet fever.

Chapter Twenty-Eight

The next few days passed in quick succession for Jonathan. He had gone about his daily business, but his thoughts were never far from Fellsworth School. For not only had little Jane continued to worsen and another young lady, Abigail Barnes, had succumbed to scarlet fever, but Miss Iverness was there.

On Friday in the early afternoon, as was his custom, he went to Kettering Hall for dinner. Normally he took his dinners in his cottage alone. But Friday nights he would venture to Kettering, if for no other reason than to spend time with Penelope. Besides their father, she was the only family he had left.

But apprehension haunted him on his walk to his boyhood home. He dreaded tonight's interaction with his father for one reason: the Bevoy.

They were no closer to finding it. And all were painfully aware of the truth. Every day that passed without the ruby increased the likelihood that they would never see it again. He and Darbin had parted on cold terms, and he had not heard from Darbin since the man had left the apothecary shop a few days prior. Jonathan had been optimistic at first, but now his hopes that they would actually recover the gem had dwindled.

His father expected him to be in London, as if that were the mystical answer to their problem. Jonathan did not share his opinion.

Reaching the hall, Jonathan hurried up the main steps, eager to be out of the gathering weather. The rain had not started, yet the warnings were all around. Thunder growled like a beast ready to pounce from its cage. Lightning simmered in the distance. Jonathan hurried inside as soon as Abbott swung the door open.

He found his father in the parlor by the fire, a pipe clenched in his teeth. This he had expected. But finding Henry Darbin in the room as well took him quite by surprise.

The men looked up as Jonathan let himself into the parlor. It was Darbin who spoke first, a crooked grin on his face. "Ah, the prodigal son returns." The words were spoken in jest, but they plucked at his already tightened nerves.

"Darbin, what brings you to Kettering Hall? I thought you were to return to London."

Darbin nodded toward the elder Gilchrist. "Your father is a very persuasive man. I have not yet returned to London. Your father convinced me to stay on at Kettering Hall for a few more days."

Jonathan cast a glance at his father, who was intently stuffing his pipe, all but ignoring the conversation between the two men. "Don't you have business to see to in London?"

Darbin cocked his head to the side. "Your father and I believe I can be of more use here."

Jonathan narrowed his eyes on the scene, unsure what to make of it. He took his seat by the fire, just as he did every Friday. It was really too warm for such a fire. The walk over had been muggy at best, and the fire made things worse.

But his father seemed oblivious. "The more the merrier, isn't that what they say? Dowden sent word that he will be joining us as well, which should please your sister. It's about time he showed himself around here again." He puffed his pipe, sending swirls of tobacco smoke into the air, pausing only when coughs racked his body.

Ian Gilchrist had never been an overly healthy man. A raucous lifestyle had aged him beyond his years. As of late his gout had troubled him increasingly, and his breathing seemed compromised as well. Physician after physician had come by, but none had been able to cure him.

Though Jonathan was not a physician, he was an experienced apothecary, working day to day with people afflicted with every manner of ailments. If asked, he thought he could help. But he knew his father. Being an apothecary was a shame to his father, and a disgraceful occupation for the heir of Kettering Hall. Accepting assistance from Jonathan would validate the occupation. Ian Gilchrist would never do that.

"I wish you would let me give you something for that cough," Jonathan ventured anyway.

His father's reply was gruff. "Don't need it."

But as yet another round of hacking assaulted his father, Jonathan sighed and leaned back against the chair.

Darbin's voice rose above the crackling fire. "I hear Miss Iverness is settled at Fellsworth School."

Jonathan noted it had not taken long for Darbin to bring her into the conversation. "She is."

"As good a place for her as any," reasoned Darbin. "Away from her father and where we can keep an eye on her."

Jonathan clenched his teeth. He was not a man prone to quick anger, but Darbin had a way of irritating him. Jonathan knew why. The man reminded him so much of Thomas that it had almost became impossible for Jonathan to separate the two. He knew it was unfair to project feelings for one person onto another, but they were so alike in their mannerisms and their ways of thinking.

Darbin fussed with his cravat. "She will be joining us for dinner, you know."

Jonathan jerked his head up. Darbin spoke as if he had some authority at Kettering Hall. It was well known that the staff at the school had very limited time off—a total of two Sunday afternoons a month. He kept his temper in check, his voice, even. "No, I did not know. It is Friday. I am surprised the school could spare her."

"Penelope paid the school a visit and spoke with Mr. Langsby directly," his father said. "You know your sister and how persuasive she can be. What she wants, she gets. Is that not right?"

"Did I hear my name?" His sister sauntered into the room.

"Uncanny," Jonathan breathed. "We speak of you and you appear. Penelope, Father was just remarking that you have the incredible ability to get what you want."

Penelope looked to her father innocently. "What is he talking about?"

"We just informed him that Miss Iverness is joining us for dinner," he recounted. "He was surprised the school could spare her."

Penelope flounced onto the sofa opposite Jonathan. She rolled her eyes. "Really, Jonathan. Do not look so sour."

"I do not think you should interfere. She is settling into a new life. Let her be about her business in peace."

Penelope's lips formed that familiar pout. "Perhaps I am interfering, Jonathan, but I want to get this ruby back. And you

234

are sitting there like a dunce, doing nothing. You speak of her new life. But what about my new life? You may not mind being poor and living in the village, but I do. The ruby is of utmost importance to me."

Jonathan shook his head in disgust. He suspected a trap. Miss Iverness was coming to dinner, undoubtedly expecting companionship, and these three would use that expectation in an attempt to extract information from her.

Jonathan wanted to know the truth as well. Nothing would be more satisfying after all this time than to have the right answers. But this was not the way.

"She knows nothing," Jonathan stated. "You should leave her alone, Darbin, and do what we have hired you to do."

Penelope jumped to Darbin's defense. "Is it truly possible for someone as clever as you to be deceived by a pretty face? Mr. Darbin is *trying* to do his job. You are not going to be of any assistance, so you might as well step down and let him do his work."

Jonathan wanted to wash his hands of this group—to leave Kettering Hall once and for all and leave the entire mess behind him. But one thing kept him tied to his chair. He would not leave Miss Iverness to face them alone.

But Penelope was not finished. "I do hope that you are not allowing any personal feelings to cloud your judgment."

Jonathan lifted his eyebrows. "Personal feelings?"

"I have seen the way you look at her," she shot back. "All glassy-eyed like a schoolboy. Miss Iverness is quite a beauty, I'll allow. And what better way to hide a secret than to flirt with the very man she is trying to keep it from. I think you are allowing an infatuation to sway your common sense."

Jonathan could feel his face reddening, his self-control slipping through his fingers. He had expected this sort of behavior from Darbin and even his father, but not from Penelope. He had thought her more compassionate than to waylay a poor girl who had done nothing wrong. Her panic over losing the dowry must be great indeed.

Penelope continued, her words terse. "Since you seem so lily-livered about this, I will take it in hand myself. You may be fine and well with losing everything, but Father has worked too hard to see it all go downhill. If you will not fight for the Bevoy, then I will. And Mr. Darbin will help me."

Chapter Twenty-Nine

Camille had been thrilled to receive an invitation for dinner at Kettering Hall.

Of course, the invitation had raised eyebrows, for Miss Penelope Gilchrist never entered the school, and her personal visit to Mr. Langsby to request Camille's presence had set tongues wagging. And it seemed odd that Mr. Langsby never asked Camille if she would accept the invitation, but told her she was to attend. Clearly the relationship between the school and the Gilchrist family was deep-seated and complicated, if just a visit from the daughter could excuse one of the teachers from her nightly duties.

But at the moment, Camille did not care. Her first days of teaching had been exciting but tiring, and she was eager to be in the company of friends once again—especially since, if she were to be called upon to nurse the sick children, she might not leave the building again for quite some time.

The Gilchrists had sent a carriage for her, and now that carriage rumbled across the countryside. Flecks of rain splattered the side of the window while purple clouds mounted in the east, gilded by momentary flashes of lightning. Camille kept her eyes focused on the window for the entire ride. She never wanted to take this beauty for granted. Never.

Camille smoothed her gown and folded her gloved hands in

her lap. She had chosen to wear her plain black teaching gown and her black kid boots. No doubt Miss Gilchrist would expect her to wear one of the gowns she had loaned her, but at least the one she was wearing was officially hers by right. She had bundled all the items that Penelope had lent her into the borrowed valise and would return it tonight. She was already in debt to the Gilchrists for so many things. She did not want to live off their charity indefinitely.

Upon her arrival, the butler took the valise from her and led the way into the parlor. A wave of excitement coursed through her. She felt unusually comfortable, as if she were coming home to a place where she belonged.

When the butler announced Camille, Miss Gilchrist jumped up from the sofa, a vision in shimmering pink sateen. She rushed over and gathered Camille's hands in her own, carefully dressed curls bouncing with each slippered step. "Miss Iverness, you are here at last. I do hope that you do not mind my asking Mr. Langsby to send you over for dinner tonight. It was presumptuous, I know, but I could not bear waiting until your free Sunday."

"It is I who am grateful." Camille quickly scanned the room. The gentlemen in the parlor had all stood when she entered. The elder Mr. Gilchrist. Mr. Darbin. A man she did not know. Jonathan Gilchrist. Her breath caught at the sight of the latter.

She had been concerned that the younger Mr. Gilchrist might not be joining them, especially given the illness at the school. But at the sight of him, her happiness felt complete. She wondered if she would ever be able to see him without feeling this way. It was childish, really. She had often read of infatuations but had never experienced one. Most men, in her experience, were rough and selfish, dangerous and cruel.

But not her grandfather, of course. And not Mr. Gilchrist.

Miss Gilchrist, obviously comfortable in the role as hostess, took Camille's arm in hers and ushered her to the center of the room. "Do come over here and warm yourself by the fire. The rain did not make your dress damp, did it?" She then turned to face the men. "I believe you know everyone present, with the exception of Mr. Dowden? Miss Iverness, this is my betrothed, Mr. Alfred Dowden. Mr. Dowden, this is Miss Iverness, the one I have told you so much about."

Miss Gilchrist broke away from Camille and stepped over next to the man, who bowed deeply. "Miss Iverness. It is a pleasure to make your acquaintance."

Camille curtsied in return.

She could have guessed Mr. Dowden's identity before the introduction. In truth, Miss Gilchrist had only mentioned him a few times, but the affectionate glances she threw his way made her feelings for him clear. He seemed to take them as his due. Mr. Dowden was not the tallest man in the room, nor the most handsome, but his deep barrel chest and sober countenance lent him an intimidating presence.

"Please be seated, Miss Iverness," chattered Miss Gilchrist, taking Camille by the arm. "I do want to hear all about your first few days at Fellsworth School."

Camille followed Miss Gilchrist's bidding and took a seat on the sofa. "Everyone at the school has been very kind and welcoming. And they are all so very complimentary of your family."

"They should be," growled the elder Mr. Gilchrist, adjusting his position in the chair and wincing as he repositioned his leg. "We've given them money to keep that school afloat more times than I can count."

"Father!" scolded Miss Gilchrist. "That is not at all gracious."

"But it is the truth."

"Be that as it may, it never does to say such things."

Camille lifted her eyes to the younger Mr. Gilchrist to ascertain his view on the topic. He seemed abnormally quiet, and he was the only one of the party not sitting. Instead, he stood at the fire, leaning with his elbow against the chimneypiece. His eyes were fixed on her, but his expression seemed more severe than she could recall. Normally there was a softness in his expression. But now he seemed hard. Almost angry.

Miss Gilchrist had moved on to ask about Mr. Darbin's recent stay in London, but Camille found herself distracted. Had she done something to upset Mr. Gilchrist? Had something been said to him by the school?

She set the thoughts aside and forced herself to smile. The past two days had been trying enough. She was determined to enjoy a pleasant evening.

Jonathan pushed his stewed spinach with his fork, too angry and frustrated to eat. He wanted to throw Darbin from Kettering Hall and insist he never return. But instead, he clamped his teeth over his lower lip.

He watched as his sister and Mr. Darbin petted and praised Miss Iverness. Penelope was seated on her left, Mr. Darbin on her right. Mr. Dowden, seated next Jonathan, focused mostly on his meal, while Jonathan's father, at the opposite end of the table, kept unusually quiet.

If Penelope's purpose was to make Miss Iverness feel at

home, she was certainly accomplishing the goal. She inquired after Miss Iverness's chambers at the school and about her students. She wanted to know whether or not Miss Iverness was getting enough to eat, and she pronounced it a shame that the school did not serve the teachers hot chocolate each morning.

But Darbin was worse. The way he flattered Miss Iverness was nauseating.

Jonathan knew he was sulking. But he also knew that if he were to open his mouth, he may not be able to control what came out.

It was Penelope's previous comments regarding his feelings toward Miss Iverness that bothered him the most. If he were honest, it was partly because they were true.

He did care for Miss Iverness. How could he not? And watching another man flirt shamelessly with her incited a rage within him that he had never known.

But irrespective of his personal feelings, he also felt responsible for her and did not want to see her led astray. Though wise in the ways of Blinkett Street and adept in dealing with people from a rougher walk of life, she was new to the more genteel brutalities of the country set. Yet surely she was astute enough to realize what Penelope and Darbin were up to.

Jonathan took a sip of the wine before him, the taste bitter against the back of his throat. Miss Iverness was seated across from him, dressed in a black gown of the sort he had seen on the school's teachers for years. But the plainness of it only seemed to enhance Miss Iverness's dusky complexion. The candlelight sparkled off her brilliant eyes, and she seemed infinitely happy. She smiled, and a soft dimple formed in her rosy cheek.

Yes, he had feelings for her.

And those feelings intensified his anger against his sister's ridiculous charade.

As he was contemplating, he almost failed to notice that Miss Iverness had turned to him.

"Mr. Gilchrist, are you well?"

The sound of his name on her lips snapped him from his thoughts. "Oh, yes. Very well."

Miss Iverness shook her head, her eyes cast down to his plate. "But you've barely eaten at all."

A smirk crossed Penelope's lips. "Jonathan is just out of sorts. Are you not, Jonathan?"

But Miss Iverness seemed to ignore his sister's jab. "I did not see you at the school yesterday, but I understand from Miss Brathay that you were there."

"Yes, I was there," he said, ignoring the strange flutter in his chest when she mentioned she had noticed his absence.

Miss Iverness frowned, her gaze fixed firmly on him. "And how did you find Miss Sonten this afternoon?"

He should give her a simple one-word answer. But he elaborated, his eyes on his sister. "She is about the same. Miss Barnes, I fear, is a little worse. Let us hope there are no further cases."

Penelope lowered her fork, refusing to be left out of the conversation. "And who, may I ask, are these young ladies?"

Jonathan locked eyes with his sister. "Young students at Fellsworth School. Both have contracted scarlet fever."

Penelope's expression darkened at his words, as he had known it would. She cast a glance at Dowden, then she fell silent.

Jonathan had known very well how a mere mention of the illness affected his sister, the memory it conjured. And he had done it purposefully, hoping to distract her from her cruel intentions toward Miss Iverness.

But he felt no satisfaction at momentarily quieting her. For the memory burned just as dark for him as it did for her.

Chapter Thirty

*I*n the parlor following dinner, candles lit every corner of
the room, the light sparkling off the gilded frames and
brass statues. The men had stayed behind in the dining room
for port while Miss Gilchrist and Camille took coffee in the
parlor. The men joined them shortly afterward, then the elder
Mr. Gilchrist announced that he would retire, leaving the young
people to entertain themselves.

It was a pleasant room, providing a warm reprieve from the
rainy weather outside. Camille settled on the sofa, enjoying this
time to relax with people she was quickly becoming to think of
as friends. Miss Gilchrist sat on one side of her, and Mr. Darbin
took the chair opposite.

Mr. Darbin leaned forward. "What say you to a game of
piquet or whist, Miss Iverness?"

Camille shook her head. "I am afraid I will have to pass on
that offer, Mr. Darbin. I do not know how to play either."

"It is simple." He waved his hand dismissively in the air. "I
shall have you playing like an expert in no time. Do say you will."

Camille shook her head. "Perhaps you should ask Mr.
Gilchrist. I am sure he is well acquainted with the rules. I would
surely slow the game down."

Mr. Darbin cut his eyes toward Mr. Gilchrist, who was
seated by the fire. "I daresay Miss Gilchrist would prefer Mr.

Dowden as a partner, for he is not only her intended, but is far more clever than I. And even if you do not know the game, you are a much prettier partner than Gilchrist and therefore a much more pleasant partner. I am willing to take the chance."

She could feel the blush rush to her cheeks at the compliment.

"I am not sure, Darbin," exclaimed Dowden, his expression cool and indifferent. "The game can be quite bothersome for a new player. Perhaps we could play something else."

"Oh, I do not think so," chimed in Miss Gilchrist. "Miss Iverness is quite adept. Besides, we cannot let the gentlemen have all the fun. Please, Miss Iverness, say you will play. It will be the perfect diversion on such a rainy night. I shall get the whist tokens."

Camille smiled in agreement. She knew that whist was a game that the genteel classes played. She had heard it referenced several times but never imagined she would be learning it.

After a quick tutorial, Mr. Darbin dealt each player thirteen cards, and the game began. Over the next few hours, Camille found herself enjoying Mr. Darbin's amusing company. Even Mr. Dowden cracked a smile from time to time. She began to see another side of Miss Gilchrist, a charming, humorous side that Camille actually enjoyed. For the first time in a very long time, Camille laughed a genuine, unguarded laugh. It felt wonderful. And she and her partner won every hand but one.

Mr. Jonathan Gilchrist had been reading the entire time. Camille couldn't help looking over to him occasionally, wondering what was wrong. But despite his sulking, it was nice to put the cares of the day aside and enjoy the company—and the attentions—of others.

Mr. Darbin stood and offered his hand to help Camille

from her chair. "Miss Iverness, you must be my charm, my lucky pence. Perhaps you will also bring me good fortune as I continue my hunt for the Bevoy."

At this Camille instantly sobered. It was the first time the stolen ruby had been mentioned all evening.

She hoped the topic would pass on by, the mention of it just an afterthought. But then Mr. Darbin took her by the elbow and escorted her to the sofa. She frowned. It seemed odd that he should pull her away from the others. Alarm pricked her and crept warmly up her neck as he bid her to take a seat and then sat next to her. The disturbing sense that something was about to happen nudged her, sharpening her sense of perception. She did not miss the glance exchanged by Mr. Darbin and Miss Gilchrist. She shifted on the plush cushion and wiped her palms on her gown.

Mr. Darbin's voice remained low, as if he was taking her into confidence. "I do hope you know you can trust me, Miss Iverness."

She tilted her head to the side and focused on the coarse fabric of her skirt, not sure how to interpret the strange comment. But before she could respond, he continued. "You have had a very rough go of it lately. And I hope you know that I am here to help you. I can help your father too. But first you must be willing to confide in me. To share what you know."

Then, suddenly, it all made sense.

The unexpected dinner invitation.

The flattery and attention.

The flirting.

She stared at Mr. Darbin, almost forgetting to breathe.

She cut her eyes over to Miss Gilchrist. Her head was tilted toward Mr. Dowden and she was saying something, but their eyes were fixed on her.

They were baiting her. Trying to get her to tell them something.

For just a few moments, she had forgotten about the dirty curiosity shop on Blinkett Street. The fact that her father knew she had been injured and did not care. That he was probably involved in unsavory business and had not bothered to warn her. But Darbin's question opened a floodgate, letting in all of the memories.

She never would have considered herself gullible, not with her intuitions sharpened on Blinkett Street. But here she had let her guard down. She had allowed herself to think that these people were different than those she normally encountered, simply because of their fancy dress and elegant speech.

What a fool she had been.

Mr. Darbin must have interpreted her reaction correctly, for lines creased his brow. "I meant no offense."

Camille rose to her feet and stumbled back from the sofa, staring first at Mr. Darbin and then at Miss Gilchrist. Had she really been so hungry for acceptance that she had actually believed they enjoyed her company?

She didn't know whether to lash out in anger or to run from the room and never look back. The candlelit parlor, which just moments ago had seemed so welcoming, now seemed dark and tainted.

"Mr. Darbin, you must believe me when I say I know nothing about the ruby. Nothing." Her voice was firm. Direct. "You seem convinced that I do, that I am keeping from you a secret that, when told, will unlock the information you seek."

"But surely you must know something," protested Mr. Darbin, his very words betraying his attempt to hide the fact he sought information. "I cannot believe that you worked at that shop all those years and know nothing of it."

Camille's defenses began to rise. Heat flushed her neck. Her cheeks. "I am not a liar, Mr. Darbin. And regardless of how many times you ask me, my answer will not change."

She looked to Mr. Gilchrist. His expression no longer seemed angry. Instead he leaned forward. Interested. Observant.

Camille whirled to face Miss Gilchrist, ignoring her injured pout. "I thank you for your kind invitation and for a lovely dinner. But I do believe it is time for me to return to Fellsworth School."

Darbin stepped forward and took her by the arm. "But we were having such a wonderful time. Please forgive me. I will not bring up the Bevoy again. I did not expect the mention of it to upset you so."

Camille jerked her arm away, biting back the sharp comment that sprang to her mind. She had tried so hard to remain on her best behavior, to conform to this genteel environment by concealing the rough aspects of her personality. But there was nothing genteel about Henry Darbin at the moment—or Miss Gilchrist, for that matter. It was not the mention of the ruby that had upset her, but the tactics they had employed to convince her to speak of it.

"Thank you, but I must return to the school."

"At least let me escort you to the carriage."

Mr. Darbin was relentless. All she wanted to do was run from the room. She tried to inch back, but the sofa prevented it.

Then Mr. Gilchrist caught her eye. He was walking toward her.

"No need, Darbin," he said. "I shall see you to the carriage, Miss Iverness."

The sudden interjection surprised her. But she swallowed, grateful once again for his assistance.

Mr. Darbin frowned, his brow furrowing as if he had been injured.

She made her hasty farewells and abruptly thanked her host and hostess. Mr. Gilchrist extended his arm. She rested her hand atop his sleeve.

She could feel eyes on her as she departed. The knowledge that they were watching her flamed her cheeks.

Would she never learn? She had thought she was well-acquainted with the world. So experienced. And yet, she had let herself be ambushed, and she had not even seen it coming.

The cooler air rushed her cheeks as Mr. Gilchrist led her in silence through the main hall. She could not get out of Kettering Hall soon enough. Humiliation burned bright, not so much for anything she had or hadn't said, but because she had thought, even for a moment, that they had welcomed her as a friend.

Suddenly, Mr. Gilchrist's cool composure and austere presence made sense. There was no mistaking it—he had known all along what was going to happen. He must think her a fool. A naïve fool.

Neither said a word as they made their way through the hall and out to the main entrance. The tense muscles in her arm twitched as the door swung open. The rain had settled in.

The carriage was only a few steps away. One of the horses pawed impatiently at the ground, as if sensing her desire to be far away, and the driver and footmen prepared for her to enter.

She wanted him to say something as much as she feared it.

He had borne witness to the remarkable changes in her life that had occurred since the day they met. It seemed absurd that she could keep any secrets from him. And yet she did.

She did not look at him as she spoke. "Thank you, Mr. Gilchrist." She started to step down the steps to the drive, but his voice stopped her.

"Miss Iverness."

She turned to him. But he was looking at her too deeply—as if he could read her thoughts and sense every insecurity.

She needed to put an end to this.

"Let's not forget who I am, Mr. Gilchrist. I am well aware that tonight's dinner was a ruse to find out what I know about the ruby. I may be only a shopkeeper's daughter, but I am not blind to the ways of the world."

He drew his eyebrows together. "Surely you do not think that I—"

She held up her hand, silencing him. "Please, sir, hear me out. For once and for all, please believe me. I know nothing about a ruby, nothing about a Bevoy. I had never heard of it before your family first spoke of it, and I hope I never hear of it again. And if your kindness to me has been based on the belief that I have a secret answer to help you, then you are sadly mistaken. Do not misconstrue my bluntness for ingratitude, but I must set the record straight."

Her chest heaved as a result of her explosion of emotion.

"I believe you, Miss Iverness." His response was calm. "And it is not because of the Bevoy that I care about you and what happens to you."

Had she heard him correctly? Or was this more of the same tactics, an attempt to trick her into something?

He stepped closer, his musky scent of Sandalwood confusing her senses. "At first I thought you were someone who needed rescuing, I confess it. But the more I am in your company, the more I realize I was wrong. You are strong, Miss Iverness. You do not need our approval, and you owe no explanation for the situation at hand."

She did not respond, fearing that if she did, words might slip. Words that hinted at insecurity or weakness. She had forced herself to believe for so long that if she were confident enough, she would not feel pain when offended. But it was not true.

"About what happened in there—I am sorry. I should have intervened sooner."

She could not stop herself from staring at him. After tonight's events, she realized how she had been tricked by Mr. Darbin and even Miss Gilchrist. She had noticed how standoffish Mr. Gilchrist had been. Did he not approve of his sister and friend's actions?

She had been hurt by her father, injured by her mother's rejection, and the fact that Miss Gilchrist and Mr. Darbin had wanted her company only as a means of obtaining information pained her as well. But Mr. Gilchrist seemed to pose the most dangerous threat to her. For he had found a way around the stone walls she had built around the quiet places of her heart. The places that still glimmered with hope and trust.

She wanted to tell him how she felt. If she did, she sensed, he would not turn her away. But old beliefs and defenses die hard.

Her chin was beginning to tremble. She stepped back, distancing herself from him. She climbed into the carriage without a word.

Chapter Thirty-One

After a restless night's sleep, Camille awoke to someone shaking her shoulder. She opened her eyes to see Mrs. Langsby.

Camille rubbed her eyes and looked to the window to assess the hour. The light was still gray. "What time is it?"

"It is early, but Mr. Langsby has asked to speak with you right away."

Camille sat up and rubbed her hand over her face. "Did he give a reason?"

"No, he just said he wanted to speak with you as soon as possible."

Memory of the previous night came rushing back. No doubt she had angered the Gilchrists, and she knew how much influence they had over the school. Fear she was going to be dismissed wound its way around her thoughts and squeezed.

Molly flinched and rolled over in the bed as the door closed behind Mrs. Langsby. "What did she want?"

"Mr. Langsby wants to speak with me right away."

Sleep marks creased the side of Molly's face, and she brushed her hair out of her eyes. "I wonder why."

Camille swung her legs over the side of the bed. "I do not

know, but I had best not keep him waiting. Will you help me with my stays?"

With Molly's help, Camille dressed quickly. She ran her brush through her hair.

"Did you have a nice time at Kettering Hall?" Molly asked. "How I should like to be invited there."

Camille slowed her brushing. The evening, which had started out so pleasantly, had left a sour taste in her mouth. Mr. Darbin had flirted with her, only to press her for knowledge about the ruby. And had Miss Gilchrist ever really been a friend? But in truth, neither of their opinions mattered as much as that of Mr. Gilchrist.

"It was lovely," Camille lied, not wanting to rehash the night's events.

"When you return I want to hear all about it—what you ate, what Miss Gilchrist wore, and every single detail. Do you promise?"

Camille smiled at the woman who was quickly becoming a friend. "I promise."

She made her way down to the superintendent's study. Through the windows lining the stairs she saw that it was still raining. Yesterday evening's thunder and lightning had ushered in a storm that had continued to this day and, judging by the thickness of the clouds, would not dissipate any time soon.

Camille tapped on the heavy paneled door of Mr. Langsby's study. At his greeting, she entered the room.

"Ah, Miss Iverness," he exclaimed, lowering his quill to its holder.

"Good morning, Mr. Langsby."

"And how was your visit to Kettering Hall?" He pushed his papers aside and focused his attention on her.

She forced a smile. "The dinner was quite enjoyable. The Gilchrists are gracious hosts."

"I am not surprised. They are the most generous of people. Please, do sit."

She sat down, unable to stop her knees from wobbling.

"I had a visit from the younger Mr. Gilchrist earlier this morning, in the predawn hours. As you know, two of our children have become ill with scarlet fever, and now we might have a third. Miss Brathay indicated that you had the fever when you were a child. Since it is unlikely you will get it twice, would you be willing to help care for the children until they are well?"

Camille swallowed. The thought of a child suffering tugged at her. "Of course. I would be happy to be of any service I can."

He smiled, satisfied with her answer. "Good. If you are certain, I will assign you temporarily to the sickroom. Miss Redburn is up there now. She has been doing nurse duty since the beginning. I am sure she will be relieved to have some assistance."

"Thank you, sir." Camille dropped a curtsy and left the superintendent's study. Following his instructions, she headed for the kitchen and the back stairwell that led up to the sickroom.

Part of her felt relieved at this development. She had not left Kettering Hall on a positive note, but at least her fear of losing her position had not come to fruition. She could not feel completely relieved, however, for now she would likely be in close quarters with Mr. Gilchrist.

She closed her eyes and gave her head a quick shake as if to dislodge yesterday's memory of him from her mind. He had been so quiet and standoffish for most of the evening. But his parting words echoed in the recesses of her mind: *I care about you.*

Could he have really meant what he said?

She had not stayed to find out. She had not even responded to him, but instead had left in a flustered hurry. And now she would face him again.

When she arrived in the sickroom, the gray light filtered through the open window. Fresh, cool air laced with moisture puffed through the opening. She sighed with relief to see that Mr. Gilchrist was not present. Three of the beds were occupied by sleeping girls, and Miss Redburn, who had been caring for Jane from the beginning, sat in the corner, sleeping in the chair.

She crept over to Miss Redburn and shook her shoulder to tell her she was relieving her for the time being. At first she did not respond. Camille shook her shoulder again.

It was only when the woman finally woke and shifted that Camille noted the telltale redness on the woman's brow.

Chapter Thirty-Two ———————

When Jonathan arrived at Fellsworth School in the afternoon, his worse fear had been confirmed: two new cases of scarlet fever. One of newly stricken was a teacher—Miss Redburn, who had been assisting with the sick children from the beginning. Miss Iverness had replaced her. And so far she had proved a dutiful nurse.

She wore her teaching dress of black linen, just as she had last night at Kettering Hall, only today she wore an apron of white mull over her gown. As always, the shiny watch was pinned to her bodice. But instead of a chignon, her hair had been woven into a long braid over her shoulder. Long ebony wisps had pulled loose from the plait, and she looked much more like the woman he had rescued. The long sleeves of her gown were rolled up to her elbows, and the thinner bandage on her forearm shone white against her tawny skin.

Earlier, when the children were awake, she had sat on a chair among them and read them stories. But now two children and Miss Redburn slept, and Miss Iverness was leaning over the third, a girl named Laura, wiping the child's brow with a cool cloth.

As he worked alongside her during the afternoon, Jonathan tried to keep his thoughts focused on his work, not on the night before. It had been a difficult evening for him. He had wanted to strangle both Darbin and his sister for the manner in which they treated Miss Iverness. Even now, he could not keep from chastising himself for not intervening sooner.

But what he wanted even more to forget was their interaction right before she quitted Kettering Hall. For he had slipped. He had uttered the words "I care for you." And she had not believed him. Worse, she had assumed his declaration was just another ploy to get information from her. How could she help thinking thus?

Miss Iverness had been much quieter than normal that afternoon and had rarely made eye contact. For long spans of time throughout the day it had been just the two of them working with the patients, and he found himself missing her good-natured chatter. Clearly the events of the previous evening had affected her—and her opinion of him.

She stood from her chair next to Laura's bed and returned her cloth to the basin. She looked at him. "What else can I do?"

He walked over and looked down at the child. Red bumps still covered her face, but she was sleeping peacefully. "I think that rest is the best thing for her. Let's hope the worst has passed."

Miss Iverness brushed her hair from her face and tucked several loose strands behind her ear. "I feel for the child. She is so young."

He thought he saw a window of opportunity to engage her. "How old did you say you were when you had scarlet fever, Miss Iverness?"

"I believe I was five. It was so long ago."

"And it seems you made a full recovery."

She nodded. "I understand it was quite a difficult time for my family, though I do not remember much of it. I do recall that many others were stricken as well."

"I would imagine so. Scarlet fever can travel very quickly. Let's hope it does not spread any further here." He reached over to the candle lamp on the table and brought it to the center of the room for more light. "It is getting late, and tomorrow could be another long day. If you want to go get some sleep, I can sit up with the patients for a while."

"I am weary," she admitted, rubbing her hand down the side of her face, "but I do not want to leave you here alone with this task. I can call Miss Smith if you like."

"I do not mind, Miss Iverness. Besides, I am well acquainted with scarlet fever. There are some very subtle signs that suggest a patient might take a turn for the worse, and I wish to be on alert for them."

She straightened the clean linens that were stacked on a nearby table. "It seems to me that being an apothecary would be a difficult profession. There is so much one needs to know."

"One learns it over time. But concerning scarlet fever, there was an outbreak in Fellsworth four years ago, and unfortunately I learned a great deal about the disease then. The experience is still very fresh in my mind."

"Oh, really?" She brushed her hair away from her forehead with the back of her hand. "I had not heard that mentioned."

"It was quite devastating. There were five deaths in the village and two here at the school. And a death at Kettering Hall."

Miss Iverness's eyes widened. "At Kettering Hall?"

"Yes. That is when my mother died."

"Oh." Her voice was gentle, her eyes full of compassion. "I did not know."

He could hardly believe that he had shared this memory with her so freely, for it was something that was rarely spoken of, even within the family. At the same time, it felt good to be able to share a bit of himself with her.

He continued. "Perhaps you have noticed, Miss Iverness, that my father is not very pleased with my profession."

She looked to the floor. "I have heard it mentioned."

"Of course, my father thinks such work is beneath a man who will inherit Kettering Hall. But there is another reason. When my mother was dying, she relied solely on the local apothecary—her brother, my uncle—and refused to allow my father's personal physician to see her. In the end there was nothing that could be done; the fever had done its work. But instead of accepting her death, my father chose to blame my uncle."

He paused to adjust the blanket on one of the girls. "My mother was a wonderful woman. Thoughtful and gentle. I think you would have liked her very much. In fact, you remind me of her in many ways."

"I take that as a compliment." Her voice was soft. "I have heard many of the teachers here sing her praises."

"She was a student here before she was a teacher. In fact, that was how she met my father. My grandfather was a patron of the school, and as such, my father was often here. It angered my grandfather to no end that he should fall in love with a person of such low birth. But Father, as I am sure you can imagine, made up his own mind about such things."

"Such a romantic story." She smiled. "See, there are more layers to your father than you want to admit."

He gave a sharp shrug. "I wish I could call it romantic, but I fear he was mostly determined to spite my grandfather. And truth be told, the marriage was a difficult one. Be that as it may, however, my mother remained attached to the school. She spent many hours here, helping. In fact, that is how she contracted scarlet fever. She was here caring for one of the students when it struck. That is why I was relieved when you mentioned you had already had it. As you know, it rarely afflicts a person twice."

"And you?" She tilted her head. "Have you had it?"

"No." He adjusted his boot on the floor.

"Do you not worry for your own health?"

"No. But I have been doing this for a long time now, so I must assume I am somehow immune." He changed the subject. "You have never mentioned your own mother to me. Is she still living?"

"Yes. I told your sister about her. She is from Portugal and she lives there now."

"Portugal?" That explained the dark complexion, those entrancing dark eyes. "That is quite a journey from Blinkett Street."

"Yes. She has been there for several years."

"But why, if I may ask?"

With a sigh, she absently fussed with the edge of her apron. "Quite a few years ago now my grandmother, who lives there, fell very ill. My mother traveled there to assist her and, well, she never returned."

"How terrible for a young girl. You must miss her immensely."

"I suppose."

"You suppose?" he repeated. "Do you not know it?"

Her jaw clenched ever so slightly before she responded. "She chose to leave, and she chose to not come back. I did miss her dreadfully at first, but eventually it became easier simply to accept that she would not return. That way I would not be disappointed."

"Did she make no effort to contact you since her departure?"

Miss Iverness shrugged. "She writes to me periodically. I rarely read the letters, though."

"You don't read them?" The idea sounded ludicrous. "Why?"

"I don't really know."

"But you might learn something from them that will make your separation easier to bear. People are people, and everyone makes mistakes. Do you not think—"

Jonathan ended his question in midthought, noting that she seemed to be growing anxious. He picked up several jars that were lying about and added them to his apothecary's box, then tried another line of inquiry. "Do you miss London?"

"Miss London?" she repeated. "No. I do not. But if you are politely trying to ask me if I miss my father . . ." Her voice trailed off.

Jonathan looked up, surprised that she had brought up her father on her own. Then he noticed the sorrow in her dark eyes. Up until now she had seemed so brave. So strong. Feisty, even, especially when provoked. But now she had the appearance of a bewildered child.

She managed to smile, though her eyes shimmered with moisture. She looked over to Miss Smith to make sure she was sleeping. "He was not always as he is now, Mr. Gilchrist. You saw him at his worst. Indeed, that is the worst I have ever seen him. There was a time when I was very young that he was happy and thoughtful. I always fancied him adventurous and brave. But when my mother left and did not return, he began to change. I watched him crumble. It was slow and hardly noticeable in the beginning, but he crumbled nonetheless.

"I was his constant reminder that Mama left—he told me that on more than one occasion. That I was his punishment, destined to remind him of my mother until one of us perished. I look very much like her, you see, or at least that is what he told me. And now I hardly recognize him."

Unaccountably moved, Jonathan fell silent. He found it touching that she had opened herself up to him in this way. There was a depth to this woman, so unlike that of most women he knew. Compared to Miss Iverness, Penelope and her friends—the lovely Miss Marbury included—seemed so simple, so uninteresting.

"It is refreshing to talk with you, Miss Iverness," he finally said.

"You have seen my darkest secrets, Mr. Gilchrist. And you have been unfailingly kind to me. I have nothing else to hide from you."

In this moment he could believe her. He was convinced that she was completely innocent, absolutely uninvolved with the robbery. Yet at the same time he felt a sensation he had never experienced—an ache within his chest that made him question his own perceptions.

For Miss Camille Iverness was either celestially beautiful, an angelic creature awaiting redemption, or she was a siren, luring him to a tragic fate, completely blinding him to who and what she really was.

Darbin's words echoed their warning. But now, with her so close and her emotions so raw, he found he could pay them no heed.

He needed to change the subject, lest his feelings overwhelm him. He cleared his throat. "How is your arm?"

Miss Iverness looked down at the bandage. "It is doing well, I believe."

"Have you changed the dressing recently?"

"Not since yesterday."

"If you'll allow me, I will change it for you."

She nodded and extended her arm as he collected his supplies. Her sleeve was already rolled up to the elbow. He removed the bandage carefully. The wound was healing—slowly. But it would scar.

It was a shame. Her lovely skin marred unnecessarily.

He touched her arm to steady it, just as he done several times before. But with this touch a streak of fire shot through him. For now he was no longer just touching a woman he was helping. No. An inexplicable connection drew her to him.

She stood before him, arm extended, her head bowed over the wound. He rubbed liniment over her cut, and she winced.

She looked up, her face inches below his. Her eyes flicked from his eyes to his lips and back to her arm. In that instant he knew she sensed it too.

She drew a shaky breath, and her lower lip quivered.

She was close. So close that with one step forward, one movement of his hand, she could be in his arms.

But then, as quickly as the moment had flamed from a simple dressing change, one of the children stirred.

Miss Iverness jumped back, eyes focused on the ground.

Jonathan said nothing more. He wanted her to stay, but he was not sure he trusted himself. He was in uncharted territory. But he now knew one thing beyond a doubt.

He could no longer deny that Miss Iverness, charming and spirited Miss Iverness, had worked her way into his heart.

Chapter Thirty-Three

That night Camille sat alone in her chamber, a single candle's light reflecting on the bare plaster walls. Since Camille had been working in such close quarters with the sick children, Mrs. Brathay had thought it best for Molly to sleep in another room until the danger had fully passed.

But sleep would not come for Camille. As tired as her body was, as much as she longed to recline on the bed and drift off to sleep, her mind remained as awake and active as if it were midday.

And truth be told, she did not want to be in this chamber. She wanted to be back in the sickroom. Back with Mr. Gilchrist.

She wanted to be anywhere that did not require her to be alone with her feelings and her memories.

Perhaps it was that afternoon's conversation with Mr. Gilchrist that had her so unsettled. She could still feel his feather-light touch on her arm as he tended her wound. He had cared for it before, and the sensation had not been there. But tonight the simple touch had awakened feelings she had been doing her best to deny.

A tremor shot through her of the memory of his face so close to her.

It would be so easy to succumb to a schoolgirl infatuation

with him, as Molly had mentioned just days ago. After all, he had rescued her. Protected her. Helped her.

But then she remembered the hot embarrassment she had endured at Kettering Hall the previous night, and she felt her face flame anew. She so wanted to be able to trust the man. But in a world where nothing was as it seemed, she feared she could not even trust her own heart.

She reprimanded herself for telling him so much about her family. But when he told his own family stories, she had seen how similar many of their struggles had been, regardless of the differences in their backgrounds.

She did not know what had compelled her to speak so openly. But there was something about him that made her want to share her heart. To tell him everything.

She needed to be very careful about that.

She thought about Mr. Gilchrist's words when she admitted to not reading her mother's letters: *You might learn something from them that will make your separation easier to bear. People are people, and everyone makes mistakes.*

It seemed so strange. If she kept her thoughts and feelings about her family locked up inside, they seemed manageable. Pretending that they didn't exist made the pain easier to bear. But if she thought about one particular memory and allowed herself to examine it fully, it was like opening a floodgate or pulling a loose thread on a tapestry.

She could not think about Papa without thinking about how his words hurt. And she could not think about Papa without thinking of Mama. And little by little, her true feelings would begin bubbling to the surface.

And where would she be then?

By now her thoughts were coursing through her like nervous energy. She jumped up from her seat. She paced the tiny room, walking from the window to the door. Back and forth.

But then she stopped next to the bureau and opened the top drawer.

The letter from her mother was in there, still wrapped in her apron with her other possessions.

She stared at it for several seconds. As long as that letter remained sealed, its contents could not hurt her. Perhaps Mr. Gilchrist was right. Maybe there was something within the lines that would make the pain of separation and rejection easier to bear.

But what if there wasn't?

She pushed her new hairbrush aside and lifted the bundle. Holding it against her chest, she sat down on the bed and untied the apron strings. She spread the contents out on the bed.

The scissors. The puzzle box that she had never sent to her mother. The coins. And the letter, now crumpled and battered.

Camille eyed the letter carefully. How innocent and unimportant it looked, lying there on the faded coverlet.

She assessed the wax, melted against the paper, pressed with her maternal family's seal. As long as it remained intact, her feelings were safe—or so she had told herself.

She picked the letter up. She set it down. But then she picked it up again.

Her life was changing, and every recent decision had pushed her in a new direction. Reading this letter would, no doubt, change her world again.

Perhaps it was from being so tired. Or just from wanting

answers. She ran her finger underneath the seal, popping it free from the paper. At the simple motion, her stomach lurched within her. Her heart pounded against her ribs.

She drew a deep breath, summoned every bit of courage, then lifted the letter to eye level. The script was so familiar, as familiar as if it had been a voice or spoken words. In fact, she could hear her mother's words, her heavily accented English, just as she sometimes heard it in her dreams.

She drew another deep breath. If she kept breathing that way, she would not cry. It had been so long since she had cried over her mother. She refused to start now.

Camille,

I wonder if you have received my letters. Your father assures me he has given them all to you, yet I have yet to receive a letter in your own hand.

He also informs me that you are angry with me for my absence and blame me for many things. I will not attempt to explain my actions or the reasoning behind them. One day you will understand that at some point every person must make choices. Continue to be angry if you must, but bear in mind that my absence has afforded you much opportunity. The skills you have learned in the shop will secure your future if you remain diligent and loyal to our family. You will always be able to support yourself, and you never need be dependent upon another. I may not have given you much as a mother, but this security and independence is the most important thing I could provide.

Perhaps one day we shall be reunited, perhaps not. But

you must put aside your feelings, for the betterment of our family and our business. One day all shall be known, but for the time being, heed my words.

Camille lowered the letter.

Now that the letter had been read, it could not be unread.

She stared once more at the familiar penmanship, the precise strokes blurring into mere curls and lines.

She blinked away the moisture in her eyes and raised her chin. Yes, the tone had been curt. No, there had been no hint of affection. But what was a letter but a bit of paper and ink and wax? It had no power over her. She had spent far too much time during the past few years healing from her mother's rejection for these mere words to affect her.

And the idea that her mother had done her a favor by giving her a trade? That was simply nonsensical. What child prefers an occupation over a mother?

She resisted the urge to tear the letter to bits. Instead, she folded it in half and stuffed it back into the apron pocket. Then she picked up the box. In a sense, it was the last thing that tied her to Papa, just as the letter had been her last tie to her mother.

She held the trinket up to the light and studied the carved elephants with their large ears and sharp tusks. The palm trees with their feathered fronds. The wood was hard, the carvings full of points and edges. Something about it felt exotic and dangerous.

She had encountered several puzzle boxes over the years. In her younger days she had welcomed the challenge they posed. But her previous attempt to open this one had proved to be a failure. Now she sat cross-legged on the bed and studied the bottom of the box, debating whether she should try again.

She repeated all the tricks she had tried before. Pushing the corners in at the same time. Twisting the top and bottom of the box in opposite directions. Opening it from the bottom. Nothing worked. Then she turned her attention to the carvings on the sides. With her fingers she explored the carvings, looking for any sections that might give way. Finally, when she pushed on the heads of the elephants that were carved on both sides, something inside the box clicked.

She froze, head tilted. Had she figured it out?

She pushed harder on the elephant heads, to the point that she was sure she was getting nowhere. But then another loud pop echoed in the tiny room and the top of the box sprang upward.

Breathless, Camille twisted the top, and the entire lid gave way.

Inside was a rough piece of white linen folded into a bundle. She plucked it out and placed it on the bed. Corner by corner, she pulled back the fabric.

And then she gasped.

Before her lay a stone. Though its surface was bumpy and unpolished, it seemed to glow from within—a deep blood red.

A cry escaped Camille's lips and her hands clamped over her mouth.

There could be no denying it.

She jumped up from the bed as if the box had held a snake instead of a jewel and took several panicked steps back.

The Bevoy. She had been in possession of the Bevoy the entire time. The very object that Mr. Gilchrist had been seeking had been on her person all along.

Her head grew light, and she feared her heart might explode.

She rubbed her forehead. Calm. She had to stay calm.

She paced the room, trying to figure out her options for this impossible situation.

She could give the Bevoy to Mr. Gilchrist, but then she would be exposing Papa. Her own father. And there was no way he or his family would ever believe she had had the ruby in her possession without knowing it. She scarcely believed that herself. If Mr. Gilchrist had any feelings for her at all—and she was beginning to think he did—this would surely douse them.

But returning the piece to Papa was out of the question. There was no denying he had obtained it through ill-gotten means. Surely that is why he had been so insistent that she send the package to her mother—to make it more difficult to trace.

But that raised still another question. Why Mama? Papa had agents and colleagues throughout the country and the continent. Why not use one of them? Did he really intend the stone as a gift for Mama?

Sadly, she doubted it.

Footsteps echoed in the hall. Camille snatched the ruby off the bed and quickly shoved both ruby and box in the drawer.

The footsteps continued past her door, and Camille realized she was holding her breath.

She exhaled and reopened the drawer, replacing the ruby in the box and putting the lid back on the same way she had removed it. Then she wrapped the apron around the box once more.

A tear of frustration—and fear—slipped down her cheek as she stepped back from the bureau.

Miss Gilchrist's warning of curses crackled in her ears.

Cursed, indeed.

Chapter Thirty-Four ──────────

Camille waited in her room for what seemed like hours, waiting for the sun to rise—and dreading the dawn. Sleep came eventually, but it arrived in fitful reprieves of consciousness marred by dark dreams, unsettling thoughts, and an onslaught of unwelcome memories.

She awakened to a knock. Even though Molly was sleeping in another chamber, she had come to help Camille dress. She also brought news. "I hear that two of the girls are on the mend. And I think Miss Redburn is better too. I heard Miss Brathay talking in the corridor."

Camille almost laughed with relief. She had grown fond of little Jane and Laura, and she was even beginning to warm to Abigail Barnes, whose brash personality had set her nerves on edge during her first days at Fellsworth School.

Camille turned to let Molly help her with her stays. "Is Mr. Gilchrist present this morning?" she asked, careful to keep her voice neutral.

"He was here until late last night, but he seemed satisfied with their progress and he left." Molly helped Camille guide the gown over her head and down over her petticoat. "He'll probably go to church this morning in the village, but I assume he'll be by later today."

Camille's heart dropped. But as much as she longed to see

him, she also dreaded being in his presence. For now that she knew the Bevoy's location, how could she possibly look Mr. Gilchrist in the eye? How could she speak and work with him as if nothing had changed? The man's very demeanor, the intensity of his expression, had a way of extracting the truth from her. She feared that the words would fly from her lips the moment she beheld him.

The Bevoy was important to the Gilchrist family. It belonged to them. And Camille had made up her mind to tell Mr. Gilchrist she had it. But she was still working on a way to explain *why* she had it without incriminating her father—or herself.

After Camille was dressed and her hair arranged, Molly left. Camille pinned her watch to her dress and started through the door as well. Then she hesitated, remembering she had an incredibly valuable gem in her bureau drawer. Now that she knew it was there, she did not know whether to leave it where it was or take it with her.

Finally she unwound her apron bundle, made sure the small box was in her pocket, and tied the apron strings around her waist.

⁂

Jonathan's walk from the apothecary's cottage to the village church was a short one. The church was an ancient structure, one of the oldest in the area, and it had been a haven for him as long as he could remember. His mother had taken him to services there when he was a small child, and as he grew older he had continued to attend—at first to please her, but then because it was something he wanted to do.

He made his way to his family's oaken pew at the front of the church and sat down. He had grown accustomed to sitting alone in the pew on Sundays. After his mother's death, his father had attended only rarely. Since Thomas's death, he had never come at all.

The church bells pealed, their mellow tone signaling the start of the service. All around him, familiar faces were filling the empty seats. He had known most of the congregants his entire life. But a strange sensation tugged at him as he sat in this room full of people.

He glanced behind, noting that the women in attendance wore gowns of every color of the rainbow. But there were no young women dressed in the school's rough black linen.

The teachers and students of Fellsworth School attended chapel on the school grounds. There were so many students, both male and female, that fitting them all into this little stone church would be impossible. Yet Jonathan felt their absence—especially that of a particular woman.

He nodded a greeting to a passing farmer, and as he turned to face forward, something caught his eye.

His father stood in the doorway of the church.

The sight took Jonathan completely by surprise. How many years had it been since his father had been inside these walls? Two? Three?

His father's expression was hard, even annoyed. The villagers were staring, for everyone knew who Mr. Gilchrist was, but they rarely saw him unless they had reason to venture out to Kettering Hall.

A hush of whispers circled the nave, one person alerting another until all eyes were on Ian Gilchrist. The old man's lips were set in a firm line, his bushy eyebrows drawn together. His wiry hair was pulled back in a neat queue, a testament to his valet's insistence, and secured with a bright red ribbon. Beneath his gold-trimmed emerald coat he wore a waistcoat of yellow with brightly embroidered flowers, and his shaky hand leaned heavily on a cane embellished with ornately carved parrots.

The people stared at the bright man coming, and the path cleared. With his cane clutched tightly in his hand, the elder Mr. Gilchrist made his way down the narrow aisle to the family pew. As he approached the seat, he pointed at Jonathan with his cane. "That is where I sit."

Jonathan, still in shock at his father's presence, scooted down the polished pew.

His father settled in the spot he had vacated and leaned forward, resting his hands on his cane. His eyes, pale and so like Jonathan's, scanned the church from under his hooded eyelids.

"I'm surprised to see you here, Father," whispered Jonathan.

"Why should you be surprised?" he growled back, his rheumy eyes fixed on the stained-glass window before them. "A man can come to service any time he likes."

Jonathan masked a smile. "You are quite right. I am glad you came."

The service passed quickly, but Jonathan heard very little of it. He was too distracted by questions concerning his father's unexpected behavior. Had the old man finally entered his dotage? Had he suddenly developed a thirst for spiritual things? Or could this visit just be another attempt to hide his precarious financial position by playing the part of local benefactor?

After the service, as the villagers were beginning to leave, his father turned to him. "I want to talk to you, Jonathan."

Jonathan straightened. "Very well."

"But not here."

"My shop and cottage is just across the way. Would you like to go there?"

His father hesitated. "That will do."

Jonathan gestured toward the entrance. "Did you bring the carriage?"

After his father nodded, Jonathan said, "I will ask them to wait for you here."

It had been years since his father had come to the apothecary's cottage. In fact, Jonathan could not recall the last time he had visited. As they crossed the village square to the apothecary shop, Jonathan could feel curious eyes on both of them. He slowed his steps to match his father's shuffling gait, but the old man was quite out of breath by the time they reached their destination.

Jonathan pushed the door to the cottage open and moved aside. His father hesitated but then stepped over the threshold, casting his eyes up to the dark wooden beams running the length of the ceiling. "I cannot believe you actually choose to live here."

"Come now, Father. It isn't so bad." Jonathan set about lighting a candle lamp and brushed aside a stack of newspapers, wishing he had thought to tidy the cottage before he left for church.

"It is a cottage, Jonathan. A tradesman's cottage. You are heir to Kettering Hall. You deserve better than this."

Jonathan raised an eyebrow at the word *deserve*. His father had always given the impression that he did not think Jonathan worthy of much at all. The masked praise sent a shot of warmth through him.

"This suits me well," he said, surveying the cramped room. "I need no more space than this. Besides, I find I do not spend a great deal of time at home anyway. I am far too busy in the shop and the village."

His father moved to the wooden table and pushed out one of the chairs with his cane. His hobbled form cast a crooked shadow on the far wall as he sat down. "I want to talk to you, boy."

Jonathan winced. He hated it when his father called him "boy." But he said nothing about it. Something seemed different with the old man, and Jonathan was curious to learn what it was.

Ian Gilchrist rested his cane atop the table and ran his finger over the carved feathers on its side. "I want to talk to you about the Bevoy."

Jonathan shrugged. He was growing quite immune to the word *Bevoy*. At first the very mention of the stolen gem had incited a strange tremor of anxiety. That sensation had gradually transitioned into one of annoyance. But now the word was becoming just that—a word.

Ian Gilchrist fixed his eyes firmly on his son. "Do you know why the Bevoy is so important to me?"

Jonathan pulled out the chair next to his father and sat down. He repeated the reasoning he had heard a thousand times over. "It is valuable. You want to sell it."

"Yes, but it is more than that. All of my treasures are."

Jonathan had often rolled his eyes when his father referred to his collection as "treasures." But today he sat still and quiet, giving his father the room to say what needed to be said.

"I started collecting when I was but a boy. It started with things I would find on the grounds of the estate—unusual rocks and such. But then one day, when I was no more than seven or eight, I found a metal box in the forest, just beyond the stables. It was a rather small box, no longer than my arm, and in all likelihood it had fallen from a rider's pack. And there was a lock on it."

His father adjusted his sore leg with a grimace. "It was winter at the time of my discovery, and the gardener was not using the shed out behind the south gardens. So I took my box and hid it there. Every afternoon I would go out to the shed and try to pick the lock. I became quite obsessed with it, for it had been such an unexpected find—something unpredicted in the midst of my very predictable routine."

Jonathan knew exactly the shed his father was referring to. It was the one at the back of the garden where the gardener stored pruning items. Jonathan himself had played in it as a boy. Now he found himself eager to hear the rest of the story.

"One day, I finally got the lock open. I still remember the excitement of opening that box and discovering a set of woodcarver's tools. It was old, and several pieces were missing, but to me it might as well have been a king's ransom. The discovery of it set me down a path of trying to recreate that excitement, that sense of wonder.

"I still have that set, which to most people might not seem like much—just rusty tools and some chunks of wood. But I never forgot the thrill of anticipation as I worked to acquire it, the adventurous feeling of opening that box to find out what was within, the satisfaction of reviewing what I had managed to acquire.

"In subsequent years I sought that feeling, that excitement, wherever I could. You of all people know that life at Kettering Hall can be tedious, far too quiet for a young man. I was to be the master one day, but other than that had no real duties, served no real purpose. So I created my own adventures, searched for my own treasures. It's possible I did so unwisely. For now I am an old man, with quite a treasure trove amassed, but not much else to show for it."

Those last words resonated powerfully with Jonathan. He sat silent, weighing their significance. Never before had his father allowed him to see this side of him, one that admitted a shred of doubt or regret.

Jonathan studied his father—really studied him. Surely his showy clothing and ostentatious cane served essentially the same purpose as the armor now lining Kettering's walls. It hid the man beneath—the real man, with flaws and fears like those of any other.

Jonathan assessed his father's withered cheek, the bushy eyebrows, and those painfully familiar light eyes. His father feared transparency as much as Jonathan yearned for it. And yet, for some reason, he had chosen today to lower his armor.

"In my quest for novelty, I fear," the man went on, "I have made decisions that now threaten the life we know. I have gambled and lost. And the reason the Bevoy matters so much to me is that I need to pay for my offenses. You and your sister deserve better than what I can bequeath to you without it."

He grabbed his cane from the table and planted it on the floor, leaning toward Jonathan with intensity in his eyes. "I do not want to be the broken link in the Gilchrist chain. I do not want to be the person who dissolves the hard work of my fathers before me. That ruby is the one thing I own that is valuable enough to right my many wrongs."

Jonathan remained silent, fearful of breaking his father's

concentration and this unusual ribbon of truth. But at length he spoke. "I understand."

"And this business with the Iverness girl—"

At the mention of Miss Iverness, Jonathan felt his pulse increase, racing through him with unbridled interest.

"I am not so old that I did not see what your sister and Darbin were doing the other evening." He shook his head, his eyebrows drawn in what appeared to be genuine sorrow. "Is this what our lives have come to—tricking a young woman into sharing her secrets? Well, perhaps I am growing daft or soft in my old age, but I do believe we should be above such things. I think you see it. Perhaps you will be a positive influence on your sister.

"And now I must go." Ian Gilchrist lurched to his feet as if he were trying to outrun the words that had just come from his mouth. "There is much I must do today."

Jonathan could only stare as his father limped to the doorway. What could he say in response to such a speech?

A strange sense of loss settled over him like a damp woolen cloak after his father left the cottage. Part of him wanted the old man to stay, to tell him more. He was hungry, much hungrier than he had thought, to connect with his father—to find some evidence of a bond between them. For the first time in his life, he sensed that his father hungered for the same thing.

After all these years, Ian Gilchrist had consented to step, even if grudgingly, into his younger son's world and to share something of his experience. Jonathan liked this side of his father. And perhaps this gate, now left ajar, could open the way to heal some of the hurt that had accumulated between father and son.

Chapter Thirty-Five

"May I please get up?" Little Jane sat up in her bed, her face rosy, her words strung together in a pitiful sing-song voice. "I am so tired of lying in this room."

Camille tucked the covers around the little girl's legs. "No, not yet. You have been a very ill young lady, and Mr. Gilchrist says you must stay abed for a few more days."

"But my throat hardly hurts anymore. Hear how good my voice sounds? And it is fine out. Do you not think I could go on just a little walk?"

Camille sat down next to Jane and put her finger to her lips. "Shh. You must keep your voice low. You do not want to wake Abigail or Laura or Miss Smith. Besides, you do not want to get up and move around too soon. The fever might come back, or you might give it to someone else. You wouldn't want that, would you?"

The little girl sighed. "No."

"I didn't think so." Camille reached down and pulled out a picture book from a basket beside the bed. "Would you like to read this? I brought it up from the library earlier today. I thought you might enjoy it."

With a sigh, the little girl took the book and opened the cover.

Even though Jane was not pleased with staying in bed, it was good to see her alert and her eyes bright. Camille reached over to the tray of Mr. Gilchrist's special tea and poured Jane a cup. "Drink this, my dear. You need your strength."

Jane took the cup from her hands, and Camille felt a small thrill of satisfaction. She had not expected to spend her days at Fellsworth School as a nurse. But as the days passed, she was beginning to see how Mr. Gilchrist found such satisfaction in helping others and why he was so determined to continue his work despite his father's disapproval.

She turned to the open window. A curl of a breeze swirled through it, its crispness reminding her faintly of autumn. She could not help but think of the maid's comment to her that first morning at Kettering Hall—about how the trees turned yellow and the woods seemed to be on fire.

So much had changed for her in such a short span of time. What would her life be like when autumn arrived?

The afternoon had grown late, and the children were enjoying some free time on the opposite side of the yard. She watched them running and playing and could not help but wonder what it would have been like to grow up with such freedom.

She was just about to turn back to her tray when she caught sight of a man, tall and straight, striding into the yard. He was dressed in a green coat and tan breeches and carried a large box.

Mr. Gilchrist.

He had come by the school every day since the children had fallen ill, but his visit today seemed much later than usual—a fact which left Camille conflicted.

How she wanted to enjoy his company, but ever since she had discovered the Bevoy three days prior, she had been unable to relax in his presence. In fact, her concern that she might say or do something to betray herself was so strong that she had avoided him whenever she could.

She returned to her seat next to Jane. With the child now awake and alert, the hours passed a little more quickly, and Camille was finding that being around children was not quite as difficult as she had thought. In fact, she was starting to enjoy it.

She and Jane looked through the drawings of elephants and giraffes together. Then she walked down the row of beds and changed the cool cloth on Laura's forehead and adjusted Miss Redburn's blankets.

A tap of knuckles on the door drew Camille's attention, and she turned. Little Jane broke into a wide smile. "Mr. Gilchrist!"

Mr. Gilchrist's eyes met Camille's briefly before he set down his box and turned his attention to the child. "Well, Miss Jane. And how are you today?"

She ignored his question. "You are so late today, Mr. Gilchrist. The day is almost over."

"It could not be helped." He sat on the chair next to her bed. "But you hardly need me anymore. Look at you. You are almost as good as new!"

"That is what I told Miss Iverness, but she said I must stay in bed."

"And you should listen to Miss Iverness, for she is absolutely right. You would not want to get up and about too early and risk getting sick again, would you? Not after you have spent so much time getting well."

"No, sir." Jane shook her head from side to side.

"That is what I thought. Now, what is this?" He picked up the book that was resting atop her covers. "This looks quite interesting."

"Miss Iverness brought that for me."

"That was very kind of her. And I have a surprise for you as well. Would you like to see it?"

Jane's golden eyes widened, and she nodded enthusiastically.

He gave her a grin, which incited a giggle. Then he opened his coat and produced a wriggling white kitten.

Jane squealed. "How lovely!" She reached for the kitten and nuzzled it close.

"Did I not tell you the first day we met that I would bring a kitten for a visit? But see, it took me all this time to catch one. I told you, I am not very good at catching kittens."

She giggled again. "Thank you, Mr. Gilchrist."

He continued. "I do not think Mr. Langsby would be very pleased with me if he knew I brought a kitten into the school, so I will have to take her back home with me. But I was hoping you and Laura could care for her while I am here. Can you assist me with this?"

She nodded enthusiastically, laughing as the kitten tried to crawl from her lap.

"Now, you be still and get rest, all right? And drink that tea until it is gone."

He stood up from the chair and turned his attention to Camille. He had brought in with him the spicy scent of the outdoors and fresh air, and his hair had been tousled by the breeze. He walked over to where she stood. "And you, Miss Iverness? How are you today?"

"I am well, Mr. Gilchrist. The kitten is adorable. What a thoughtful gesture." The gift was indeed a kind one, but the words felt thick and foreign on her tongue.

His eyes narrowed on her, and he folded his arms across

his chest. "You look pale, Miss Iverness. You are not falling ill, are you?"

"No, sir, I am quite well."

His concern wrenched her. For no, she was not ill. But she could not tell him what plagued her, what haunted her waking moments. She was keeping a monstrous secret from the only person in the world from whom she wanted to keep nothing.

Mr. Gilchrist stepped closer, studying her more intently. She felt for certain that he could see the lie in her eyes. She blinked and looked away.

"I am not sure you are all right."

The more he tried to help her, the more interest he showed, the tighter the noose pulled. The air around her, which just moments ago had seemed cool and refreshing, now seemed fetid and stifling.

"Well, you know how I should like for you to remain in my company, Miss Iverness, but I would feel better if you were to go lie down a bit. Perhaps you have been working too hard of late."

She latched on to her opportunity to escape the room. "I think that is just what I need."

"Mrs. Langsby should be coming for the evening shift soon. I will ask her to check in on you and bring you some broth or tea. The last thing we want is for you to fall ill as well."

"Please do not overly concern yourself with me, Mr. Gilchrist. But I do think I will go lie down for a little while."

She could feel his gaze on her as she walked from the room. Her shoulders felt heavy. This was an impossible situation.

The air in the corridor felt much cooler, and she paused to lean her back against the wall and draw a deep, steadying breath.

She stole several moments there, breathing deeply, trying to cool the simmering frustration burning within her.

Mr. Gilchrist had suggested that she lie down, but her heart was too restless. She felt the need to be out of the confines of the school, among the trees and meadows that had become the marker of her new life.

She hurried to her room for her bonnet to guard against the breeze and took the back steps, the ones usually used only by the staff, down to the back entrance, exiting by the kitchen garden. She made her way through rows of beans and cabbages to the walking path that led to the main walkway by the forest. But the sound of her name soon halted her steps.

"Miss Iverness! Miss Iverness. Wait!" Camille shielded her eyes against the late-afternoon light to see Molly weaving her way through the bushes. With one hand she gathered up her gray wool skirt to avoid the low-lying bushes, and with the other she waved toward Camille.

"Molly, whatever is the matter?" Camille asked once her friend was close enough.

Molly stopped a few feet in front of Camille, huffing for air. "Oh my, I have been searching everywhere for you!"

Molly's flushed cheeks concerned Camille. "What is the matter?"

"I just had the oddest encounter, and I wanted to inform you of it right away. I was walking with some of the older girls from the chapel when a man, an older man, stopped and asked me if I knew who you were. Of course I asked who he was, but he would not say. He asked if you were inside, and I told him if he had any questions he would have to go speak with Mr. Langsby, and then he walked back down the road. I did not like it, Miss Iverness. I did not like it one bit."

A ribbon of alarm rode in with the freshening breeze. Camille did not doubt her friend's word. It seemed her past was determined to find her.

Molly wrung her hands in front of her. "I was about to go straight to Mr. Langsby, but then I saw you first."

Camille wanted to put her friend at ease. "Thank you so much for your concern, but please do not fret on my account. It might have been someone from Kettering Hall. I cannot think who else would possibly be looking for me."

"But this man was not from around here," Molly protested. "I know most of the people from Kettering Hall, and he was not from there."

"What did he look like?"

Molly held her hand to a height equal to her own. "He was short—about this tall—with gray hair and the start of a beard. Oh, and he had the strangest green eyes that pierced quite through one. I am certain that I would know him if I had ever seen him before."

Camille forced her face to remain calm. But as Molly began her description, she knew who had come looking for her.

Papa.

She looked over her shoulder to the right, then the left. Her skin began to prickle, the sensation running from the top of her head down her limbs to her toes and fingertips. The breeze sweeping in from the forest seemed to have dropped several degrees as they stood there.

Molly appeared not to notice. "What are you doing out here?"

"I-I was just about to go for a walk."

"I would feel much better if you would simply return to the school. I do not like the idea of a stranger lurking about. Besides . . ." Molly squinted skyward. "Just look at those clouds. I just know it will rain soon."

Camille followed her gaze. Molly was right. Pewter clouds were quickly blowing in from the horizon. But she simply could not face going inside. Not yet. "I promise to keep to the grounds. I will not go far."

"You are braver than I am."

Camille watched her friend walk away. Part of her wanted to call after Molly and beg her not to leave her alone. There had been a time when solitude had felt like a fortress for her. Now, faced with uncertainty, she longed for companionship.

She trusted Molly. How she wanted to tell her everything, to completely unburden herself of the secrets she had kept so close. But for Molly's own sake, she couldn't do that.

The door closed behind Molly as she entered the school. Camille rubbed her hands over her arms, noting how her injury no longer ached. So much about her had changed in the short time since she left London. In some ways she felt stronger, more confident than ever. Yet she also felt softer, more fearful. As if she had more to lose.

Camille reached her hand into the pocket of her apron. The carved puzzle box felt sharp and hard beneath her fingers. She was growing to hate that box. She wanted to throw it and the gemstone it held as far as she could into the depths of the forest.

The teasing breeze from the forest had stiffened into a brisk wind. As if sensing her frustration, it howled through the leaves, pushing the clouds closer. A fresh gust peppered her with drops of rain.

A walk would not do. Her restless soul would have to be content with the indoors. She must find some way to conceal and contain the swirling emotion within her.

The drops fell harder, heavier, as she hurried back to the building. The interior was noisy—full of children and activity as the staff prepared for the evening meal. Camille found herself grateful for the chaos, the brightness—grateful for anything to distract her unsettled mind and force her thoughts in another direction.

She had thought she could pull up roots, outrun her past, fit into a world that was not her own. She had thought that if she wanted a new life badly enough, she could reach out and grab it.

But this storm had blown in an inevitable truth—she could never escape her past. Never be other than what she was.

Her hand was shaking as she reached for the brass knob to her bedchamber. She wrapped her fingers around the oblong metal, squeezed, and turned. She stepped into her room, pushed the door closed behind her, and leaned against the door, her eyes shut. A tear, hot and fiery, escaped the corner of her right eye and trickled down her cheek, hugging the contour of her chin.

When she opened her eyes, she jumped in shock.

"Hello, Daughter."

Chapter Thirty-Six ——————————

*E*arly the next morning, Jonathan walked up the path from the village to the school, just as he had so many mornings over the past several weeks. As he walked along the forest's edge, the spicy scent of damp leaves enhanced each breath, and the wind's soft whistle through the leaves pushed him forward.

He heaved a deep sigh of relief and satisfaction. Miss Redburn and all three children had turned a corner. No one else at the school showed any signs of scarlet fever. They might have just skirted disaster in that regard.

But it was Miss Gilchrist who concerned him at the moment. The previous afternoon she had appeared tired. Her cheeks, which normally boasted a rosy hue, were pale. Her eyes had seemed lackluster. She had not denied him when he suggested that she rest.

He quickened his steps. He would be much more comfortable when he knew she was well.

But as he rounded the bend and approached the school's tall iron gates, he found himself even more unsettled than before. The grounds were unusually active for such an early hour. Both adults and children scurried about with great haste. The school's carriage had been pulled around to the front, and some of the boys were tending to the horses.

Jonathan adjusted the box in his arms and stepped through the gates, pausing to survey the activity around him. Miss McKinney, who was talking to another teacher, looked up and gathered her skirts to run toward him.

"Mr. Gilchrist, have you heard?"

He noted with alarm that the younger woman's cheeks were flushed, her eyes wide with panic.

"Heard what?"

"It is Miss Iverness. She is gone!"

"What?" he shot back. "Why, that is not possible."

"I assure you it is." Miss McKinney lifted a hand to push her wind-blown hair from her face. "She did not arrive to watch the sickroom as she normally does, so I went to her room, and imagine my astonishment when she was not there. Or anywhere. Oh, it is too dreadful."

Jonathan shook his head, trying to attach meaning to the words he was hearing. "What do you mean, she was not there?"

"Just what I said. Her bed has not been slept in. Her bureau drawer is empty. She is not to be found anywhere in the building. I am so terribly worried. We have been searching for her all morning."

Jonathan clenched his jaw. The thought of Miss Iverness's leaving sent a tremor through him, starting in his heart and racing to his limbs. His head. He had sensed something was amiss with her, especially after the dinner at Kettering Hall, but he had never expected her to disappear without a word.

"Mr. Langsby tells me not to worry," continued Miss McKinney, "but yesterday there was that strange man asking after her. I just do not know what to make of it. This is not good, Mr. Gilchrist. Not good at all."

Jonathan's head jerked at the mention of a stranger. People

rarely traveled to Fellsworth without a clear purpose. "A strange man, you say?"

Miss McKinney clutched her shawl tightly. "Yes. I was out walking with the children, and a short man approached me. He had gray hair and a beard and the most piercing green eyes. And he asked about Miss Iverness. I warned her to be wary, and now she is gone! Oh, I should have told Mr. Langsby."

Jonathan's stomach tightened. Except for the beard, she was describing James Iverness. And a beard could easily have grown in the days that had passed. He rested his hand on her shoulder in an act of comfort. "Do not worry, Miss McKinney," he said, as much to reassure himself as the teacher. "I am sure she is well. Where is Mr. Langsby? I should like to speak with him."

"I believe he is in his study."

Alarm pushed Jonathan forward. He bowed in parting to Miss McKinney, then hurried up the path to the main entrance. He forced his feet to stay at a walk, though they wanted to break into a jog. Jonathan wanted answers, and he could not get them soon enough.

The gray clouds made everything inside the building seem dark and ominous. Jonathan stomped down the familiar hall, leaned his shoulder against the study door to open it, and stepped inside.

"Good morning, Mr. Gilchrist. You are quite early today, are you not?"

Jonathan was in no mood for small talk. "Miss Iverness is gone?"

Mr. Langsby looked up from his book. "It appears she is."

"Do you know where she is?"

The older man shook his head, his expression controlled.

His calm demeanor was in sharp contrast to Miss McKinney's. Her alarm at Miss Iverness's disappearance had bordered on panic, whereas Mr. Langsby seemed almost unaffected.

"No I do not," he said. "I believe our Miss McKinney went to wake her this morning and her things were gone. We've no note. No anything."

The air seemed too thin to breathe. "Something must be wrong. She would not simply leave."

Mr. Langsby shrugged. "She is a free woman, Mr. Gilchrist, free to come and go as she pleases. It isn't the first time that one of ours has left in such a fashion, and I daresay it will not be the last. 'Tis a pity, though. We were becoming quite fond of her, and we thought she was content here in our quiet school. But apparently she had other plans."

Jonathan fought to control his rapid breathing, his annoyance with the man's indifference growing brighter with each breath. Something was obviously not right. Miss Iverness would not simply leave, not without saying a word.

Or would she?

She had tried to tell him several times that she was not as she seemed. Is this what she had meant? Had her words been a warning?

Unable to control the energy racing within him, he began to pace. "But surely you must understand. She came here on my recommendation. I feel responsible on some level, and I just want to make sure she is well."

"I would not fret." Mr. Langsby removed his glasses and placed them on the desk before him. "In my assessment, she was a very sweet woman, but also quite a capable one. I have no doubt that she can take care of herself."

Chapter Thirty-Seven

*B*efore Camille opened her eyes, she knew where she was. The air was thick with soot, and the familiar scent of smoke awakened a part of her memory that had almost fallen asleep.

Blinkett Street.

She pressed her eyes shut, trying to recall the view from her window at the Fellsworth School, with its wide green lawn and the sounds of children playing on the grounds below. But the vision would not form.

Panic rose as she opened her eyes. The dark, cramped upstairs room that had once been her solace now seemed like a prison, and the painting on the wall that had once brought comfort now seemed to taunt her, its careful brushstrokes and vibrant hues a cruel reminder of the world she craved.

She sat up, still fully clothed in her black linen gown, kid boots, and even her apron. She had refused to change out of them, not ready to let another bit of that world slip from her. Already her mind was churning, plotting her next step. She would not stay here. She couldn't—not now that she had tasted life beyond the boundaries of Blinkett Street.

It would be impossible for her to return to Fellsworth, of course. There would be no hiding from Papa there. Nowhere familiar would be safe. And if she did return to the school, how could she possibly explain her sudden absence? They would either turn her away for neglecting her responsibilities or, if the truth became known, reject her because of the character of her family.

She felt the box in her apron pocket. By some miracle, she had been able to conceal the ruby from Papa. Somehow he had made his way into the school unnoticed and found her room. He had searched every nook and cranny of her chamber at Fellsworth, but he had failed to check her person.

The ruby belonged to the Gilchrists, and somehow she would get it back to them. She should have returned it to Mr. Gilchrist when she had a chance, but regret would do little for her now. She needed to act. And although she had been unable to discern the correct course of action while still at Fellsworth, she could see it now.

She hurried over to her trunk and knelt before it. She ran her fingers across the rough wood and uneven edges before lifting the lid, careful to prevent it from squeaking in the silence. The trunk contained the treasures of her life before her time in Fellsworth—less than two weeks previous, but it seemed a lifetime ago. She pushed aside a winter cloak and heavy shawl and reached down to the back left corner. She exhaled in relief when her fingers brushed velvet. She gripped the fabric pouch and pulled it free. After freeing the string, she looked inside. Both coins and paper money were tucked neatly within. She tucked the pouch into her bodice and gathered a few other personal effects. Her shawl. A clean dress and underthings. Everything she thought she would need but that was light enough to carry in her battered satchel.

She would go to Fellsworth long enough to return the Bevoy

to its rightful owner. And then she would disappear. Somehow. Somewhere.

As far from Blinkett Street as she could possibly travel.

※ ※

There was no doubt in Jonathan's mind what needed to be done.

Mr. Langsby's lack of concern regarding Miss Iverness's disappearance came as no surprise, especially since Mr. Langsby was not familiar with her history.

Jonathan was, and he could not ignore it.

He needed to return to London and the sordid length of Blinkett Street.

And fast.

From the school he headed to Kettering Hall, leaving his apothecary's box in the sickroom. He had arrived at the school on foot, so he ran the familiar path from the village to Kettering, ignoring the burning in his chest and the rain that was starting to sprinkle from the heavens.

Jonathan did not wait for a welcome once at Kettering Hall. Rainwater showered from his coat as he crossed the threshold. He paid it no mind.

He wanted—no, needed—to speak with his father. A shift had occurred yesterday morning in his cottage. The rift between them had not been mended—time had rendered it far too deep and jagged to be set to rights so quickly. But at present, he felt his request would be acknowledged, if not welcomed.

For the first time that Jonathan could remember, he did not wait for an invitation to enter his father's private sanctum. He ran across the entryway to the main hall, his boots sliding on the smooth marble, then crossed to his father's study. He placed his hand on the curved brass handle and pushed it open with a force that extracted squawks of surprise from the caged bird in the corner.

Ian Gilchrist jerked his head upward, his face twisted into a scowl, his eyebrows drawn in apparent irritation. "Jonathan! What is the meaning of—"

"Miss Iverness is gone," Jonathan blurted, his voice little more than a gasp for air.

His father stood in a slow, deliberate motion. "Gone? What do you mean?"

Jonathan closed the door behind him and stepped over several crates, ignoring the bird's beady eyes and how they followed him. "I went to the school today for my regular visit, and upon my arrival I was informed that she had disappeared. Her bed had not been slept in, and her things were all missing."

His father sunk slowly back in his chair, as if his mind were mapping the significance of the news. "This cannot be a good development."

His father was referring to the Bevoy, to be sure, but for Jonathan Miss Iverness's absence signified something far more personal. He tugged the hat from his head and forced his fingers through his wet hair. "I intend to go after her. I just came by to tell you that I am taking a horse from Kettering's stable and will set off for London immediately."

Ian Gilchrist nodded. "Take Zion. I've never ridden him, but the stablemaster claims he's a steady mount."

"Thank you."

His father's reaction took Jonathan a bit by surprise. He had expected indifference or perhaps even anger that a possible clue to the whereabouts of the Bevoy had slipped through their fingers. Instead, an expression akin to concern tugged at his father's mouth.

The older man ran his fingers over his chin. "Do you know where you are going?"

Jonathan gave a sharp nod. "One of the teachers said that a short man with gray hair and green eyes was asking about her the other day. It has to be James Iverness."

"Be careful," warned his father. "Iverness is a shifty character."

A strange warmth sparked in Jonathan's chest. Was his father concerned for his safety? "I will."

Jonathan turned to leave, but his father's words halted him. "Take this."

He pulled a polished chest from a nearby trunk and set it on the desk. He opened it to reveal a set of dueling pistols and a set of matching knives. "I know this goes against your convictions, but here. You might need them."

When Jonathan hesitated, the old man thrust the chest into his arms. "Don't argue," he growled. "Just take them."

Chapter Thirty-Eight

_C_amille hoped the earliness of the hour would work in her favor.

Her father was not one to rise before noon if he could possibly help it. He was a creature of the night, active when most of the good people of the world slumbered. So there was a good chance he was still snoring in the chamber across the hall.

Experience had made her well acquainted with every creaky floorboard of her room and the corridor outside. She held her breath and avoided them as she left her cramped chamber, satchel in hand.

Her heart beat wildly as if attempting to warn her of a danger she was already all too familiar with. Hurt and betrayal mingled with the fear and trepidation within her, but she banished them with practiced skill to make room for clarity and confidence—both of which she would need. Camille patted her pocket, ensuring that the box and letter were still in their place.

She made it to the landing and down the narrow stairs. The morning sounds of Blinkett Street were audible through the thin walls. She was so close to freedom, for once she was free of their shop she could blend into the masses, and disappearing would be easy.

But then she heard voices—male voices, then one that sounded female. She couldn't tell where they were coming from.

Camille's heart pounded with such intensity that she felt certain that everyone within a mile's radius could hear. She drew a deep breath and bit her lip. Those voices could only spell danger.

Camille stepped to the right side of the staircase, knowing that the left side had a tendency to squeak under her weight. She considered her options once she reached the bottom of the curved stairwell. If the voices were indeed coming from the back room, she would want to turn right and exit from the shop's front entrance. If they were in the shop, she would need to turn left and make her way through the back room to the alley.

If all went well she could slip into the shop without being seen or heard. And all was going well until her satchel slid from her shoulder and banged against the wall.

She froze.

Then the sound of toenails echoed on the wooden floor.

Tevy.

The voices in the other room stopped.

Tevy's thick tail thudded against the thin walls. The sound of his panting drew closer. There would be no stopping the animal if he wanted to find her. She needed either to run back upstairs or make a dash for the door.

But then the voices resumed. Tevy's sounds ceased, and her breath released with shaky relief.

Just as her confidence was returning, however, a black nose nudged the door at the bottom of the stairs. Tevy had found her.

Her heart burst at the sight of him. His gold eyes brightened, and his tail wagged against the wall.

She wanted to run to the dog—her constant childhood companion—and throw her arms around him. Instead she held out her hands to signal silence.

Too late.

Heavy boots thudded on the floor, followed by muffled grumbling. A hand reached around the door and grabbed the dog by the collar.

Papa.

His face looked sinister in the morning shadows. She had never really been terrified of him before, had never really thought him capable of physically harming her. But now everything was different.

How she wished Tevy would come to her. She would feel much safer. But even though she knew the dog loved her, he was even more loyal to her father.

Camille drew a sharp breath, trying to appear normal. "Good morning, Papa."

"Well, now, what it is that you are up to?" He eyed the satchel in her hand. "You wouldn't be trying to leave your Papa without saying a proper farewell, would you?"

She lifted her chin with practiced bravado. "Of course not."

"Well then, you won't mind handing over what is in the satchel, will you?"

She pressed her lips together. She was trapped. Papa stood at the bottom of the stairs, completely blocking her escape. Tevy sat at his feet, his pink tongue hanging from the side of his mouth.

Clearly she had no choice. Camille pulled the satchel from her shoulder and tossed it down the rest of the stairs. Then, deciding to act as if everything were normal, she spoke brightly. "Perhaps I should go and get us some bread from the baker."

She started to brush past him, but he grabbed her arm. "You'll not be going anywhere. Not until we get this straightened out."

She frowned, feigning innocence. "Get what straightened out?"

He nodded toward the shop and stepped back, a silent indication that he wanted her to go that way. She descended the rest of the stairs and turned right. It was then she got her first glance at the shop. Her breath caught in her throat.

The damage from the night the shop was vandalized had obviously not been set right. The shattered front window had been boarded up, but in the dim light from the other window she could see that the room was void of merchandise. It had all been removed. The shelves were empty and falling from the walls. Tables were turned. Broken glass and splintered wood littered the floor.

Camille's stomach clenched. It wasn't the state of the room that shocked her, nor the stale odor that permeated it. It was quite another matter entirely.

She spotted him immediately in the corner of the shop. His dark eyes were fixed on her, and a crooked grin spread over his face.

Mr. Darbin.

The man's lip curled into a smile. He bowed with dramatic flourish, his dark hair falling thick over his forehead.

A sinister chill traveled Camille's spine.

He stepped forward, his voice oozing with amused gentility. "My dear Miss Iverness. How much more pleasant it was to spend time with you in the comfort of Kettering Hall. But how the tides have changed."

He stepped closer, the scent of his tobacco reaching her before he did. She wanted to shrink back, to look away. But she did neither.

"You picked up whist so quickly, I am surprised that you did not see the game that was being played beneath your very nose." Mr. Darbin spoke to her with the same easy familiarity he had used when they met at Kettering Hall. But the smile which at one time had held such warmth now dripped with contempt. "We know you have the Bevoy. Do not protest, for I saw the puzzle box in your hand that very morning at Kettering Hall. So if you'll just kindly tell us where it is, all can go back as it was."

She pinned him with her stare and spoke slowly. "As I told you before, I know nothing of the Bevoy, and I certainly know nothing of its whereabouts. But if I did, I certainly would not share such information with you."

"Come now, Camille. Is that any way to speak to our guest?"

The words were spoken by a woman.

A coldness draped over Camille like a veil of ice and snow. She knew the voice. Despite the years that had passed, none could be more familiar.

She turned slowly, as if it were a ghost standing behind her instead of a person of flesh and blood.

"Mama," she gasped, her voice barely above a whisper.

Camille had wondered a million times what it would be like to have her mother home, but she had never imagined it like this. For this felt wrong. Very wrong.

The woman standing before her was very much like the woman Camille remembered. Time's paintbrush had barely touched her beauty. Her hair still shone ebony, without a trace of gray. Her skin was a darker shade of tawny, and her dark eyes flashed in the shadows, focused steadily on her daughter.

The child in Camille wanted to throw herself into her mother's arms. She wanted to fling her arms around her neck and believe that everything that had happened was somehow a mistake. But something held her back from moving. For the expression that met her gaze was not the expression she remembered.

Hardness lined her mother's face. She did not smile or move to embrace Camille. She stepped forward, her arms folded in front of her, one long forefinger tapping the fabric of the opposite sleeve. She lifted her chin and looked down her nose at Camille. No warmth lit her eyes.

Camille pressed her lips together as her mother circled her with slow, deliberate steps. When she was finished with her assessment, she stopped in front of Camille.

"All this black you wear. You look to be in mourning."

Camille's chin began to tremble, but she did not respond to the odd statement. She was acutely aware of all the eyes on her. Papa's. Mama's. Mr. Darbin's. She had to be prudent.

Her mother stepped even closer. Her scent of mint and lavender triggered familiar memories, but now it seemed to reach fingers around Camille's throat and squeeze. She remained perfectly still as Mama reached out and tilted her chin to the side with a cold finger. "You are a beauty, as your father said you were," she said in her heavily accented English.

Camille did not blink. "What are you doing here?"

Her mother dropped her hand and adjusted the shawl around her shoulders. "I hear you have been giving your father quite the difficult time."

Camille straightened her posture as if any bit of added height would give her an advantage. "And that news is what finally brought you back to England?" She made no attempt to contain her sarcasm.

"Quiet, girl," growled Papa. "You'll not be taking that tone with her, nor with me."

Her mother lifted her hand to silence her father. To Camille's amazement, he backed down.

"No, it isn't what prompted me to return. Other matters of business incited my journey weeks ago. But what a shame to hear that you have been behaving like such a wild thing, after all the advantages you were given." Her mother began to circle Camille again with slow steps. The very act made Camille feel like a caged animal.

At length her mother spoke again. "When I left, you were young, Camille, too young to understand the intricacies of family balance. I do not blame you for being angry with me for my absence. I expect it. But I will not accept your insolence. You are still my daughter, and I will have your respect."

She finished her circle and stopped, her gaze burning into Camille's. "At present, the importance of our family's business troubles far outweighs any hurt feelings or anger you might have. If you know anything of the Bevoy, I expect you to speak now and quickly. Now is not the time for selfishness. And there is no time to waste. Your father and I have toiled far too long on this project to see it crumble at this stage, long before you were given the box. So tell me. Where is the stone?"

Camille practically heard the click in her mind as all the pieces of the puzzle finally shifted into place. Her father's little gifts to her mother had not been a ploy to get her back, as Camille had thought all these years. He must have been sending her valuable English items—perhaps stolen ones—to sell somewhere on the continent.

How could she not have seen it? It made perfect sense.

Her father dealt in imports. Why not exports as well—even smuggled, illegal ones? And how much better if his agent in a foreign country was a woman well acquainted with the culture and landscape?

The full implication of this realization took a little longer to sink in, but it hit Camille harder than the first, triggering a sense of lonely bereavement she had not felt in years.

Her mother had left her not out of hard necessity. Not out of tender familial obligation. But for money.

For several moments, no one spoke. Then suddenly, violently, her mother reached out and grabbed Camille's arm, the fingernails digging through the fabric of her uniform. "Where is it, girl?" The words were forced through gritted teeth.

At the contact, Tevy lunged forward and swished against Camille's skirt in an act of protection, a snarl curling his lip, but her father jerked him back by the collar.

The sudden motion jolted Camille, and her heart beat wildly in her chest. She fixed her eyes again on her mother.

So this was the truth of her circumstances. Her father, her mother, and the Gilchrists' hired investigator were all working together—against her.

Camille stood straight, doing her best to show no emotion. She could feel the bulge of the box in her apron pocket. And she felt another click, this one deep in her soul. Stubbornness coursed through her, powered by years of pent-up frustration and pain. She would never hand the Bevoy over willingly, not when she knew its true owner.

Never.

Chapter Thirty-Nine

Camille winced as the rough rope rubbed against the tender flesh of her wrists and ankles. She adjusted her position against the wall so that most of her weight was on her hip instead of her backside, careful to make sure that the box stayed in her apron pocket and out of sight. Once she was a little more comfortable, she leaned her head against the shop's rough wall and fixed her eyes on Mama.

She was still struggling to comprehend that her mother was really here in London after all these years. When she was younger she had often imagined what this day would feel like, how it would feel to behold the woman who had left her family with nothing more than the empty promise of a quick return.

But the woman in the room was not the mother she remembered. Her mother had never been overly affectionate, but this woman seemed completely heartless.

Camille spoke up. "These ropes are not necessary."

Mama looked up from the jar of pocket watches she was sorting. "Your father believes they are."

"And what of you? Do you believe it necessary to tie your only daughter like an animal?"

Mama set down a watch beside the jar, her dark eyes narrowing on Camille. "I told you I will not have your insolence."

But Camille would not cower to anyone, especially this

woman who had abandoned her. "You never answered my question. Why did you return?"

Mama returned to the watches as if bored with the topic. "Your father needed help with the business."

"So it was not to see Papa—or me, for that matter. It was about the business."

Mama's voice deepened. "I will not take your judgment."

"It isn't judgment." Camille shook her head. "I cannot pretend to understand why you would stay away all this time. But now, knowing that you can go about your business while I am trussed up on the floor, I can deduce that any motherly affection you once had for me disappeared long ago."

Mama stepped out from behind the counter. "You brought this on yourself."

"And how did I do that?"

"The Bevoy, Camille. You know how important it is to our business, and yet you do your best to thwart your father's plans."

"The Bevoy does not belong to Father. Did you know that?"

"Are you accusing your father of stealing?"

"No. I just think you do not have all of the facts."

"Mr. Darbin saw you with the box, Camille. Your father placed it in your hand. So until its whereabouts are determined, we must take every precaution."

"Binding my hands is a precaution?"

Mama stepped even closer, her lips pressed into a tight line. Her distinctive scent of lavender wafted closer to Camille. "Do not question what you do not understand, child."

"I am not a child, Mama. I may have been a child when you left, but time has changed everything."

Mama pointed a finger in Camille's direction. "I had no

choice but to leave. This world is very unpredictable. I saw what I needed to do to secure my future, and I continue to do that to this day."

"But you had Papa. And this shop. And me."

She huffed. "If I had left this shop in the hands of your father, it would have been bankrupt within a month. He is a trader, an adventurer, not a businessman. But you—even when you were very young I saw that you could do it. You could manage the day-to-day business while I took care of our operations in my homeland."

"I was just a child."

"You were strong enough—bright enough. I could handle things in my country that neither of you could. And you had a knack for influencing your father." She gazed down her nose at Camille and gave a barely perceptible sniff. "I tell you, I did what I had to do to keep the family going."

"If that is the case, then why did you not come home after you succeeded in your efforts? You could have come at least once or twice. And if you thought I could handle the business, why lie to me about why you were in Portugal? You could have explained."

"It is not that simple."

"It sounds pretty simple to me."

Mama gave an exasperated snort. "We did what we did to protect you, Camille. Why can you not understand that? For your own safety, it was best for you to not know the intricacies of our business dealings. Besides, you were a child. It would have been far too easy for you to slip and say the wrong thing to the wrong person."

Camille had no answer for that, just a sense of weary sadness. She closed her eyes and leaned her head back against the wall.

"One day, maybe you will understand." Mama's words hung heavy in the air like dust motes. "One day—you will see—the world will be unkind to you. There will be a point when you have to make a decision that you may or may not be content with. Then you will have to live with that decision, as I have done. And you will do what is necessary to thrive."

Thrive? Camille thought back over her past life in the shop. The lonely days and the fearful nights. The sense that she was worth no more to her mother than an occasional letter. *Were we thriving?*

"I have already had to make such decisions, Mama. And I still don't understand."

Her mother didn't answer, merely turned back to her watches, her face still void of emotion. But whereas her mother could remain void of emotion, Camille could not. Her mother's apparent lack of affection and her lack of regret over the time they had spent apart ripped at her already aching heart.

With a wrenching effort she attempted to adjust her view, to face reality.

This was not a family, at least not at the moment. And she was not a daughter, but a prisoner. A hostage. A means to an end.

Whatever relationship she and her parents had shared had been badly ruptured, and Camille sensed it might never be repaired.

"So you are still wearing that old watch of your grandfather's?" Mama nodded toward the brooch, condescension dripping in her voice.

Camille glanced down at the timepiece. "I am."

Her mother huffed and turned back to her counting. "The old man was a fool. That was far too valuable a gift to give to a child."

Sarah E. Ladd

The malice in her mother's tone struck Camille momentarily speechless, then angered her. "You will notice that despite my young age I managed to take good care of it. Grandfather showed me kindness, and I treasure this keepsake from him."

"Of course you thought him kind. He showered you with gifts. You were young when he died; you didn't have time to learn his true character. If you had known him better, you would have known that he was very much like your father. He squandered that whole estate. No mind for business."

Camille bristled. "And why is a mind for business so very important?"

Mama stared at her as if she had grown a third arm. "How else is one to secure one's way in the world? Tsk. With a question like that, it is hard to believe that you are my daughter."

Camille gave up reaching an understanding with her mother. "How long do you intend to keep me here?"

"As long as it takes."

The ride from Fellsworth to London was a long one. Normally the journey passed quickly on horseback, but today heavy rain blurred Jonathan's vision and mud slowed his pace.

When he finally reached the city, Jonathan rode as close to Blinkett Street as he dared before renting a stall at a city stable block and paying a boy to tend to Zion. With cautious steps and a watchful eye he wound his way to the unpleasant little corner of London that, like it or not, had become an important location in his life.

310

Already familiar with the maze of streets and alleys protruding from Blinkett Street, Jonathan ducked down a side street, taking the back way to James Iverness's shop. The rain mingled with smoke and soot clung to him. The moisture intensified the musky stench of manure and wet animals. Jonathan crept along the jagged wall, blending in with the constant motion of carts and people. He was reminded of a similar venture several weeks ago, when he had first laid eyes on the little shop. But his motives then had been far different.

After a quick glance from the right to the left, Jonathan pulled his hat low over his eyes and stepped from the side street onto Blinkett Street. He walked slowly, waiting for a cart to pass, before he stepped to the front of the shop.

The shattered shop window had been boarded up, but the other window was intact. He looked inside and his breath caught in his throat. For through the dirty glass he could barely see Miss Iverness seated on the floor. She was propped against the wall, her head leaning back. Her eyes were closed.

Jonathan took a step back, his fist balled at his side. Every instinct within him screamed to force open the door and go to her rescue. But he had done that once and had ended up causing her harm. He needed a better sense of the situation before he attempted such action.

Forcing his breath through gritted teeth, he took a cautious step closer and peered deeper into the room.

She appeared to be alone.

It seemed far too simple that all he had to do was open the door, grab Miss Iverness, and run, but at the moment that seemed the best solution. His heart raced as he inched closer to the door, careful not to attract attention to himself. The shabby crowd shuffled past him, seemingly oblivious. Despite the coolness of the damp air, perspiration gathered under the brim of his hat.

He licked his lips and focused his gaze on the brass handle just an arm's length away. He needed to act quickly, before his window of opportunity shattered. She might be alone now, but who knew how much longer?

He reached out his hand, the brass cold beneath his fingertips. The broken door swung open easily, but it scraped against the floor.

Miss Iverness jerked her head up. Black wisps of hair framed her narrow face, and her complexion glowed pale. Her eyes widened in surprise, but then she jerked her head toward the curtain that led to the back of the store.

He nodded. Eyes scanning the space for signs of trouble, he stepped over the boxes until he was quite close to her. He took careful note of his surroundings. Debris throughout the store. A curtained doorway behind the counter. A hall or stairwell opening off the adjacent wall. Laughter coming from somewhere—perhaps from behind the curtain. And as he drew near he realized with a gulp that Miss Iverness's hands were bound behind her back. Her feet were tied together as well.

He immediately knelt and pulled the knife from his waist to untether her legs.

"That can wait," she whispered, her voice barely audible. "Quickly—reach into the pocket of my apron."

"What?" Jonathan struggled with the second bit of rope. "I cannot. I—"

"Do it," she hissed. "Quickly. Please. There is a box in there. You must take it."

The rope around her ankles gave way. He reached to help her lean forward so he could reach her hands, but she pivoted to give him better access to the pocket.

"Take it. Now."

He reached into the pocket, and his fingers brushed against something wooden. Some kind of carved box. He pulled it out and stared at it.

"It's a puzzle box," she whispered urgently, "and the Bevoy is inside. Push the elephant heads simultaneously to open it. Press as hard as you can. But I need you to take it now and go. As quickly as you can."

The sudden onslaught of information hit him, each bit of it battling for dominance. He looked down at the small box with its carvings of elephants and trees.

"Please go," she urged, her voice thin with desperation. "Please, please go."

"I am not leaving without you." Jonathan reached for the ropes binding her wrists.

"There is no time," she protested. "They are in the other room. And they are dangerous people. I have no doubt they will harm you or even us both if they find you here. Please, please take the stone and leave now."

"I didn't come here for the Bevoy, Camille." Jonathan paused in his task long enough to lock gazes with her. "I came here for you."

At this she finally stopped resisting and pivoted to give him a better angle. Tears filled her eyes, and she shook her head slowly. "You do not understand. I am not what you think I am."

"You are exactly what I think you are." The rope gave way, and she rubbed her wrists. Still kneeling, he leaned closer to her.

313

"You are strong and kind and compassionate. And you are the woman I love. And I refuse to leave here without you."

She said nothing, but a tear slipped down her cheek. He had never seen her cry. He touched it and brushed it away.

Her words came in a rush, with renewed fervor. "But, you must know—"

"You can tell me later."

She nodded and looked toward the door. "Then we must hurry."

He stood and helped her to her feet. She seemed unsteady, no doubt as a result of sitting for so long. Laughter intensified in the back room. She rose to her feet and headed toward the half-open front door. He started to follow her, but as he took a step two men came bursting through the curtained opening.

Jonathan pulled one of his father's pistols from his waistband. He was already aiming the barrel before he saw their faces clearly.

James Iverness.

And Henry Darbin.

Nothing could have shocked him more than to see Darbin here. And yet on some level he was not surprised.

"Darbin," Jonathan breathed.

Darbin's dark eyes widened, then a smile stretched his thin lips. "Jonathan Gilchrist. You are the last person I expected to see here. I wish I could say it was a pleasure."

Jonathan scrambled, trying to line up the pieces of the puzzle before him. What was Darbin doing here?

It was then that Jonathan noticed that Darbin had a pistol as well. It was pointed straight at his chest. And there they stood, their pistols pointed at one another.

A standoff.

At that moment, James Iverness propped his hands on his hips, his demeanor calm as if he were out for a Sunday stroll. A giant brown dog circled round his master's feet, his yellow eyes locked on Jonathan. "Jonathan Gilchrist, eh? So this is the pup that has caused me all this trouble."

"Aye, 'tis." Darbin's voice was as smooth as ever, and his pistol remained locked on Jonathan, his demeanor steady and cool. "I had an inkling—a small one, mind you—that you had affections for the lovely Miss Iverness here. Can't say that I blame you, pretty lass that she is. But I must say I am surprised you would go to all this trouble for her. After all, you are a Gilchrist. I would think that fact alone would render you above such weak emotion."

Jonathan drew a sharp breath. His gaze flicked toward Camille. Her dark eyes flashed with fear. He steadied his focus—and his pistol—on Darbin. "I suppose I misunderstood your intentions, Darbin. I had thought you to be a friend of the family. Clearly I was mistaken."

Darbin's voice rang with confidence. "You trust far too easily, Gilchrist—a trait you did not learn from your brother, I might add, but one you might be wise to develop."

"We had an agreement."

"Exactly. But need I remind you that you contacted me, not the other way around? You brought me into this on a completely different level. And I was happy to comply."

Another bit of the puzzle clicked into place. Darbin had been involved with the robbery from the beginning. Who else would have such intimate knowledge of the Gilchrist home? Darbin had been one of Thomas's best friends and a frequent guest at

Kettering Hall. Of course he had knowledge of the home's layout, of the location of his father's study. And if he had taken up with Iverness, he no doubt knew that the ruby was at Kettering, most likely in the study.

With each passing moment, more questions catapulted through Jonathan's mind. "And that business with McCready?"

"Aha. A scene, my friend. A ruse. Quite the actor, that one. He could have a career on the stage, could he not? That was to throw you off our trail. Worked like a charm too. But who would have thought you would believe I could find a thief so quickly? Although I appreciate your confidence in my abilities, you do overestimate my skills."

"Miss Iverness could have been killed," challenged Jonathan. "Never pegged you to be a murderer."

Darbin shrugged as if bored with the conversation. "She needed to believe it too. Come on, my friend. Do not be so gullible. Too many people knowing the truth about such transactions can be far too complicated. Mr. Iverness taught me that. It was his idea."

The idea that any man would knowingly put his daughter in harm's way turned Jonathan's stomach. But now it all made sense. Darbin's disappearance the night the store was robbed. His ongoing interest in Camille's whereabouts. Iverness's harshness toward his—

At that moment a tall, slender woman stepped through the curtained doorway. There was no denying who she was, for she and Camille shared a remarkable likeness. Surely this was her mother. But there seemed to be nothing motherly about this woman. The lines of her face were hard, her expression scornful.

Jonathan wanted clarification, but he knew he would not get

it. Not here, and possibly not ever. All that mattered was getting Miss Iverness—his Camille—away from this shop. Somehow she was connected with everyone here. But he didn't care. Any relationship that tied her up with them was one that had to be severed. He began to circle toward Camille, who stood close to the shop's front door.

But then Darbin did the unexpected. In a very small movement, he pointed his pistol away from Jonathan and directly at Camille.

Jonathan's blood ran cold, and his stomach turned within him. He adjusted his aim. "Let her go, Darbin. She is not what you want."

"And how can you be so sure? Did I not tell you there is more to Miss Iverness than what meets the eye? I did try to warn you, you know. For Thomas's sake."

Sweat gathered on Jonathon's brow. The air seemed too thick to breathe. But for the first time that day all was clear to him.

He had the one thing that they wanted.

And they were threatening the only person who mattered to him.

Darbin's voice rang out far too confidently. "And this is an interesting position we find ourselves in, you with a pistol pointed at my chest, and I with a pistol pointed at Miss Iverness. What are we to do?" His words issued a challenge.

Jonathan knew he had the advantage. The Bevoy was in his possession. But still he asked the question: "What is it you want, Darbin?"

"You know what I want," the man hissed. "And I know full well that Miss Iverness has more information about it than what she is sharing with me."

Sarah E. Ladd

Jonathan shifted his weight carefully as he listened. "Now, I have a bit of information to share with you. Miss Iverness does not have the ruby, so you might as well take your pistol off her."

"You are bluffing," snorted Darbin, casting a glance toward James Iverness before latching his gaze back on Jonathan.

Jonathan pressed his lips together. This was the moment.

He had a choice, and the choice he made at this moment would define his life from this moment forward.

He could back out of this dusty, cluttered little shop with the ruby securely in his pocket. He could give it to his father and win his praise. He could save the estate.

Or, he could turn the ruby over and free Camille.

She had never declared love for him. He did not even know if she would leave the shop and return to Fellsworth with him. But in his mind, there was no question.

The box was in his hand.

It was worth the risk.

Jonathan held the puzzle box up. "Release her, and the ruby is yours."

At last the older woman spoke. "That's it." Her words rushed forth hungrily. "The Bevoy is in that box."

Jonathan heard Camille gasp, but he did not look her way. Instead he steadied his eyes on Darbin. He repeated himself. "Let Miss Iverness go, and this is yours. You have my word as a gentleman."

Iverness and Darbin exchanged glances again. Jonathan could read their thoughts, interpret the look that bounced between them. Once in their possession, the gem would be sold, and if they were working together, it would be gone in the blink of an eye. If he had learned anything, it was that Iverness likely had a buyer lined up before Camille ever left with the ruby.

Pistol still aimed, Jonathan set the box on the counter to his left. The clatter of wood against wood echoed through the shop.

"This is my proposal." Jonathan's voice was steady. "Miss Iverness and I will leave. The ruby will stay."

An incredulous look crossed Darbin's narrow face. "You would hand it over? For the likes of her?"

Jonathan did not answer the question—not directly. He just repeated his terms. "I will give you the ruby. You will make no effort to detain us further, and you will never contact Miss Iverness again."

"He's bluffing," breathed Iverness, kicking the dog away from his feet and taking a step forward. His green eyes bored into Jonathan, unblinking.

"I swear it on my brother's grave," Jonathan countered. "I will give up all rights to the ruby. And you never contact her or my family again."

James Iverness looked at his daughter, and for a fleeting moment, a spark of emotion glimmered. His eyebrows drew together, and his lips seemed to fall into a frown. But just as quickly as it appeared, the expression disappeared.

"And if we don't agree?" asked Darbin.

Jonathan straightened his aim. "I will pull the trigger."

"You may kill me, but my colleague has a knife. And you will have nothing, no time to reload."

"What do you care?" Jonathan shot back. "Because when I pull this trigger, I will not miss. If you think my brother was a good shot, think it through. For we were taught by the same master, and I was a far better pupil than he. Now, I think Miss Iverness needs to leave this discussion, don't you?"

Darbin dropped his hand.

Jonathan did not move his eyes away from the men. "Leave, Miss Iverness."

When she did not move, he glanced at her over his shoulder. She looked from her mother to her father, whose gaze was fixed firmly ahead. Jonathan did not miss the flash of shock, of daughterly sadness. But as quickly as that expression wrote itself on her face, she gathered herself and raced for the door. The dog, who had been sitting at Iverness's feet, gave a sudden bark and ran after her.

James Iverness lunged forward, seized the box from the counter, and twisted the top a certain way to pop it open. He held the gem up to the dirty sliver of light squeezing through the door window.

Jonathan looked at the ruby. It looked black and dull to him. But the woman lunged forward and ripped the gem from James Iverness's hand.

All of this . . . for a stone?

"We have a deal, then," Jonathan confirmed. "You have what you want. You will leave Miss Iverness alone. The relationship is severed."

A crooked grin crossed Darbin's face. "You are more like your brother than I thought."

"I am not at all like my brother." Jonathan backed out of the shop, pistol still pointed. But the other three occupants of the room were too interested in the prize to notice his retreat.

Chapter Forty

Jonathan burst from the shop onto Blinkett Street. He filled his lungs, but instead of the fresh air they so desperately needed, he inhaled rain and smoke and the scent of filth.

He tucked the pistol at his waist, still unable to believe what had transpired and how willing James Iverness and his wife had been to trade their daughter for a ruby. Their greed sickened him. But he had no more interest in them at the moment.

He adjusted his coat to hide the firearm and looked to his right, then his left.

Camille was nowhere to be seen.

Momentary panic struck him. He had told her he had feelings for her, that she was the woman he loved. But she had never said as much to him. For all he knew, she cared nothing for him. Perhaps she had already disappeared into the crowded streets of London, never to be seen again.

He pushed his way through the crowd toward the nearest side road. The rain blurred his view, dripping from the brim of his hat to his face. Fear pushed his pace harder until he was jogging through the streets. He paused at each alley, peering through gates and down the narrow spaces. But he found nothing.

He was not sure how long it was before he stopped running and came to a halt, gasping. She was gone. For if she had wanted him to find her, surely she would have made her presence known.

His chest heaved with the exertion of the past several minutes, but the real pain was in his heart and soul.

Gone.

Then, almost on a whim, he looked down one last alley. And there, leaning against the wall, head bent, was Camille. The brown dog from the shop was sitting at her feet, his tongue hanging from the side of his mouth. But when the dog noticed him, he stood. He growled.

Camille turned toward Jonathan. Her eyes were rimmed with red, her face shiny with rain and tears. Her dress was soaked, and her black hair, loosed from its pins, hung down her back in sodden ropes. She touched the dog, and he sat back down. Her breath came out in sobs, and her shoulders trembled.

He jogged toward her until he was so close he could feel the heat radiating from her. There were so many things he wanted to say to her, but in the moment, his mouth could form no words.

She wiped her face with the back of her hand. But then came the outburst—more demand than question. "Why did you do that?"

"Do what?" he asked, confused by the intensity of her voice.

"The Bevoy belongs to your father, not to them." Tears choked her voice. "You gave them the Bevoy to free me. You should not have done that."

He drew a deep breath, his own breathing calm in contrast to her heaving gasps. "Did I not tell you," he whispered, "that I came to London for you, not the Bevoy."

She shook her head, her dark eyes locked on his, her breath slowing. "But you need it. Your father needs it. I would be fine, I would—"

"Camille."

She heard him not. "That was my mother. My mother! After all these years! I—"

Her rush of words dissolved into deeper sobs. The display of such anguish was enough to trigger emotion of his own.

He pulled her to him and wrapped his arms tightly around her—tightly enough so she knew he would not let go. Tightly enough that she would never again doubt that there was someone to protect her. To love her.

Someone who expected nothing from her in return.

After several moments she pulled away. She looked from his hair to his eyes to his lips. And that was all the encouragement he needed.

"Camille." He reached his hand forward and gently smoothed her hair from her forehead.

She shuddered as she drew a breath, and then she cast her eyes downward.

Jonathan gave a chuckle, letting his finger linger on the soft curve of her cheek. "My father was right, you know."

"What do you mean?"

He smiled at her. In fact, he could not stop smiling now, even if he wanted to. "I am beginning to believe that the Bevoy was cursed. And now that it is gone, out of our lives, there are far better things ahead of us."

"Us?" She gazed up at him, meeting his eyes once more.

"Yes, us. If you'll have me." The raindrops fell on her forehead, and he brushed them away with his thumb. "When I thought you were gone, it was as if you had taken my very soul with you. I never want to be apart from you. Never again."

He let his hand fall from her face to her shoulder to her arm.

She leaned toward him, and she drew a shaky breath. "I must tell you something."

Her words were spoken in such a solemn tone that he almost feared what she was about to say.

She pulled away, her eyes downcast. "I had the Bevoy the whole time. It was in that little package I carried in my apron. My father gave it to me, but I never dreamed the ruby was in there. I swear to you, I did not know. All that time, all of your trouble, and all the time it was in my possession. I am so sorry. The Bevoy belongs with your family, and I—"

How could he make her understand? He wanted to silence her on the matter, wanted never to hear the word *Bevoy* cross her lips again.

So he did the only thing he could think to do.

Jonathan reached out and pulled her to him. She felt small and warm in his embrace, but just the nearness of her infused him with confidence. "I care nothing about the Bevoy," he said, his voice barely above a whisper. "I care about you."

He tilted her chin up to his and kissed her, tenderly at first. Then, as his senses took over, he drew her closer still.

He had taken her by surprise. At first she stiffened, and he thought for a moment she might pull away. Intense longing commandeered his senses, and he deepened the kiss—brazenly, without apology. Every emotion he'd experienced over the past several weeks fused into a desire unlike any he had ever known.

He pulled away, and the expression in her eyes, the complete trust he found there, wound its way around every fiber of his being. "My Camille. I want to take you away from this. Marry me. Please, please, my darling, marry me. Never leave me again."

He waited, half fearing her reaction. Then a smile, the first smile he had seen from her today, curved her lips.

"Yes, Jonathan," she told him. "Yes!"

She flung her arms around his neck and returned his kiss with a passion fully equal to his. And Jonathan knew he had found his home—the only estate to which he had ever aspired.

It was wherever Camille was.

He held her close, wanting to memorize the feel of her in his arms. He kissed her forehead. Her cheek. Her lips. And then he leaned down to rest his forehead against hers. "I am sorry to say, however, that today's events will seal the fate of Kettering Hall. I fear it will not be able to remain in the Gilchrist family. I hope it will not disappoint you to not be the mistress of the estate."

She smiled. "I have always wanted to be an apothecary's wife. Nothing could make me more complete."

Chapter Forty-One

$\mathcal{J}$onathan propped his fists on his hips and looked around Kettering Hall's parlor for the last time. It had been six months since he handed the Bevoy over to Darbin. Six months since he and Camille had left London together, and one month since she became his bride. In many respects, with her at his side, he was happier than he had ever been. But now, gazing around the familiar room, he sobered. He had thought it would be easier to say good-bye to his childhood home, where lukewarm and painful memories far outweighed the pleasant.

In many respects, he had failed his family. He had not recovered the Bevoy. Not permanently. True, he had held it in his hands. But then he had given it away. And the repercussions of that action had come swiftly and fully for his family. The relationship between Penelope and her Alfred Dowden, already strained, had dissolved completely. Jonathan's father had sold the lion's share of his beloved collection and generated enough funds to retain the London house. But as predicted, Kettering Hall had been sold.

All around him stood furniture covered with white sheets. Heavy drapes blocked out light from the windows. Chimneypieces that had boasted fires at all hours were dark. No servants bustled, eager to help.

Kettering Hall was like a ghost house, dark and gloomy and

haunted with memories. But then Camille came around the corner, bringing with her a brightness that could not be diminished.

The soles of her boots echoed on the wooden floor. She smiled as she approached him, an easy, comfortable smile, and slid her hand into the crook of his arm. But she sighed as she looked around the stark room. "I fear I will always feel guilty about Kettering Hall."

He covered her warm hand with his own. "And why is that?"

"If it weren't for me, you would have had the Bevoy. Then your sister would have married, and your father would have his collection still."

Jonathan shook his head. "And I cannot allow you to accept guilt over such a thing."

"Even though he does not say as much, I do believe your father blames me."

"Kettering Hall is being sold because my father lost our money, not because of anything that you did. Had we lost the estate for the sake of a stolen ruby only, then we did not have the funds to sustain it in the first place. Besides, I am the one who stands to inherit, and you are worth more to me than a thousand Kettering Halls." He leaned over and kissed her forehead.

Camille smiled at the display of affection. "I wonder what the new owners will be like."

"I've no doubt we will meet them at some point since our cottage is so near."

A horse's whinny rose above the sounds of the morning as if summoning the travelers for their impending journey. "It sounds as if they are about ready to depart. We should bid them farewell."

He cast one last, long look around the silent room, then led

Camille to the main drive, where footmen scurried around and horses jingled their harnesses. Tevy, who had accompanied them from London all those months ago, ran out from around the carriage and loped happily toward Camille.

"He loves the country as much as I do." Camille leaned down to scratch the big dog's ears, then straightened and pulled her shawl closer around her shoulders. She nodded toward the small courtyard in front of the drive. "Penelope is over there. I should like to speak with her before she leaves."

Jonathan watched her head across the drive, then turned his attention back to the carriages. There were two of them—one for the family and another for the few members of staff who were to go with them to the London home. Three footmen worked to lift the bright bird's cage onto a separate wagon, inciting an onslaught of protesting squawks. Jonathan stepped closer to his father, who was watching the odd event with interest.

"I never thought I would see the day Kettering Hall would leave the Gilchrist family." The old man drew a deep breath as Jonathan approached, his eyes not leaving the bird. "And there is none to blame but myself."

A breeze swept down from the forest, carrying with it late autumn's spicy scent. Gone were October's golden hues. Instead, drab gray and brown covered the landscape, broken by patches of early snow. Jonathan kept his eyes fixed firmly on the landscape as he spoke. "As you always say, the Gilchrists will prevail. A minor setback, 'tis all."

His father chuckled and shook his head, finally looking away from the bird. "I've seen my fair share of minor setbacks. I don't think we will recover in quite the same way with this one."

"I do wish things could have ended differently." Jonathan flipped his collar up to guard against the damp wind.

"Time and folly have caught up with me, my boy. The time has come to reap what I sowed. Your mother warned me of such. I've been a fool to let it go on this long. Now 'tis time to face the proverbial music."

The mention of his mother had jerked Jonathan's head upright. His father almost never mentioned her, and hearing a reference to her pass the man's lips both pained and comforted Jonathan. It brought to mind dozens of memories of the woman who had been gone for so very long.

His father continued, leaning heavily on the head of his parrot cane. "Even if you had brought home the Bevoy, it was only a matter of time. One cannot erase a lifetime of imprudence with one such action."

The men stood in silence as the immaculately dressed footmen carried the remnant of the Gilchrist treasures to the carriage one last time.

"I fear this is the end of an era," remarked his father solemnly.

Jonathan clasped his hand on his father's shoulder. "But the beginning of another."

⁂

With Tevy bouncing along beside her, Camille walked down the garden steps and over to the small bench her new sister-in-law occupied. Penelope, clad in a blue cloak trimmed with fur, had her back to Kettering Hall, but she turned as Camille and the dog approached.

She wrinkled her nose as Tevy approached her. "I can't believe you aren't afraid of that beast."

Tevy panted from his recent burst of activity, his tongue lolling from the side of his mouth. Camille bent down and scratched behind the floppy brown ears. "I can see how he might frighten you, but really, he is quite the gentle giant."

"Gentle giant indeed." Penelope pulled her hand back as the dog nudged it, begging for attention.

"If you think Tevy is frightening, you would not have cared for Link, our shop cat."

"I do not see how a cat could be more frightening than a dog."

"Link was a champion mouser. He had one eye and could be as cantankerous as they come. Sometimes he made Tevy seem like an angel by contrast. But he was my friend, and I loved him."

"How different your childhood was from mine," Penelope mused. After a reluctant pause, she gave the dog a single pat on the head with her gloved hand. "You'll have to come to London to see me, for I think I'll not return to Fellsworth."

Camille sank down on the bench beside her. "Never is a long time."

"How could I return here?" Penelope shook her head, her elegantly arranged curls bouncing about her face. "And not because I care what the villagers say. You know I couldn't care less about the gossiping and the staring."

Camille bit her tongue to keep from responding to that statement, supposing the opposite to be true. Instead she gently asked, "Then what would prevent you?"

Penelope lifted her head, the breeze blowing in her blond hair, her deep blue eyes fixed on some distant point in the horizon. "It isn't my home anymore."

Camille sat with her for several moments in silence. How she could relate to that feeling of not knowing where she belonged. "But you have your father. He loves you. And of course you have Jonathan and me. You will always have a home, Penelope. Never you fear about that."

But she knew that was not what Penelope ached to hear. Sadness etched itself in the tiny creases around her sister-in-law's eyes. A frown formed on her lips, but it was not the pretty pout that Camille had witnessed her employing on several occasions. No coy light lit her eyes. For she had tasted the bitterness of disappointed love.

Camille had never known that particular pain. But she did know what it was to be rejected by a loved one, and her heart ached for the woman sitting next to her.

After a moment's thought she reached for her brooch. It had been given to her by a family member, intended to encourage her.

Now another family member needed encouragement.

"We are sisters now, are we not?"

Penelope nodded.

"I want you to take this."

Penelope's eyes widened. "I couldn't."

"I know it is not as fine as what you are used to, but I—"

"No, please do not misunderstand. It is a lovely brooch, a true treasure. But it belongs to you. I cannot take it. Especially after . . ." She faltered, unable to continue.

Camille rubbed her thumb over the smooth metal. She recognized the feeling of fumbling for words, unable to express what she truly felt. An aching heart was an aching heart, regardless of how or why. Even now, in her supreme happiness, she felt a nagging ache, a constant sense of loss.

She extended the brooch to Penelope. "Read the inscription on the back."

Penelope took the piece and turned it over. " 'All things work together for good to them that love the Lord.' "

"My grandfather gave it to me when I was young. I never really understood it before, what it meant, but I think I am starting to. One day I shall share with you the extent of my own journey, but there were many times when I felt all was lost and this piece brought me comfort. I hope when you look at it, you will know you are loved. And I believe, in the end, that everything really will work out for the best."

Tears brimmed Penelope's eyes, making them appear even brighter and bluer in the afternoon light. "I loved Mr. Dowden. Truly, I did."

Camille patted Penelope's gloved hand with her own. "I know you did."

"But he loved my dowry. He loved Father's money. Not me."

"And you shall find someone, a new man, who will love you for you. All will be well, you will see. This move is simply a new adventure."

Chapter Forty-Two —————————

*M*rs. Camille Gilchrist sat in her chair by the fire in her new home, the apothecary's cottage. Outside a quiet morning snow fell gently on the lanes of Fellsworth, and inside a warm fire crackled and simmered in the fireplace. Tevy, who had grown quite accustomed to long naps, slumbered at her feet. In her hands she held the ledger to her husband's shop.

It was a task she had no need to perform. Jonathan was quite capable of handling his own professional affairs. And there had been a point in her life when she had thought that if she never saw one more ledger book it would be too soon. But now she found herself wanting to help. Asking to help.

Somehow she had always known she would end up working in a shop. After all, she had spent her entire life preparing for it. But never would she have imagined she would be working alongside her husband—someone who loved and cherished her, who valued her opinions and contributions and praised her.

The door opened, and Jonathan shook the snow off his coat before stepping through the door that led from the shop.

"Good day, Mrs. Gilchrist." A boyish grin flashed, his cheeks ruddy from the cold.

She returned her quill to the holder and stood, unable to prevent the smile that rushed to her own lips. "Good day, Mr. Gilchrist."

He took off his greatcoat and hung it on the hook next to the door, then removed his hat. "Feels good in here. Getting awfully cold outside."

He rubbed his hands together before reaching his hand out to her, and she closed the distance. His hand felt cold in her warm one and brought a flutter to her heart.

Jonathan wrapped his arms around her, the scent of cold and snow still clinging to him. As she rested her head against her husband's shoulder, a peace unlike any she had ever known settled upon her. The image of her grandfather's watch rushed her, along with the inscription.

All things work together.

It was true what she had told Penelope. For so long the words had not resonated with her. But now as she stood with her husband, happy, content, and peaceful, she began to understand. Every difficult situation, every broken moment, every tear had made her the person she was supposed to become and put her in the arms of the person who would make her complete.

She looked at Jonathan, whose strong character and quiet strength had given her the confidence to open her heart and receive love.

"Welcome home, dearest." Camille stood on her tiptoes to give him a kiss. "Welcome home."

Acknowledgments

$\mathcal{T}$o my husband and daughter—it is because of your love and encouragement that I am able to follow my passion for storytelling. Thank you for sharing this dream with me.

To my parents, Ann and Wayne—through prayer and counsel you have helped me find my path. And to my sisters, Sally and Angie—thank you for always cheering for me.

To my first readers, Ann and Sally—thank you for brainstorming with me and helping me get the story just right!

To my agent, Tamela Hancock Murray—you are not only my agent, but a trusted friend. Thank you for dreaming big!

To my fabulous editor, Becky Monds—thank you for caring so much about my story and for inspiring me. And to the rest of the team at HarperCollins Christian Publishing—from marketing to design, from to production to sales, I am in awe of the work you do!

As a writer, I am blessed to get to work with other writers who share the same passion for story. To my accountability partners, Carrie, Julie, and Melanie—thank you for being such a source for support and encouragement. To my writing "sister" Kim—I am so blessed to call you friend! To the ladies of "The Grove"—Katherine, Kristy, Cara, Katie, Melissa, Courtney, and Beth—thank you for sharing your gifts and inspiring others to tell their stories.

I am so grateful for each and every one of you!

Discussion Questions

1. Which character in this novel do you identify with the most? Why?

2. If you could give Camille one piece of advice, what would it be? What advice would you give Jonathan?

3. What words would you use to describe Penelope? Do you think Penelope influenced Jonathan? What impact does Penelope's behavior have on Camille?

4. In what ways is Camille different at the end of the novel than she is in the beginning? What does she learn about herself throughout the course of the story?

5. How do you think the fact that Camille's mother moved out of the country affected Camille? How would Camille be different if her mother had never left?

6. Did Jonathan betray his family by trading the ruby for Camille's safety? Why or why not?

7. It's your turn! What comes next for Camille and Jonathan? What would you like to see happen to these characters in the future?

WHISPERS ON THE MOORS

JOIN AMELIA, PATIENCE, AND CECILY ON THEIR ADVENTURES IN REGENCY ENGLAND.

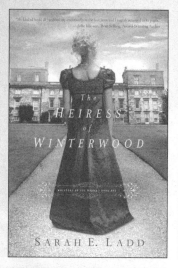

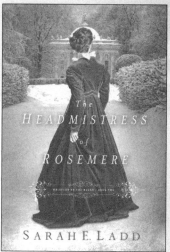

"Ladd proves yet again she's a superior novelist, creating unforgettable characters and sympathetically portraying their merits, flaws and all-too-human struggles with doubt, hope and faith."

—*Romantic Times*,
4-STAR REVIEW OF
A Lady at Willowgrove Hall

ABOUT THE AUTHOR

$\mathcal{S}$arah E. Ladd received the 2011 Genesis Award in historical romance for *The Heiress of Winterwood*. She is a graduate of Ball State University and has more than ten years of marketing experience. Sarah lives in Indiana with her amazing husband, sweet daughter, and spunky Golden Retriever.

Visit her website at www.sarahladd.com
Facebook: SarahLaddAuthor
Twitter: @SarahLaddAuthor